STAR TREK

THE NEXT GENERATION

D1325197

STAR TREK:
THE NEXT GENERATION NOVELS

STAR TREK:
THE NEXT GENERATION GIANT NOVELS

STAR TREK ®
THE NEXT GENERATION

GHOST SHIP

DIANE CAREY

TITAN BOOKS
LONDON

STAR TREK **THE NEXT GENERATION 1:**
GHOST SHIP
ISBN 1 85286 067 7

Published by
Titan Books Ltd
19 Valentine Place
London SE1 8QH

First Titan Edition July 1988
10 9 8 7 6 5 4

British edition by arrangement with Pocket Books, a division of Simon
and Schuster, Inc., Under Exclusive Licence from Paramount Pictures
Corporation, The Trademark Owner.

Printed and bound in Great Britain by Cox and Wyman Ltd, Reading,
Berkshire.

To Captain Frank R. Carey, U.S.M.C., I.R., for providing all the right details. Thanks, Dad.

To Jack Lifton, my own private physical chemist and international intelligence source. (By the way—Clive? Eat your heart out.)

To David Forsmark, for helping hammer out the tough ethical questions—the ones with no easy answers—without which our books would be just more noise. Great minds and all that.

To Nicole Harsch, expert in space psychology—you found all the right articles and led us through them unerringly. Ever tried swordfighting?

And to Star Trek editor Dave Stern—saving the best for last. You make all the editorial arm-wrestling easier to tolerate, and I appreciate you.

Gregory . . . you did it again.

These are the kind of people I'm talking about when readers ask me how I manage to write scientific, military and philosophical passages with accuracy. They are the people I mean when I cagily answer, "Oh . . . I have my sources."

Life is an offensive, directed against
the repetitious mechanism of the universe.

—Alfred North Whitehead

GHOST SHIP

Chapter One

THE *SERGEI G. GORSHKOV* moved through the water as though the sea had been made solely to carry such ships. As every sailor knew in his deepest soul, there had been no ocean before there were ships, and the ocean had only gotten so large because ships of such bulk came to chase its farthest shorelines, to push its hem forever back, to conquer its lengths and breadths with their intrepid spirit. The ships, ever bigger, ever more powerful, ever more majestic, were the badge of spirit for mankind.

At least . . . sailors think so.

For bakers, it's the bread that rises in their ovens that mankind should pay attention to.

Point of view.

Arkady Reykov unbuttoned the dark blue overcoat of the Soviet navy and shook the heavy outerwear from his shoulders. His petty officer was there to catch the coat and store it away. Reykov did not acknowledge the service, but simply strode onto the bridge, coatless, authority intact. Today the eyes of the Politburo were on him and this vessel.

1

His executive officer met him immediately, with a dogged reliability that Reykov found slightly annoying but somehow always welcome. The two men nodded at each other, then turned at the same moment and the same angle to look out over the stunning landing deck of the Soviet Union's second full-deck carrier. The shipbuilding facility at Nikolayev was far behind them. Before them lay the open expanse of the Black Sea. Around them in a several-mile radius, the carrier support group plunged through the sea, barely out of sight. There were four heavy cruisers and six destroyers in the carrier group. The tanker force would catch up tomorrow.

Reykov was a large man, straight-shouldered and inclined to staidness, the type of Soviet man that appears in comedy-dramas when typecasting is necessary to the story, except that he didn't have the obligatory mustache. Executive Officer Timofei Vasska was thinner, fairer, and younger, but both were handsome men—which, truth be told, didn't come in very handy in their particular vocation. But at least it was easier to get up in the morning.

One wanted to look good when one piloted a ship like this, this nuclear mountain upon the sea. It had taken a long time to store up the expertise to build a carrier. No one could become a naval architect just like that, and even if he could, where would he get the economic structure to support his knowledge? It takes a vast technology, ideas, factories, machining, measuring, weighing, thinking, knowing, production, and counterproduction even to make a ballpoint pen. And a carrier is a little more expensive.

Reykov was proud of this Lenin-class *Gorshkov*. She was big, and the Soviets liked big. And she carried a weapon that was the first and only of its kind. Their

2

pride and joy. Something even the Amerikanskis didn't have.

Reykov inflated his chest with a deep breath. His ship. Well, he could pretend it was his.

He felt the pulses of the five thousand men in his crew, throbbing with metronome steadiness beneath him as he stood on the bridge in the carrier's tower.

"Approaching maneuver area, Comrade Captain," Vasska said, his voice carrying more lilt than those words required.

Reykov acknowledged him with a quick look. "Signal the flight officer to begin launching the MiGs for tracking practice."

He felt a little shiver of thrill as he gave that order, for it was the first time the new MiGs would be launched from an aircraft carrier during an actual demonstration for dignitaries. Until now, only military eyes had seen this. The Soviet Union had finally learned how to work titanium instead of steel, and now there was a new class of MiGs light enough to be used on carriers. For years the motherland had sold its titanium to the U.S. while Soviet planes were still made of steel. Too heavy, too much fuel. It was with great pleasure that Arkady Reykov watched as the MiGs sheared off the end of the flight deck and took to the sky, one after another—seven of them.

"Have the fighters go out fifty miles and come in on various unannounced attack runs at the ship. Prepare for demonstration of laser tracking and radar to show we could knock out each of the fighters as it appears. And advise the political commissar to get the dignitaries out of their beds. They'll want to be red instead of green today for a change."

Vasska put up a valiant fight as he dictated these

orders to the appropriate stations, but despite himself his cheeks turned rosy and his shoulders shook. "They *have* been green, haven't they, Comrade Captain?" he muttered toward Reykov, keeping his voice low and his eye on the other bridge officers.

The captain smiled. "And tell them to be sure to get dressed before they come out on deck. Those American satellites can count your leg hairs."

"Haven't you heard the latest intelligence?" Vasska tossed back. "Bureaucrats have no leg hair."

Reykov leaned toward him in a manner so natural it had almost become unnoticeable after their years together. "They should put the bureaucrats in a gulag. Then things might get done."

Vasska smirked at him and gave him a delicate glance. "You used to be one of those."

"Yes," the captain said, "and they should've gagged me. Perhaps by now you'd be captain and I'd be on the Politburo."

"I don't want to be captain. When all the shooting starts, I like somebody to hide behind."

Reykov turned up one corner of his mouth. "That's all right. It's my secret desire never to sit on the Politburo. Are the drone targets operational for the tests? Have they been checked?"

"Several of them. We sent out two this morning, and one malfunctioned. Let's hope we have better odds for the demonstrations."

"In the old days," Reykov commented with his usual dryness, "there would've been self-destructs on the targets. Just in case we missed."

The two men shared a chuckle.

"The Teardrop missiles have been checked and rechecked. This batch is probably going to fire as it's supposed to, I hope. All this target practice and

4

nothing to shoot at," Vasska said as he watched the sea crash past *Gorshkov's* vast prow.

"Mmmm," Reykov agreed, his lips pressed flat. "You know, Timofei, I've served almost thirty years and I've never been fired at even once."

Vasska straightened, his boyish face tight with a restrained grin. "Then how do you know you won't break under attack?"

"You've met my wife."

Vasska clasped his hands behind his back and lowered his voice again. "What's the situation with Borka?"

"I talked to him . . . I got him alone."

"Did you make progress?"

Reykov bobbed his brows and shrugged. "He can't be watched every minute. It's those times he's out of sight that make me worry."

"What have you tried?"

"Reasoning . . . threats . . . rewards . . . nothing works. I'm afraid the time is coming for severe action."

Vasska nodded sympathetically. "Be firm, Kady. I wish I could be there. This is what comes from too much permissiveness. Rebellion. Time will take care of it, though. Borka will eventually make his own decision, and then you can proudly say your grandson isn't wearing diapers anymore."

Even as he said it, Vasska fixed his eyes on his captain's thick dark hair with its tinge of silver just over his left brow, and had difficulty imagining Arkady Reykov as a grandfather. The captain's face was almost unlined, his eyes every bit as clear and vital as the day Vasska first saw him eight—or was it nine?—years ago, while Vasska was still a pilot and Reykov was flight officer on the small carrier *Moscow*.

5

It hadn't been a bad eight years, at least not after the first two, when they finally believed they could speak candidly to each other. That is a day which in many relationships never comes at all.

"Be sure there are no other aircraft in the area, Comrade Vasska. Launch the target aircraft and let's proceed with this performance before we all get hungry and can't do our jobs."

"Shall we wait until the political commissar notifies us that the dignitaries are watching?"

A reed-thin smile stretched across Reykov's face as he measured and tasted each alternative several times before finally narrowing his eyes on his privilege as captain. He leaned toward Vasska for another of those private exchanges. "Let's *not.*"

Vasska's cheeks tightened as he imagined the dignitaries hitting the ceilings of their staterooms when the gunnery practice began. He made his back straight and firmly announced to the duty officer, "Signal tracking maneuvers, Comrade Myakishev."

The performance with live fighters went shiningly well, primarily because it was all "on paper." There was no firing of weapons until the unmanned drones were launched to circle out wide across the expanse of the Black Sea and come back to harass the *Gorshkov* as had been carefully arranged and rearranged. The dummy missiles were bombarded with a hail of depleted-uranium slugs whose weight alone would be enough to press off an attacking missile if it hit at sufficient distance. There were dignitaries on board, and nothing was being left to chance. There were a few misfires, a few misses, and a few false starts, but while not a perfect performance, it was a performance that could be *interpreted* as perfect, if the right language were used. Reykov was certain the language would be selected as carefully as a mother clips her infant's fingernails.

That immutable fact about Soviet coverage was little comfort, however, as Reykov turned to Timofei Vasska and quietly spoke words that chained them to their seats. "Prepare demonstration of the E.M.P."

With the last hour's weapons' displays still booming in his ears, Vasska's skin shrank from the order, though he let none of his apprehension show. Such a device. The first of its kind to be mounted on a moving unit. Even the stationary ones prior to this one had been nothing more than a few isolated test guns. This one was real, mounted permanently at the center of *Gorshkov*'s gunnery shroud. E.M.P. . . . controlled electromagnetic pulse.

"Signal the *Vladivostok* to begin firing dummy Teardrops. And Vasska," Reykov added quickly, raising a finger, "be sure they only fire one at a time and give us forty seconds to reenergize the pulse."

Vasska shook his head and said, "Won't it be wonderful if our enemies are so cooperative as to never fire more than one missile at a time?"

Reykov shrugged his big shoulders and said, "We're working on it. It'll be good enough if we can scramble the guidance systems one by one. Let's not ask for trouble. Just don't make fools of the designers."

Vasska nodded to Myakishev, who relayed the order out into the distance.

"Inbound," came the dry announcement a few moments later. "One Teardrop missile, heading four-zero true."

"Visual range?"

"In six seconds, sir."

"When it becomes visible, we'll fire the E.M.P. on my order."

"Yes, Comrade Captain. Visibility in three . . . two . . . one . . . *mark.*"

They squinted into the crisp blue atmosphere and saw the incoming dummy missile. Hardly more than a silver glint against the sky, even the dud caused a hard ball in the pit of every stomach. Reykov imagined the dignitaries' skin crawling right about now.

"Fire the E.M.P."

Myakishev touched his control panel, and below them on the tower a twelve-foot-wide antenna swiveled toward the inbound. They all flinched when the pulse fired—

There was a near-simultaneous *snap* and a white flash. At first it seemed the snap came first, but now that it was over they weren't sure.

In the distant sky, the Teardrop skittered on its trajectory, corkscrewed to one side, and plunged into the sea far off its mark, victim of a fizzled guidance system.

The bridge broke into cheers.

Reykov pumped a sigh of relief from his lungs. "Reenergize the pulse, Comrade Vasska."

"Recharging now, Comrade Captain."

"Good boy, good boy . . ." Reykov inhaled deeply and tried to make the sensation of trouble go away. He wasn't really nervous, but for some reason his hands were cold.

"Comrade Captain . . ." Myakishev bent over the officer's shoulders at the radar screen.

"Comrade?" Reykov prodded, his hands dropping to his sides.

8

Vasska, having heard something in Myakishev's tone, was also bending over the radar station.

"We have an inbound . . . and it's not one of ours."

Vasska dove for the TBS phone and had it to his ear as Reykov barked, "Contact the *Vladivostok.*"

"Sir, Captain Feklenko reports they did not fire. They did *not* fire on us."

"Then what is it?"

"I don't know."

"What is it? Is it American?"

"Doesn't appear to be."

"Then what? Is it French? Is it British? Albanian? Do the Africans have missiles? Whose is it?"

"Sir, there's no log of this . . . I'm not even certain it's a missile," Vasska said, snapping his fingers to other manned positions in silent orders.

Reykov pressed up against Myakishev's shoulder. "Billions of rubles for you geniuses and you can't tell me what it is. I want to know whose is it. What is coming in?"

"It's headed directly toward us!"

Reykov straightened, his eyes narrowing on the distant sky. For the first time in his life, he made the kind of decision he hoped never to have to make.

"Turn the E.M.P. on it. Fire when ready."

The wide rectangular antenna swiveled like the head of some unlikely insect, and once again the terrible *snap-flash* came as the electromagnetic pulse pumped through the atmosphere with scientific coldness.

It should have worked. It should have scrambled the guidance controls on any kind of missile or aircraft, any kind at all.

Any kind at all.

"It's homing in on the beam—accelerating now!" Myakishev's voice clattered against his throat.

Vasska whispered, "Even the Americans don't have anything like that . . ."

Reykov twisted around and plowed through the bridge crew to the chilly windowsill. He stared out over the Black Sea.

There was something there. It wasn't a missile.

On the horizon, making child's play of the distance between itself and *Gorshkov,* was a wall.

An electrical wall. It sizzled and crackled, made colors against the sky, shapeless and ugly—the phenomenon looked, more than anything, like an infrared false-color image. Colors inside colors. But there was no basic shape. It was crawling across the water, the size of a skyscraper.

Behind him, Myakishev choked, "Radar is out. Communications out now—we're getting feedback—"

Reykov gasped twice before he could speak. "Full about! General quarters! General—"

His voice went away. Around him, every piece of instrumentation went dead. As though molasses had been poured over the bridge, all mechanisms failed. There wasn't even the reassuring sound of malfunction. In fact, there was no sound at all.

Then a sound did come—an electrical scream cutting across the water and swallowing the whole ship as the false-color bogey roared up to the carrier's starboard bow and sucked the ship into itself. It was three times the size of the ship itself. *Three times.*

Reykov's last move as a human being was to turn toward the radar station. He looked at Timofei Vasska, who straightened up to stare at his captain, both hands clasped over his ears, and the two men

10

were locked in a gaze, frozen, held. It felt as though all their blood were clotting at once.

Reykov's last perception was of Vasska's eyebrows drawing slightly together as the two men shared the wholeness of that final moment before obliteration.

Then Vasska's face was covered with the false-color image, and Reykov's mind, mercifully, stopped operating.

The false-color phenomenon drenched the aircraft carrier in its electrical wash. Within moments, there were no more life-forms on board. The immense vessel had been wiped clean of organisms, from the horde of humans to the smallest cockroach hiding in the cook's shoe. Even the leather on the seats in the captain's stateroom was gone.

There was only steel and wire and aluminum and titanium and the various fabrics—tarps and uniforms —that were recognizable as inert. The *Gorshkov* sat on the open water, empty.

The hull and the airfield it supported began to rumble, to vibrate. Ripples shot out from the hull at the waterline, creating patterns on the sea, and with every passing second the intensity of these vibrations mounted until *Gorshkov* was actually creating waves on the Black Sea.

The ship shook like a toy, shuddered, and was ripped in half as though made of chocolate cake. The shriek of tearing metal blared across the entire sea. Each piece of the ship became an individual explosion, a splotch of color inside the electrical vortex, and blew up like so many fragmentation grenades.

Ninety thousand gross tons of scrap metal rained across the waters of the Black Sea.

* * *

"Captain's on the bridge."

The U.S.S. *Theodore Roosevelt* (CVN-71) churned through the sea at the center of the six cruisers and seventeen destroyers that made up its carrier group. From where he came to a stop beside the navigation station on the bridge, Captain Leon Ruszkowski could easily see two of the Aegis cruisers plowing along at a distance of four miles off their forward and port beams.

"Nice," he murmured. "Blue sky, warm day, waters of the exotic Mediterranean beneath, and a song in our hearts. Ah, to be in Paris. Or Athens . . . hell, pick a city."

"Will coffee do?" Executive Officer David Galanter appeared, and sure enough the mocha scent of coffee, sugar/no cream, came with him.

The captain took the china mug and said, "Dave, you'll make a hell of a headwaiter someday. We'll all retire and open up a Greek restaurant in east L.A. Admiral Harper could be maître d' . . . Annalise can cook. . . ."

Air Wing Commander Annalise Drumm broke off her enchantment with the flattop and looked his way. "Do I get free breakfast?"

"Poached octopus on whole-wheat toast, our specialty."

She smiled and rolled her eyes. "After a while we could replace the octopus with those little pink erasers that come on the tops of navy pencils. Nobody'd know the difference."

"We'd probably get a write-up in *Connoisseur*. Dave, what's that blip?"

"Sorry, sir . . . one minute. Compton, check that."

The captain moved closer, squinting. "Gone now. What was it?"

12

Galanter shook his dark head and frowned. "Not sure, sir. All stations, verify integrity of the area."

A very subtle change came over the bridge. Highly trained crewmen moved into action so smoothly that the series of exercises was barely distinguishable from what went on when they were doing nothing.

Then the radar officer calmly said, "Picking up six blips, skipper . . . correction—seven blips. Seem to be fighters."

"Fighters from where? Annalise, you got hardware in the air I don't know about?"

Annalise crowded him at the monitor, suddenly possessive of their airspace. "No, sir, all fixed-wings are in."

The captain's brows drew closer. "And the *Dwight Eisenhower*'s three thousand miles away. Get an ID, Compton."

"They seem to be seven MiGs, sir. Signature radar says configuration is MiG-33B, Naval Version."

"Are we under attack?"

"No, sir. Their missile radar is not on."

"What are MiG-33s doing here? What happened? Who speaks Russian?"

"I do, sir," Compton said without taking his eyes from his screen.

The captain didn't hesitate. "Get on there and find out what's up."

"Uh, yessir." He bantered into his comm set in Russian, and within seconds came back with, "Skipper, Soviet CAP is requesting permission to land on our flattop. Says they're out of fuel. Coming in at high warble. Very agitated."

Commander Drumm and the exec crowded the captain as he frowned and muttered, "Seven MiG-33s want to land on a U.S. CVN? Must be some bitchin' reason. I don't suppose we better wait for a note from Mother on this one."

Galanter agreed with a cautious nod. "Out of fuel's out of fuel."

The captain watched the status boards and said, "Tell the Soviet squadron leader to dump all their missiles and bombs and empty their guns completely. Annalise, scramble four Tomcats to escort them in."

"Aye, skipper." She dashed for the exit so fast that they almost didn't notice her leave until she was gone.

But the captain knew—he didn't even bother to look. "Sound general quarters."

Galanter's voice got stiff. "Aye, sir. Bos'n, sound general quarters."

"General quarters, aye." The bosun immediately went to his broadcast intercom, pierced the ship with an alert whistle, and sent the deceptively calm order booming through the two thousand airtight chambers on the carrier. *"General quarters. General quarters. Man your battle stations. This is not a drill. Man your battle stations. This is no drill."*

Captain Ruszkowski didn't wait for the stirring announcement to stop, because that would take several minutes. Throughout the ship, thousands of trained men and women were streaking toward their posts, all blood running hot with a thrill that inevitably comes from hearing those words over the intercom. No matter how awful or how dangerous, there was always the thrill. It was part and parcel of the voodoo that made things work on a military vessel.

Ruszkowski kept quiet just a few more seconds until he heard the distinct *kksshhhhhhhoooooo* of F-14s peeling off the flight deck in succession so quick it was scary. That was a good sound, and he started breathing again. "Scan for any vessels in a thousand-mile radius. I want to know if this is a fake."

Compton turned in his chair. "Sir?"

"Go, Compton."

"Russian wing commander says three bags full, sir. They'll comply with dumping their arms and anything else you want."

"Ask the squadron leader what kind of arresting gear he has, then tell him what we've got and see if they're compatible. We'll have to know if their tailhookers are up to speed or if we have to rig a barricade."

Galanter straightened. "Should we tell them that? I mean, isn't that classified?"

"Yeah, but I don't really care. And signal our picket destroyer that they might have to go in after the MiGs if we can't hook them and they have to ditch."

"Soviet CAP leader says he's willing to comply unconditionally on all counts, sir. He sounds pretty shook up."

"Signal they have permission to land, Mr. Compton. Dave, let's bring those pilots in."

It had never in all the history of the universe been so hot. An eerie yellow light flashed on and off, picking up the roundness of tiny beads of perspiration on the woman's ivory skin. Some of the beads caught on the ends of her long black eyelashes as she lay there with her eyes tightly shut. The glow was spasmodic, on, off, on, off.

Her eyes shot open. Her hands gnawed the edges of the mattress. Her back was suddenly stiff from sitting up so quickly, yet she had absolutely no memory of having sat up. Beneath her uniform, perspiration

15

rolled down between her breasts, as though someone had dumped a beaker of glycerin over her shoulders.

"Don't fire . . . shut down all systems . . . Vasska . . . Vasska!"

She was gasping. Several seconds thundered by under the terrible flash of the yellow light before her eyes focused on the delicate floral arrangement on her dresser.

"Yellow alert . . . yellow alert . . ."

She turned her head, blinking tears from her eyes, and undone black hair moved on her shoulders, reminding her of who she was. She tried to catch at her identity as it slipped in and out of her mind, to draw it in, cling to it—

"Yellow alert . . . yellow alert . . . Counselor Troi, please report to the bridge immediately. Counselor Deanna Troi, report to the bridge please. Yellow alert . . . yellow alert . . ."

Chapter Two

"FIRE PHASERS."

Captain Picard's precise enunciation gave the order a theatrical tenor. It was followed almost immediately by the thunder of weapons powering through the big ship. A slim, magisterial man of thrifty movement, Picard stood the deck without pacing as most would, watching the latest of a series of rather tedious scientific exercises.

In the corner of his eye he saw the yellow alert light flashing, and it reminded him that stations had been manned and any quick shifts in orbital integrity could be handled without surprise now. "Orbital status, Mr. LaForge?"

As he spoke, Picard crossed the topaz carpet to bridge center and glanced over the shoulder of Geordi LaForge, ignoring—through practice—the fact that the dark young man had a metal band over his eyes that made him appear blindfolded. There was something ironic and disconcerting—to humans—about trusting the steering of a gigantic ship to a blind man.

LaForge's head moved, downward slightly and left —it was their only signal that visual tie-in to his brain was working at all. "An orbit this tight is tricky since gas giants have no true surface, sir, but we're stable and holding. I guess the Federation's going to get all the information it wants whether we like it or not."

Picard moved quietly to the other side of LaForge and placed his hand on the young officer's lounge. "When I want an editorial, I'll ask for it, Lieutenant."

LaForge stiffened. "Yes, sir. Sorry, sir."

The captain imperiously guarded his own opinion. Though the huge new starship was supposedly on an exploratory mission, the Federation was dragging its feet in letting the *Enterprise* get on with it. The ship had yet to push into truly unexplored space, and Picard was annoyed by the giant gas planet turning on the room-sized viewscreen before him. All right, it was an anomaly. Yes, it was unique. Yes, it was large. But if the Federation Science Bureau wanted to study it, surely the planet wasn't going anywhere. They needn't take up an entire Galaxy-class ship to have a look at it.

"Mr. Riker, secure from yellow alert. Go to condition three."

William Riker came to life up on the quarterdeck. "Condition three, aye, sir." He started to look toward the tactical station, where the order would be funneled through, but at the last instant left it to the officer in charge, for his own gaze was fixed on Jean-Luc Picard.

The captain regarded his bridge and its people and their task with the stateliness of a bird on a bough. Not a bird of prey, though, this captain. This one could soar in any direction, whichever way duty demanded. Not a large man or even an imposing one—a task he left to his first officer—the captain was at times unobtrusive, the bird hiding in the foliage, watching, never seen until those great wings suddenly spread. Those around him knew this could happen at any moment, this sudden peeling off across the bridge panorama like a lean sky thing. Even in repose, his presence kept them alert.

I wish I could do that, Riker thought, a little wince crossing his broad features. He tried not to watch the captain while the captain was watching the bridge, but it was hypnotic. As usual, Riker's back was hurting as he stood to starboard, too rigidly. He wished he could shake the habit of prancing, born of deep-seated little insecurities that nagged at him constantly as though to keep him in line. Later he always wished he hadn't moved so punctiliously as he got from here to there. Horrible to risk the captain's thinking he was being deliberately upstaged. Next selection: "First Officer on Parade."

But worse . . . if the first officer appeared diffident. Wasn't that worse? There was no middle ground, or at least Riker hadn't found it. He wanted to be a bulwark, but not one the captain had to climb over.

It was tiring, pretending to be completely one with a commanding officer whom he simply didn't know very well on a personal basis. Yet they faced the prospect of sharing the next few years at each other's side. Could that be done on the plane of formality that had set itself up between them?

Riker tried to pace the bridge casually yet without appearing aimless. That was the tricky part. It actually hurt sometimes—his back, his legs, aching. Like now. If not done right, the movements became pompous and ambiguous. He would become victim to the plain fact that the first officer actually had conspicuously little to do on the bridge. He worried about that all the time. Good thing he generally had command of away teams; at least he had that to make him worth-while.

Picard had it down. Quiet authority. Dependable not-quite presence. They could easily forget he was on the bridge at all. He would simply watch from his bough.

Riker forced himself to look away from the captain's coin-relief profile before he was entirely mesmerized.

"Something wrong, Mr. Riker?"

Caught.

Riker turned and drew his mouth into a grin that must have looked forced—another mistake—and said, "Not at all, sir. Everything's fine." He felt his eyes squinting and didn't want the grin to get out of hand, so he pursed his lips and pretended to be very interested in the tactical display.

Good—the captain was looking away. *Relax, Riker. Down with one shoulder. Now the other. Good soldier.*

A casual turn told him no one was looking at him. Everyone was busy with the giant.

A moment later he was hypnotized again, but this time it was not by the subdued presence of Captain Picard. Now the gas giant caught him, held him, cradled in its unparalleled blueness as it roiled before them on the wide ceiling-to-floor viewscreen.

Ah, that viewscreen. It was the only thing on this ship that truly conveyed the size of the vessel and its technological grandeur. Dominating the bridge, the screen was half a universe all by itself.

The other half was over Riker's shoulder: the new *Enterprise*. Barely broken in, swan-elegant, she spread out behind him like the wings of the bird.

Birds. Everything's birds all of a sudden, Riker thought, and he glanced at Jean-Luc Picard.

20

"Condition report, Mr. Data," the captain requested then, directing his gaze to the primary science station aft of tactical.

Riker turned aft in time to see a slender humanoid straighten at the science post. The face was still startling, its doll-like pyrite sheen softened only by its sculpted expression. Data's expression, when there was one, always carried a childlike naïveté that eased the severeness of his slicked-back hair and the cartoon colors of his skin. For the hundredth time, Riker involuntarily wondered why anybody smart enough to create an android so intricate was too stupid to paint its face the right color or put some tone on its lips. If his builders filled it with human data—pardon the pun—somewhere in the download must have been information that the palette of human skin types didn't include chrome. It was as though they went out of the way to shape him like a human, then went even further out of the way to paste him with signs that said, "Hey, I'm an android!"

Data's brushstroke brows lifted. "Readings coming in from phaser blast echoes now, sir. Absolutely lifeless—high concentrations of uncataloged chemical compounds, very compressed . . . extremely rare reactology, Captain. This information will prove valuable."

"Is there a margin of safety to attempt probing through to the gas giant's core?" Picard asked.

Data's face was framed by the black mantle of the slenderizing one-piece flightsuit, its color picked up again by the breast panel's mustard gold, a standard Starfleet color since the Big Bang. "A wide margin, sir. I recommend it."

Riker pressed his arms to his sides. There was something unreal about Data's voice. More human

21

than human, the words were rounded and spoken with an open throat, as though it was always working a little harder than necessary.

"He." Not "it." For the sake of the rest of the crew, think "he." No sense rupturing the trust others might have by accidentally pointing out the fact that he's an instrument, even if he is. Riker shook himself from his thoughts as he sensed Picard's glance, and in that moment he collected the authority he needed to carry out the captain's unspoken order.

He cleared his throat. "Increase phasers to full power. Let's see what's at the heart of this beauty."

"It is beautiful, isn't it? You don't stumble on one of these every day," Beverly Crusher commented. Folding her long arms, she sat on the bench just port of the counselor's seat, exercising a ship's surgeon's traditional right to be on the bridge when she didn't feel like being anywhere else. Dr. Crusher was yet another stroke of color against the bisque walls and carpet. Over her cobalt-and-black uniform her hair was a Cleopatra crown of pure terra cotta—and there was just *something* about a redhead. She was reedy and quick, smart and graceful, and inclined toward sensible shoes in spite of her narrow-boned loveliness. Riker liked her. So did the captain. Especially the captain.

"Yes," Captain Picard murmured, using the conversation as an excuse to move a few steps closer to her, "and it's twice the size of common gas giants. Fire phasers."

The muted *phhhiiiuuuuuu* hummed through the ship again, and on the screen an energy bolt cut downward into the surfaceless swirl.

"Reading various concentrations of gas," Data reported, "merging to liquid . . . compressing into solid masses in some areas . . . logging the compounds now, sir."

"Excellent," Picard responded. "I'm sure—"

The forward turbolift beside the captain's ready-room door opened, and Deanna Troi flew out onto the bridge, so unlike herself that she drew all eyes. She was a wreck—about as opposite her usual demeanor as she could get without mud-wrestling first. Her hair, usually knotted up in a style so tight it made other people's muscles ache, was a black mass, spilling over her shoulders and around her pearly cheeks. Her eyes, extra large with their touch of alienness, obsidian as eyes that looked out from a Greco-Roman fresco, were skewed by some terrible calamity. She was breathing hard. Had she run down every corridor?

Riker plowed through the bridge contingent to the space just below her platform. "Deanna . . . what's wrong?"

She panted out a few breaths, her pencil-perfect brows drawn inward to make two creases over her nose. "Why . . . why is there a yellow alert?"

Even now she spoke softly, her words touched with that faintly alien Betazoid accent. She was working hard to compose herself, but something was obviously pressuring her.

Riker moved a step closer, hoping to reassure her. "We're attempting close orbit around that." He made a gesture toward the viewscreen, but his mind wasn't on it any more than hers was. He parted his lips to say something else, but Data was interrupting him.

"We're firing into its atmosphere to get feedback readings. Even though its core is unignited, the planet is putting out three times the energy it should, mostly in long-wave radiation. We have to be on alert in case of shock waves or gravitational recoil—"

"Data," Riker snapped, wishing there was an off switch. He silenced the android with a sandpaper look, then turned back to Troi. "I should've told the computer to bypass standard procedure and not call you up here. It's my fault."

She put out her hand in what began as an appeasing gesture, but as she spoke it turned into the kind of move a woman makes when she wants to steady herself. "No . . . it isn't your fault. . . ."

The captain floated in at Riker's left. "What's bothering you, Counselor?" he asked, gently but with an edge of impatience.

Her kohled eyes narrowed beneath those drawn brows. "I heard something . . . in my mind. . . ."

"Can you describe it?" Riker asked. A twinge ran up his spine. Her muted telepathic talents always made him nervous. It wasn't exactly disbelief, because no one could dispute the existence of Betazoid mental traits, but it was a kind of distrust.

She backed up a step. "I'm sorry . . ." She blinked, took a deep breath, and pretended to recover. "Captain, I'm sorry for the interruption. I didn't mean to disturb your tests. Please excuse me."

Before either of the men could speak, she made a quick and nervous exit.

Riker stared at the lift doors. "I've never seen her act that way," he murmured.

Data rose and came a few steps toward the ramp. "Is Counselor Troi ill?"

"It's something else," Riker decided quietly, more to himself than to Data.

"She behaved abnormally."

Now he drew his eyes from the lift and struck Data with a look that would have bruised had it been a

24

blow. "I don't think you're anyone to judge," he barked.

Picard tilted his shoulders as he turned, saying, "Permission to leave the bridge, Number One. Temporarily."

"Thank you, sir," Riker said. "I won't be long." He had to restrain himself or he would actually have bounded for the lift. He cast one more acid glare at Data before leaving the bridge.

Picard smoothed the moment with a calm extension of the science tests. "Continue phaser bursts at regular intervals."

Data drew himself away from the stinging, confusing reaction Riker had given him and settled into his usual station at OPS on the forward deck. "Science stations are receiving continual information from the planetary core now, Captain." He lowered his voice as he had often heard humans do, and to LaForge said, "Commander Riker is annoyed with me."

LaForge shrugged. He glanced at the android, but saw not what human eyes would see. The android's bodily heat was unevenly distributed throughout the high-tech body, a body far denser than that of a human body of equal volume. The sections of infrared were localized into hot spots, more defined than the infrared blobs in a human body, and LaForge could easily discern the places where organic material was fitted in to intricate mechanics. Data gave off an electromagnetic aura, but he wasn't exactly a toaster oven.

"You could try being a little less stiff," LaForge suggested. "Learn some slang or something."

Data's lips flattened. "Slang. Colloquial jargon, nonstandard idioms, street talk . . . it's often inaccurate. I have tried to incorporate that speech into my language use, but it does not seem to flow."

"That's because you use it as though it still has quotation marks around it. You use individual words instead of the whole meaning of the phrase. You've got to try to use slang more casually."

"What purpose does it actually serve?"

LaForge leaned toward him and delicately said, "It makes you approachable. Give it a swing."

As his lips silently traced that last word, a perplexed expression overtook Data's features. Unlike the times when he worked too hard at his expressions and ended up looking like a vaudeville clown, these moments made him look much more human than any he could force, these moments when unexpected emotion simply popped up on his face. "Swing . . . a child's toy, a sweeping maneuver—oh! An effort. A try. Yes, swing. I'll swing. Computer, show me all available dictionary and dialect banks on Earth slang, rapid feed."

The computer came to life on the panel before him and its soft feminine voice, in a delivery much more at ease than Data's own, asked, *"What era's slang would you like, and what language?"*

Geordi LaForge settled back into his lounge and mumbled, "I always thought you needed a hobby."

Abruptly there was a sound on the quarterdeck, something akin to a growl, but as quickly it was gone and replaced by the resonant bass of Lieutenant Worf as he stared at his monitor.

"Not possible!"

Captain Picard drew his attention away from the blue giant and approached his own command chair, behind which the horseshoe rail arched upward and across the tactical console. Past that, Worf stood with his back to the bridge, staring at his status monitor as though his dissatisfaction could bore right through it. Of course, with a Klingon, that might very well be the case.

Pulling up the automatic extra measure of calmness he found himself using with Worf, Picard urged, "Lieutenant? Something?"

"I'm not sure I saw it," the Klingon spat.

But Security Chief Tasha Yar twisted her toned body without taking her hands off her tactical console and told him, "I saw it too."

"Saw what?" Picard demanded.

"An energy pulse, Captain." The girl pushed back a lock of her boy-cropped blond hair. "A huge one. Across the entire solar system."

Only one step carried Worf all the way forward to Tasha's side. "Very sharp and powerful, sir, a refractive scan. Like an instant sensor sweep."

"It was too quick-fire for sensors," Tasha shot back.

"Then what?" Worf boomed. "There's no trace of it now."

Picard used their argument to cloak his movement up the ramp to tactical, where he peered over the controls. There was nothing showing. "Could it have been an aberration? Feedback from our experiments?"

"Sir, it came from outside the solar system," Tasha said, her throat tightening around her voice as it always did when she let herself get excited.

"Track it."

"Nothing left to track," Worf said coarsely.

Picard raised his head. "Don't use that tone with me, Lieutenant. There is no crisis yet."

Worf's big brown face didn't look in the least apologetic, given a particularly animalistic texture by the riblike cranium of his Klinzhai racial background, the strain which had emerged dominant during the last Klingon purge. He was imposing; in fact, he was downright terrifying, because the other crew members could always see that controlling himself was plain work for him and someday he just might lose the fight.

"Sorry, sir," he rumbled. "It was there during our last phaser burst, then it was gone." He placed his big hands on the tactical board and burned a glare through the forward screen. "I don't like it. It's like being watched."

Picard stood back on his heels for a contemplative moment, his handsome eyes wedging. "Could be another vessel. Let's make sure they don't miss us. Saying hello is part of our job. Put sensors on wide scan. Lieutenant Data, you handle broadcast of standard hailing frequency with greetings in all interstellar languages and codes as well as automatic universal translation."

"I'm hopping to it."

"Lieutenant LaForge, take us out of orbit. Disband further testing of the gas giant until we ascertain the trim of the solar system."

"Aye, sir. Disengaging orbital condition." LaForge pressed his fingers to the signal controls on the beautiful board at wrist level and just that easily drew the massive starship out of the gas giant's gravitational envelope. During that maneuver, while the ship was safely under control of the navigational computer, he took a moment to glance left to Data.

When he looked at the other crew members, he saw the layerings of infrared that he could intensify as needed, he saw blood running through arteries, arterioles, capillaries, and so on, but he saw them better than a computer would because his brain acted

28

as interpreter and he was more intuitive than any computer. Over that infrared image, like a nylon stocking drawn over a mannequin, he saw skin and a hazy shine of fine skin hairs. The mannequin appeared to be lighted from within, and had a slight glow.

But Data—Data was a work of art. Geordi alone could see the exotic materials, brilliantly blended, the different levels of heat and coolness, the different densities where metal met synthetic, where synthetic met organism, and where all meshed. He saw the density of Data's body, and all the million tiny electrical impulses that kept him working and ran like swarms of insects through his body when he worked a little harder or concentrated a little more or called up more strength. But it wasn't like looking at the computer stations before them or the mechanism behind the wall at the coffee/food dispenser. Not at all. Those were machines.

LaForge sometimes got the feeling that people forgot he could hear too. He had listened to Riker's tone just before the first officer left the bridge. He had heard the flutter in Data's voice when he mentioned that Riker wasn't too pleased with him. Data was mechanical, but to Geordi LaForge he was no machine.

Geordi allowed himself an indulgent gaze at Data's face as the android glowed with concentration. He saw the structure of synthetic facial bone, tiny blood-fed fibrous ligaments attached to impulse interpreters, stockinged by the cool involucrum that was his skin. Geordi saw a handsome face, unafraid of its own features, a face that could show many feelings, from courage to calculation, confusion to compassion, to

29

those sensitive enough to see its minute changes. And Data's eyes, no matter their brimstone cast, were unfailingly gentle.

Geordi shook his head and uttered, "Machine, my ass."

Picard looked up. "Lieutenant?"

"Secure distance, sir."

"Speak up, then."

"Yes, sir."

The door's buzzer sounded clearly, but Troi didn't respond to it. Once again lights played across her face, but not the lights of yellow alert. She sat at her private desk, watching a holograph simulate the motion of a patch of blue ocean water. At the ends of the foot-wide holograph, the ocean faded and became table. Dead center on the patch of churning water was a three-dimensional image of an old military vessel. It was wedge-shaped, piled high with steel-gray metal mountings that made no sense to her. On the screen at her wrist came the simple description: *First iron screw steamship, S.S.* Great Britain.

She frowned and tapped the continue button. The 3-D image sucked in on itself as though imploded, twisted around a little, and reanimated into something utterly different, something bigger, flatter, clunkier, chugging across her table. The dark band of screen beneath it said: *Tanker,* Edmund Fitzgerald, *lost with all hands, Lake Superior, Michigan, United States, Earth 1975.*

Troi hit the button almost angrily. Those weren't right. They weren't right. A new image came almost instantly, a big black, white, and red ship, very elegant and slim this time, obviously meant to carry people. People—that was right. She looked at the display band. *Luxury liner* Queen Elizabeth II, *Cunard Line, Earth.*

No . . . no . . . Troi's mulberry-tinted lips lost their perfect shape. No. Her finger moved again.

H.M.S. Dreadnought, *battleship, Great Britain, Earth, 1906.*

She leaned forward now as she recognized some element—the color, the demeanor of this ship . . . closer. She tapped the button again, this time saying, "This type of vessel."

"This is a naval defense/offense vessel which would be used during and after World War One," the computer courteously told her.

"Continue."

The holograph winked, and she was gazing at another ship of the same kind, but from a different angle as it crashed through the little round patch of sea. Its slate-gray bow rose and fell in the sea. The computer image turned as though Troi were circling it in an aircraft, to give her a complete look at it from all angles. It had a crude kind of grace about it, certainly a strength, but it had no lights at all, no colors like the starship's sparkling yellow and white lights, its glowing reds, its vibrant electrical blues.

Aegis cruiser, built by SYSCON for the U.S. Navy, Earth, 1988.

The door buzzed again.

"Oh—yes; come in."

She let the old-style ship pierce its way through the tiny sea in front of her as she looked up to see Will Riker stride in. As soon as the door opened, his eyes were already locked with hers. How long had he been waiting out there? She faintly remembered now that the buzzer had sounded once before.

"I was worried about you," he said. He settled into

31

the other chair and leaned one elbow on the desk just short of the holograph. The bulky cruiser splashed toward him, and yet stayed right where it was. "I didn't know you were a history buff." He nodded at the Aegis. "That's nice."

Troi tilted her dark head. "I've never seen anything like this before."

So that was the end of the easy transition, Riker realized. Something in her tone told him her statement was more significant than it pretended to be.

"What happened?" he asked, no longer protecting her from her own behavior on the bridge.

She gave him an uncharacteristic shrug with one shoulder and shook her head, a self-conscious smile tugging at her lips. "Did you see what I did? I'm so embarrassed. I've never mistaken a dream for reality before. I must really have looked funny. Did anyone laugh?"

"Laugh?" Riker said saucily. "You should've seen them. Captain Picard had to be wheeled off the bridge, Worf was—"

"Oh, you!" She swatted his nearest knee and chuckled at herself again.

"I wouldn't worry about it," Riker told her, lounging his big frame back in the chair. "Everybody does something like that sooner or later. The more stoic you are, the worse the goof-up seems."

"Am I stoic?" she asked, the smile broadening again.

"I don't know, Counselor," he said. "I don't remember the last time I looked at you and only saw the professional. I've got more flowery things to remember about you."

Troi pursed her lips, leaned forward, ignoring the holograph of the ship as it continued its nonvoyage, and propped her chin on one hand. "Tell me, Bill. Make me feel better."

"No fair. Figure it out for yourself. You of all people could do it."

Settling back, she said, "That's not very comforting for a person who just dashed onto the bridge in a frenzy."

Will Riker's bright eyes flashed before her impishly. "You want comfort? How's this? I was assigned as second officer on a destroyer right after my promotion to lieutenant commander—about a thousand years ago, if memory serves. I got my assignment at Starbase Eighteen, and keyed the coordinates to the new ship into the transporter, stepped on the pad, and boom, there I was. I strutted around being the almighty second officer, puffed up just like a soufflé, and we were ten hours out of spacedock before I figured out I had beamed myself onto the wrong departing ship."

"Oh, Bill! Oh, no . . ."

"And the ship I'd landed on wasn't a destroyer, either. It was the U.S.S. *Yorktown*—an Excelsior-class starship, heading out on a two-year mission. Her captain made Picard seem like Francis of Assisi. They'd already been delayed four days by diplomatic entanglements, and here's Second Officer Riker having to report to the *real* second officer."

Her hand was clapped over her mouth by now, and she parted her fingers enough to burble, "What did they do?"

He spread his hands. "What could they do? They turned the whole ship around, this huge ship, and they came all the way back through space to rendezvous with the destroyer I was supposed to be on. So there was the destroyer, having to meet a starship just to pick up its second officer, who was supposed to have reported in ten hours before."

"Oh, dear . . ."

"So quit complaining."

"Is that a true story? You're not making it up to make me feel better?"

"Make it up? Deanna, nobody sane could make up anything that punishing. It's like a practical joke somebody plays on a bridegroom on his wedding night, except I did it to myself." Shaking his head musingly, he added, "I could never quite look at a transporter platform the same way again. I always wonder if I'm going to end up beaming into some-body's shower by mistake. And the worst was yet to come. Two years later, I really was assigned as *Yorktown*'s second officer and I had to report to that captain *again!*"

She giggled, bringing an unlikely girlishness to her demeanor. "Did he remember?"

"Remember? First thing he asked was if I'd been hiding in the hold all this time."

Their laughter entwined and filled the dim room, chasing away the discomfort.

As Riker watched her custodially, he noticed she had picked up on his feelings and was actually doing the blushing for him. At first he was tempted to draw back within himself, but he knew it didn't matter. With Deanna, holding back showed up like a beacon. There was no point. He wished he could be this relaxed with the other members of the crew.

They sat together, grinning at each other, warm in their mutual memories and the privacy of a relation-ship and a past they had allowed no one else on board to see. It was like starting fresh, with a whole new life, with their attraction to each other getting a second chance, because no one else knew. No one else on the entire ship *knew*.

Breaking his gaze at her gentle face, Riker looked at the unlikely holograph beside him and asked, "You had a nightmare?"

Her expression made his smile fall away. He forced himself not to say more, to give her a chance to answer in her own time, while he indulged in the presence of her troubled onyx eyes.

"A nightmare," she murmured. "But in this nightmare I could feel the emotions of the strangers in it. It was nothing I recognize . . . sharp images of things I know nothing about. Names I've never heard."

Riker perked up. "What names?"

She drew the memory up and forced herself to speak. "There was Vasska, Arkady, Gork . . . Gorsha . . . I don't know those sounds. And I don't understand why I would hear names. I can't do that. I can only read some emotions. I've never been able to draw complete communication."

He inched a little closer. "But you're Betazoid. What's so surprising if you can—"

"I *can't*. I never could," she insisted, wondering if she could make him comprehend. "You don't understand what it means to communicate with a silent mind. You don't know the trouble, the discomfort of dealing with races that can't shield their thoughts. It's as if a sighted person suddenly enters a world of chaotic lights and colors, or a hearing person suddenly comes into a place that was nothing but uncontrolled noises. The light would be blinding, the din maddening . . . I've worked hard to separate my own thoughts from those of others, Bill, and I've done well at it. You can see why it disturbs me that I'm experiencing something so unfamiliar."

"Deanna, it was a dream," he told her soothingly, cupping her hand under his.

Her voice dropped to a whisper. "But it wasn't," she insisted. "At least . . . not entirely."

He believed her. Deanna Troi was the quintessence of professionalism and not given to the flights of personality often displayed by her Betazoid race. Without a pause he asked, "Have you asked the computer to trace the names?"

Troi lounged back in her chair, finally relaxing. "Computer off."

The holograph gave an electrical snap, sucked down into a tiny core of light like a balloon suddenly losing all its air, and winked out.

"Have you?" he prodded.

"I suppose I'll have to."

"Why do you say it that way?"

"I don't like to give in to dreams."

Riker gazed at her, dubious.

Without giving him time to formulate a response to that, she asked, "Bill, what do you think? Do you think I might utilize my talents better in some other way?"

"You don't mean leave the ship, do you? You aren't thinking about that."

"Perhaps," she said, "if that's how I can best serve the Federation."

Desperation struck him. As much as he had—yes—avoided her, as afraid as he was that their past liaison would cloud his effectiveness as first officer, the prospect of her vanishing from his life suddenly cut him like a blade. "Don't you like it here?" he asked, careful of his tone. "Don't you like starship duty?"

"Oh, I like it very much," she said. "Oh, yes, very much. But there are times . . . can you imagine what it's like to stand on the bridge and realize I have nothing to do?"

With another shake of his head, Riker tapped a finger on the table and blurted, "Can I imagine it? I don't have to. It's the legacy of first officers the universe across. If you look up *first officer* in the marine dictionary, it says 'do not open till crisis.' Listen, it takes time for a new position to evolve. When we actually turn to exploratory missions, I think you'll find yourself up to your chin in work. Keeping us sane in deep space—that's hardly nothing. A ship's psychologist is second only to the chief surgeon on deep-space missions."

She smiled softly at his sincere effort, and murmured, "Where does that put the ship's telepath?"

To this, Riker had no ready answer.

Troi sensed his concern and forced up a partial smile to ease his worry. She fell into his wide blue eyes as she had so long ago, and crashed through them just as the holographic cruiser crashed through its patch of blue sea. How could she make him understand? Could any human understand how uneasy she was, all the time? She knew people were uncomfortable around her because they thought of her as a kind of voyeur, always peeking through the keyholes of their thoughts. Mind slut, some called her. Many avoided her, so she had always tried to be more businesslike and stoic about her extremely unbusinesslike talent—and even that practice had backfired.

Cold, they called her. An *unfeeling* mind slut.

How could she tell him that a crowded corridor was an empty place for Deanna Troi? Barren and lonely. She made such an effort to hide inside herself that she had become insulated from everything but their eyes, accused of a crime she refused to commit. Among her own people she could no longer go unrestrained; having built her discipline almost obsessively, she could no longer drop it for the short times she spent among Betazoids. Thus lost in both communities, misinterpreted by each as too aloof, she had become a woman of feelings who walked forever alone.

Even now she hid those truths from William Riker and his gentle waves of concern.

She swallowed imperceptibly and parted her lips. "Now I ask you—what's the matter? What disturbs you?" She could both sense and see him weighing whether or not to tell her what he was thinking, then almost immediately he changed his mind.

"I don't like to see you experiencing hurts that aren't your own," he admitted. "It doesn't seem fair."

"It's my nature," Troi told him. "My heritage from my mother's people. It's the nature of telepathy. Oh, I could shut my mind, become more alone, as you are, but I've found my way to be useful. I'm lucky, you see," she said, forcing a smile. "I can experience the emotions yet remain objective about them."

He thought of the strange ship that had just clicked out of being on the table beside them and shrugged. "I guess I never thought about it that way."

She pulled her hand from under his, then put it on top of his and pressed down gently. "There is more than hurt to be felt, you know. I can also feel love."

Riker allowed himself a sentimental smile. For an isolated moment they shared something that neither was completely sure still existed between them anymore. The magnetism was undeniable, but at the same instant it pierced him with its own dangers.

"I can't stay," he said. "I have to go back up there and act indispensable."

"I know."

He crooked his forefinger under her chin. "Try to relax. We all have that kind of dream sometimes. I just wanted to be sure you were all right."

Troi smiled warmly. "I'm all right."

He squeezed her hand, somehow feeling he hadn't quite accomplished what he came in here for. Well, no point dragging it out to the maudlin. Stepping toward the door, he made what he thought was a clumsy exit.

The door brushed open, then closed automatically behind him, leaving him alone in the corridor as he took a stride or two toward the bridge turbolift—

And braked hard.

There was someone in front of him. He'd sworn the corridor was empty an instant ago. The air was chilled, heavy.

The man was big, almost as big as Riker. And maybe fifteen years older. His eyes were ready for Riker's, and didn't flicker away, but remained steadily focused. A wave of silver was the only inconsistency in his thick dark hair, and there was a uniform cap tucked under his arm. Yes—he was wearing a uniform, a dark blue uniform of some kind.

Riker vaguely recognized the style, but it was almost a "racial" kind of memory rather than something from his own experience.

The man's pale lips separated without moisture. His face worked as though to speak, but there was an invisible wall between them. There was no sound, no sensation of warmth—in fact there was now a distinct chill in the corridor.

The large man, standing straight and proper, lifted a hand toward Riker, beckoning. Or perhaps asking—a gesture of entreaty—but then his handsome face crumpled, his brow knitting tightly, brackets of frustration forming on either side of his mouth.

Riker was as a man chained during those moments. He might have believed anything when the other man's form slowly turned gauzy, thinned, and disappeared.

Chapter Three

"CAPTAIN, I'M PICKING UP an energy blip. . . ."

Tasha Yar caught back her voice and grimaced at her readout board, confused. A flop of bangs had come back over her eyes as though to insist some part of her would always rebel against the discipline. Her delicate Lithuanian complexion blotched slightly around her cheekbones as she willed the instruments to start giving her sensible information, especially when Captain Picard appeared at her side and looked down at those same instruments.

"It's gone now," she told him bitterly. "How can that be? Worf, do you have anything?"

"Nothing," the Klingon thundered, redoubling her impatience. "I *don't* like it."

"Steady, both of you," Picard said. The readings looked absolutely normal. These two hotheads were dependable, but the doubting Thomas side of him wished he himself or Data or LaForge had also happened to see this flicker of energy Worf and Yar claimed had been there.

Suddenly Yar struck her board with the heels of her hands and shouted, "There it is again! But it's inside the ship!" She slammed the intercom without consulting Picard. "Security to Deck Twelve, Section A-three!"

"Inside?" Picard stepped closer. "Are you sure?"

"It's gone again!"

"Check your instruments for malfunction. Worf, do the same with long-range sensors."

Yar took a deep breath. "Aye, sir."

"Checking," Worf said, much less embarrassed than Yar was.

Picard straightened. "And call Mr. Riker to the bridge."

Troi continued to gaze thoughtfully at the empty space where the holograph ships had been chugging across her table. Her gaze was unfocused, contemplative, and though she had tried to raise her hand several times to press the Revive and Continue point on her computer board, something stopped her every time. Nor could she make herself ask the computer to continue. Continue giving in.

A dream. But not one formed within her own mind, of that much she was becoming certain.

The door opened again, this time without the polite buzzer, and Riker strode back in. Troi gained almost instant control over her troubled expression.

Teasing him with her eyes, she asked, "Have you been hiding in the hold all this time?"

"How much power are you feeding into that unit?" Riker asked her.

She blinked. "Pardon me?"

He stopped, his thigh just brushing the edge of the table. "Your holographs. They're bleeding out."

She started to respond, but was cut off by the intercom.

"Commander Riker, your presence is requested on the bridge. Report to the bridge, please."

Riker touched his insignia com. "Riker. I'll be right there."

He brought his attention back to Troi. "Your history lesson. It's bleeding out into the corridor."

Her lips touched and parted as she tried to understand what he was saying and to find the right answer. His expression, his tone somehow made her think there should be an answer and she hated to make him feel as silly as his statement sounded—but what was he talking about?

Finally she steadied herself and coolly said, "But that's not possible."

Riker shifted to his other foot. "Of course it is. You should have maintenance check the energy intake on this thing."

Working to avoid the inevitable, Troi tried not to feel responsible. "No," she said, "it can't be. Don't you remember? I turned it off before you left. I haven't turned it back on."

Without really changing very much, Riker's federal-blue eyes took on a perplexed hardness that wasn't directed toward her at all, but toward a sudden mystery. His mouth tightened over the cleft chin so slightly that she might have missed it had she not been watching for changes.

Troi knotted her hands on her lap and resisted the urge to touch him. Caught by the ominous perception in his eyes, she added, "Completely cold . . ."

"This is crazy," Yar complained. She flattened her tiny mouth into a hard ribbon and forced herself to report in a more correct manner to her waiting captain. "Security reports no unusual activity on

43

Deck Twelve at all, Captain. My instruments are in perfect working order. I don't understand this."

On the forward bridge, Captain Picard had his back to Conn and Ops and didn't see Data start to open his mouth to add his two bits, or see LaForge gesture at the android to keep quiet. Everyone else saw the motion and understood its prudence, especially when Picard raised his voice and roared, "That's quite enough of this waffling about. Next time the glitch appears, I want the computers on this vessel ready to record it. We've got the most advanced technology available to the Federation incorporated into the memory core and active matrices of this vessel, and you people are still relying on intuition and your own eyes. Now, snap to and let the ship do its job."

His tone indisputably said that he didn't mean they should let the ship do their jobs *for* them, but that they should be doing their jobs better, more completely meshing with the systems beneath their hands. Picard was simply the kind of commanding officer who didn't like to have anything out of line.

He swung around, glaring at the main viewer as though he were looking for something and couldn't find it, as though he could coerce an answer out of the darkness of space, and mused, "Too damned young."

The port turbolift came open and Riker stepped out, escorting Troi by the elbow. Odd . . . she still looked unprepared to come to the bridge, her hair still down, her casual short uniform on instead of the usual one-piece she had taken to wearing most often and the two of them stood together before Picard, their faces troubled.

"Captain," Riker asked, "may we have a word with you, sir?"

* * *

Troi's distress was no longer obvious. It had been carefully cloaked by her professionalism once again, and only those who knew her very well could tell that her hands were held a little too tightly against her lap as she sat in her lounge in the command area and told them her story of dreams. And there was only one person here who knew her that well.

Will Riker watched her, forcing himself not to interrupt, not to say anything after he too had finished describing the incident in the corridor, no matter how silly it sounded. He simply stood by, as the others focused on Troi. It hadn't been easy for her, telling the captain that she had a dream that wouldn't go away, and for Riker describing that person—or whatever he was—in the corridor had been just as strenuous. Only Captain Picard's studious attention to their silly stories told them that he'd seen enough in the galaxy not to dismiss such things as silly.

The captain stood over Troi now, absorbing the whole idea of her dream with what Riker had told him about. Earth ships, humans in uniform—somewhere there was a common denominator. He meant to find it.

"Can you describe your perceptions more specifically, Counselor?"

Troi tipped her pretty head. "I'll try to verbalize them, Captain, but I must advise you these are imprecise explanations. Telepathic impressions are sometimes too vague for interpretation."

"Do your best."

She nodded once. "My mind describes to me several different historical periods, not necessarily all of Earth, though the clearest ones seem to be human or humanoid. Perhaps that's simply because of my partly human heritage—I can't say. Some, though . . . some

45

are so alien that I don't know any words to describe what I've seen."

"Alien, you say?"

"Yes, very obviously so. But the ship I envisioned was definitely of Earth."

"Believe me, we'll get to that in a moment. Go on."

She paused, but not for long. Picard wasn't a man she cared to keep waiting. "There's a haze of apprehension . . . urgency . . . resistance. But no violent intent."

"You can't be sure of that!" Tasha interrupted from the afterdeck with her usual serenity. She caught Riker's eyes, and his disapproval, but she plugged on. "I mean . . . if they're alien sensations, then Deanna could be misinterpreting them completely. To their home beings, those impressions might be hostile, aggressive, and dangerous."

"You're too suspicious, Tasha," Riker said defensively.

"I'm doing my job," she retaliated. Not so much as a glimmer of regret marred her conviction. She knew perfectly well she was volatile—it was an advantage. Unlike Worf, who constantly worked to control his Klingon explosiveness, Tasha would stand up for the worth of her own. Riker saw that in her eyes as he looked back at her now, in the underlying ferocity beneath her face, and indeed it caused him to back down. Not until he'd been silent for several seconds did he realize how completely she had gotten her point across.

Troi picked up on the tension immediately, though she needn't have been telepathic for that. It chewed at her; her job was to keep watch over the emotions and mental states of the starship complement, to guide them through tensions and head off the truly harmful

46

contretemps that came and went in this kind of extended separation. How awful to be the cause of this . . . how terrible.

She tipped one hand up as it leaned against her thigh and said, "No . . . Tasha's right. Because though there's no perception of aggressive intent," she said, pausing then to say the one thing that truly frightened her, "doesn't change the fact that I'm receiving glimpses of violent destruction."

Not giving those ominous statements any chance to take hold on the imaginations of the bridge crew, Picard lowered into his command chair beside her, hoping to put her and everyone at ease. He was aware of the effect these little disturbances were having on the crew, especially when they saw Deanna Troi's usual poise inexplicably shattered. "Can you focus on that? Are we in danger?"

"That's what confuses me, sir," she said steadily. "While I see images of destruction, there seems to be no intent behind it, even though it's definitely the product of a mind and not natural phenomena. As I said, no violent intent."

"That's reassuring, at least."

"But, sir, you don't understand." She stopped him from rising with a light touch on his forearm. "I shouldn't be getting concrete images at all. It's simply not among my abilities to receive visions and forms. As such," she added reluctantly, "I'm not certain you should trust my judgment."

A soothing smile appeared on Picard's princely features. "I trust your interpretation, Deanna."

"But she's a telepath," Dr. Crusher pointed out. Until now the doctor had been a silent observer, fascinated both personally and professionally by Deanna Troi's story of unwelcome impressions and unfocused dreams, and as her voice cut through the distinct tension, it added a touch of common sense they needed right now. "She's not a psychic. There's an important distinction, you realize."

"Yes, that's true," Troi said, looking at her gratefully. "That's what I mean. The difference between what I can do and what I'm somehow being forced to do."

Piecing it all together and still getting a choppy mosaic at best, Picard nodded. "Tell me what you're feeling," he said, "in one word."

She didn't answer immediately. Several long and anxious minutes went by as she selected and discarded a number of possibilities. Those around her watched as each crossed her face, each perplexing her with its inadequacy.

Then she found it. Or the one that came closest. For the first time in all those minutes of searching, Troi fixed her gaze on Jean-Luc Picard and worked her lips around a word.

"Misery."

When she spoke, the misery shone in her eyes. She was caught in empathy for that instant, empathy for the beings whose impressions she was being given, or being forced to receive. It was as though she were asking, imploring, for help. After a pause she drew a breath and sighed, her lovely brows drawn tight as she realized the full impact of that word was somewhat lost on them. After all, they weren't feeling it.

Picard saw the change in her face. "Misery can be many things, Counselor," he said to her.

She nodded. "Yes," she agreed. "Clinically I would call it a kind of dysphoria. But I'd be inaccurate to say there was no physical suffering. Yet I don't perceive a sense of body. It's quite confusing, sir. I'm sorry."

"Permission to stop saying that, Counselor," Picard

48

offered. He placed his hands on his knees and stood up. "Now, let's see about these ships." He led the whole crowd up to the extra-large monitors at the aft science station, where Worf was moving aside to let everyone curve around his post. The captain spoke up immediately. "Computer, show me various military vessels from—when did you say?"

Troi stepped forward, somehow managing to stay close to Riker, to gather strength from his presence. "The most familiar one was late nineteen-eighties, Captain. An Aegis cruiser, according to records."

"Computer, engage as specified."

On the screen, almost instantly, a 2-D image of the Aegis appeared.

Picard asked, "Is this the right ship?"

"Oh, no, sir. Simply the right . . . idea. The right age."

"Computer, expound upon this index."

The Aegis was replaced by a different vessel, then another, and another, while the balmy female voice ticked off descriptions.

"*Destroyer, United States Navy . . . PT boat, United States Navy . . . computer support vessel, Royal Canadian Maritime Command . . . light amphibious transport, United States Navy . . . nuclear submarine, Navy of the Union of Soviet Socialist Republics . . . Invincible-class V/STOL carrier, Royal Navy of Great Britain . . . CV-type conventional-power aircraft carrier, United States—*"

"Stop!"

Troi drew back from her own outburst, but continued to point at the screen. "This is very close."

"Close, but . . ." Picard prodded.

"But . . . I don't know. I know very little about surface vessels."

"Computer, specify this vessel."

"*U.S.S.* Forrestal, *CV-59, commissioned October 1955, United States Navy.*"

"Very well, continue."

Another ship popped on the screen, looking much the same to the untrained eyes watching it now. "*CVN-type nuclear-powered full-deck aircraft carrier—*"

"Yes!" Troi jolted. "Yes, this!" She pressed a hand tightly over her mouth, profoundly moved by what she saw.

Picard remained subdued, capping her reaction with his own implacability. "Computer, specify."

"*U.S.S.* George Washington, CVN-73, *Enterprise-class aircraft carrier, commissioned January 1992, United States Navy.*"

Troi pulled her hand from her mouth. "This is extremely familiar to me."

A tangible discomfort blanketed the bridge. All eyes flickered, then settled on her. Of course, she felt it without looking. Self-consciously she corrected, "Rather, to the impressions I've been channeling."

"Yes," Picard murmured, glancing at Riker over Troi's dark head, "of course. You said something about names."

Troi stared at the aircraft carrier as if she feared it might disappear like all the other images. "Vasska was one. Arkady . . . and Gor . . . Gorsha—no, it's not right, not complete."

"Data, you up here, please."

Caught by surprise, Data all but hurtled to them from the lower deck, taking the seat at the science station as though he'd been deeply stung by their not asking for his help earlier. Riker moved aside a bit farther than necessary, giving in to a twinge of prejudice, but he forced himself to let it pass. Data *was* the qualified one. An instrument running an instrument.

Evidently Data was ready to guide the search through *Enterprise*'s vast memory core, focusing on the specific type of aircraft carrier and the names Troi had spoken; he didn't request that she repeat them. His fingers nearly tangled in his haste to participate and be useful amid all this talk of feelings and senses and memories.

If there was disappointment, he didn't allow it to show on his face.

"Sir," he began, "I regret this may take some time. I'll have to operate by a process of elimination. May I suggest you allow me to notify you once I pull it off."

If that was his polite way of asking them not to hang over his shoulder the whole time, it worked.

"Very well." Picard motioned the little crowd away and leaned toward Riker. "What was it he said?"

"Sir—" Tasha raised her hand in a brief gesture, and quickly drew it down when Picard turned. "I'm Lithuanian."

Picard swallowed an impulse to congratulate her and merely asked, "And?"

"And I recognize those names. They're Russian."

"Ah! Very good, Lieutenant. Mr. Data, make use of that."

"You bet," Data clipped, and didn't see Picard's double-take as he turned to his station.

"Captain . . ." Troi turned abruptly. "If I may, I'd like to return to my quarters. Perhaps I can clear my mind. Focus in on these impressions, or let them focus in on me."

Picard noticed that Data was still watching him, as though the decisions hinged upon one another—computer search and mind hunt. "That's sound strat-

51

egy," he told her, "since we don't seem to be able to zero in on it any quicker with our hardware. I want you to be careful, however. And nothing is too small to report."

"Yes, sir," she murmured, and as she pivoted toward the turbolift she caught Riker's concerned gaze. "I promise."

The bridge was wide, the walk to the turbolift uncomfortably long as Troi deliberately kept herself from showing anxiety. Riker's own legs tensed; he empathized with her every stride, wished he were going with her, that he could somehow help. Seemed like lately all he and Deanna could be to each other was a mutual distraction . . .

"She's a very competent broad," Data offered.

So innocuous. So deadpan . . .

Riker stopped breathing. Picard glowered. LaForge and Worf both stiffened in place, Tasha flushed, Bev Crusher looked away.

Troi was barely reaching the turbolift. Had she heard?

Data sat in a pool of perpetual good intentions, his chair swiveled ever so slightly toward the rest of them, and as all eyes crawled to him with that collective reprimand his expression became confused. He glanced from each to the others. "Chick? Dish?"

The turbolift doors brushed open. A preoccupied ship's counselor stepped in.

"Bird? Bun? Babe? Skirt? Fox?"

"Data!" chorused Picard, Riker, and Yar, just as the lift doors closed.

The android flinched, and closed his mouth in an almost pouting manner. His gold-leaf face took on a sudden innocence; he looked vulnerable. Under their scolding eyes, he retreated once again to his memory search through the starship's deep mainframe, and Picard noticed a definite shift of Data's shoulders when attention fell away from him.

"Stations, everyone," Picard said casually, setting the mood for the bridge to relax until there was a reason not to. The tension didn't entirely dissolve, but each officer made a laudable effort not to contribute to its increase.

From one side Picard accepted a graceful nod from his ship's chief surgeon. He recognized the decidedly medical gesture—Crusher wasn't going to offer an opinion—not yet. Not until all the cards were on the table. Not about Troi's agitated condition, not about these unclinical occurrences, not about anything.

"I'll be in sickbay, Captain," she said roundly, "whenever you need me."

Picard nodded an acknowledgment, warmed beyond logic by her words, and the past once again moved between them, the mutuality of sadness and vision that had made them acquaintances long ago yet had also stood in the way of their ever becoming close. He watched with a twinge of regret as Crusher pivoted and left the bridge.

Burying his feelings, Picard approached Riker from so practiced an angle that Riker didn't notice him until he spoke. "Mr. Riker."

"Oh—Captain . . . aye, sir? What can I do for you?"

"Better ask what you can do for yourself. Tell me again what you saw in the corridor."

Riker shifted uneasily, unhappy with the idea that he'd been "seeing things." He still held a heavy rock in his stomach, his brows still tightened over his eyes no matter how he tried to relax his face. "I wish I knew. It looked as solid to me as you do now—*he* did, rather.

When it faded, I assumed it was overbleed from Troi's holographs. But it wasn't. And I wasn't imagining it."

"How can you be sure of that?"

"Because it didn't do what I would've expected it to do. I think my imagination would make something act as I might expect it to, but this . . . man . . . reached out to me with the strangest expression. It's difficult, sir. I'd like to be more concrete—"

"Captain," Data abruptly called from above, whirling in his chair. "I have it, sir."

"Hi, Mom."

Wesley Crusher raised his head as his mother strode into their quarters off the main sickbay. His face had the typical porcelain smoothness of sixteen-year-old skin, his hair combed a little too neatly, his clothing pin-straight on his skinny frame. He'd taken to looking more like that since the captain made him acting ensign. It seemed to Beverly Crusher that Wesley was keeping himself perfectly groomed just so he wouldn't look out of place among the uniformed personnel on the bridge, and like any sixteen-year-old he carried it to extremes.

"Wes," she began, not in greeting. "I need you to do something for me."

He gladly turned away from his study tapes. "Sure, Mom. What?"

"Are you scheduled to go onto the bridge today?"

"Me? Well, not exactly. Mr. Data asked me to help him catalog some physics theories sometime this week, and I was going to use that as an excuse to go up there later—"

"Can you do that now?"

Wesley got to his feet, which made him suddenly

as tall as his tall mother. "Really? I mean, how come?"

"Baby-sit the bridge for me."

Wesley's smooth face fractured. "Huh?"

"I want you to keep an eye on things for me. There's something going on, and nobody's sure what. It's affecting Deanna Troi, and if I can't have her expertise to call upon, then I want to at least keep a jump on conditions."

Wesley grimaced. "Mom," he began, "I don't have a clue what you're talking about."

Dr. Crusher grinned sadly at him. "Call it medical intuition. Call it anything you want, but just be my spy on the bridge. I can't go up there myself because I've got a lineup of pediatric checkups this afternoon, and besides, I'd be too obvious. Will you do it?"

He shrugged, sure there was a catch somewhere. "Of course I'll do it."

She patted the side of his face as she was given to do once in a while just to remind herself that this bright, lively, *tall* fellow was still the seven-and-a-half-pound infant who hardly ever slept a night through until he was twelve years old. "Thanks, buster. I'll never forget this."

She started toward the lab entrance, but turned when Wesley asked, "Mom, just what is it I'm supposed to be watching for?"

Beverly Crusher didn't slacken her pace as she turned once again in midstride. "Use your imagination."

Riker entered Troi's quarters hesitantly. He knew he was interrupting much sooner than she expected. And there she was—so much like before, so much.

"Back again, Bill," she murmured, and she smiled at him. The dim quarters lit up just a little.

It took him by surprise, as it always did, that "Bill." Very few people called him that, and on this ship, only Troi. Only Deanna. "I'm sorry about this," he said, approaching her, but this time not sitting down. "Believe it or not, Data's already found the file. I didn't want to bug you so soon, but—"

"Don't apologize," she said. "It doesn't really suit you."

His brows went up. "Doesn't it? That's bad."

Troi shrugged. "Depends on the source."

"The source doesn't have the luxury of not knowing how to apologize," he said. "Maybe someday."

"Maybe someday *Captain* Riker. Don't you think?"

"You're digging, Deanna," he accused with a grin. "I'm just so many loose-leaf pages to you, and don't think I don't know it. I'm not ready for captaincy, but I admit—"

"That first officer is an awkward position," she completed fluidly.

Riker laughed and dropped into the nearest chair. "Quit doing that, will you?" At first he lounged back in the chair and casually waved his hand, but time was pressing, and he leaned forward again almost immediately. "I hate to rush you."

"It's all right. I'm anxious for the answer as much as for the peace. Solitude is not that welcome a companion."

Riker paused then, wondering if she could sense his empathy for her, and the inadequacy of his understanding. Ultimately, as he found himself unable to draw away from her steady unshielded gaze, he simply asked, "Why do you stay? What can it do for you to stay among humans? We must drive you crazy."

56

Troi laughed. "Oh, Bill . . . you're such a decisive fellow. Don't you know why I stay?"

"I'm on audio, Counselor. Tell me."

Her smile changed, became more wistful, and she looked down. When she looked up again, her coal eyes sparkled. "I like humans."

Riker grinned. "Do you really?"

"Yes, quite a lot. Better than I like Betazoids. But don't tell anyone." She pursed her lips conspiratorially. "Yes, I like them. Even though I make them uncomfortable, I like them very much. They're so honest, so well-meaning, they have such deep integrity as a species . . . and my human half has given me something few Betazoids possess."

"What's that?"

She squared her shoulders against the back of the chair and said, "Discipline. Self-discipline, I mean. And . . . I believe I possess an intuition Betazoids never had to develop. My mother and her people take everything at face value, and they often think it's a joke to invade the minds of others. I've learned that in the universe nothing can be taken at face value, and I learned that from humans. Do you know that as an alien hybrid, I can actually read a wider range of emotions than full Betazoids? Even though the impressions aren't clear, I can do that. I have many advantages thanks to my human side, and I'm proud of it."

Riker was appreciably silent, surprised by her generosity. He knew how often she must feel alone. He saw the glances that were cast at her as she came into a room or left one. For a long time he'd wondered if his affection for her was indeed affection or just a man's protectiveness toward what he perceives as a woman's weakness. Troi bore an excess of handicaps

57

in her position as ship's counselor, a position that was new to Starfleet, new to the Federation, and still undefined. No one really knew, or at least understood, what her purpose was on the ship. But they all knew she was here to watch them, to evaluate the overall psychological condition of the ship's complement and report to the captain as necessary. A mental guardian —or watchdog, depending on perception. Someday the Federation would be able to define the post of ship's counselor, or people would just get used to the idea, but for now Deanna Troi and the few like her would have to brook the vagueness.

"You impress me," he said spontaneously.

She laughed again. "Don't be too impressed. I cry myself to sleep more often than I'd like to admit."

Her faint Greek accent tapped the words out with the clip of a sparrow's talons hopping across marble. Riker bit his tongue and kept his inadequate reassurances to himself. She didn't need them—at least none he could voice.

"Thank you," she whispered, and he knew he'd failed to keep his feelings to himself. "I'm needed, Bill. I can make a contribution that even full Betazoids could never make. For that privilege, I'll happily pay the price. I'm not sure, though, that this is the place to make that contribution."

Riker clasped his hands and leaned his elbows on his knees, gazed down for a moment, then looked up. "Do you know how guilty you're making me feel?"

Troi flickered her eyes at him, paused, then tossed her head. "As a matter of fact, I do."

Caught off guard, Riker blushed and couldn't keep control of his smile, but she was still smiling too. Damn, she was good at that.

"To the bridge, Number One?" she suggested gently.

He stood up and reached for her hand. "To the bridge, Counselor."

"Go ahead, Mr. Data."

Picard spoke evenly as he stood on Troi's right, Riker on her left, as though their presence at her sides would help protect her from what was to come. She still looked controlled enough, considering she'd gotten no chance whatsoever even to put her head back for a moment and absorb these events. Data punched up the records he'd discovered.

"Sir, I must apologize," Data said. "The search was not as exhaustive as I first estimated. Counselor Troi's perceptions were accurate and all the information came together—"

"Let's hear it, then, Data. Don't dawdle."

"Yes, sir. As you can see on the monitor, this is a full-deck nuclear aircraft carrier from the nineteen-nineties. It was a Soviet Union vessel out on a demonstration run in the Black Sea when it mysteriously disappeared on April twenty-fourth, 1995."

"Disappeared?" Picard rumbled. "Do you have any idea the size of a nuclear-powered aircraft carrier, Commander?"

Though Picard meant the question to be rhetorical, Data had an immediate answer. "Oh, yes, sir. Up to ninety thousand tons with a personnel complement five times that of our starship."

The captain suddenly felt silly for having asked. "All right, go on. What was this ship called?"

Even Data was aware of Deanna Troi as he quietly responded, "The *Gorshkov.*"

Troi's eyes drifted closed. She steadied herself within the sounds of that word, then opened her eyes again and kept tight rein on the battery of emotions—even the grief.

"Go on, Data," Picard urged.

"Her captain was Arkady Reykov. He had a long, rocky political history before leaving that arena for the naval command. His disapproval of the Soviet system had caused him some discomfort, but his skill as a naval officer evidently overshadowed that. Such experience was at a premium in the U.S.S.R. in those days, so he was allowed to continue."

Riker listened to the simplified description of a twisted international skein, all the tugs and pulls of that volatile period, and couldn't help wondering what Reykov would have felt if he'd known the future. If he'd known he was a cog in the mechanism that led to Earth's 21st-century cataclysms.

"And this Vasska?" Picard prodded.

The response, spoken as tenuously as spider's threads snapping between two leaves, came not from Data, but from Troi.

"Timofei . . ."

They turned to her.

Troi poised herself and completed, "Timofei Vasska. I believe he was first officer."

Uneasily Picard turned to Data for confirmation.

"Yes, that is correct," Data said, just as uneasily.

"Do we have photographs of them?" Riker asked.

Data glanced at him. "Possibly . . . let me run a search. Computer, show any available visuals of Reykov or Vasska."

The computer settled into a long hum, but they didn't have to wait long until its soft feminine voice said, *"Only available visual on specified subjects is a news photograph shortly before launch of the Gorshkov. On screen."*

The screen did its best to focus a grainy photograph of some hundred or more uniformed men, apparently officers of the carrier, all standing together on the big flat deck. The figures were small and crowded together, but on the left two officers stood slightly apart and in front of the others, their faces blurred by the poor quality of the photo.

"There," Riker said, pointing. "Computer, augment the two men in the foreground."

Abruptly two faces appeared, somewhat blurred, yet their strong features and proud expressions quite clear on the screen.

"That's him," Riker murmured, pointing again, this time at the big man on the right. "That's the man I saw in the corridor."

Picard looked deeply into the Soviet officer's strong eyes and murmured, "Reykov . . ."

As he said the name, he realized his reaction was instinct. No one had told him that this was the captain of the *Gorshkov,* yet somehow he knew. Somehow there was a symbiosis, something in the face that he, as a captain, understood.

He turned to Deanna Troi. "Counselor?"

She steadied herself, gazing into the faces on the screen. "Yes," she said quietly. "Reykov and Vasska."

"Data," the captain said, "do you have anything more on these two?"

The android nodded and said, "A little, sir. Timofei Vasska was thirty-five, a longtime exec of Reykov's. Records are incomplete, but a few articles on the incident speculated that the two men were friends and

61

may have plotted together to defect with some new technology."

"What technology?" Riker blurted, not caring if he was out of order. He felt the tightness of Troi's exquisite body beside him and might have done anything at that moment to ease her fear. He felt it so strongly that he might as well have been the telepath.

Data was about to answer when the lift door parted and Wesley Crusher strode onto the bridge, his long legs going like wheel spokes, and he grated to a stop as all eyes struck him. The placid expression dropped away under a slap of surprise—why were they all bundled together around the science station?

He hovered in place for a moment, then waved clumsily and smiled. "Hi, everybody . . ."

The captain straightened. "What are you doing up here at this hour, Mr. Crusher?"

Wesley's mouth dried up. Funny, but it all sounded so easy when his mother talked about this. "I . . . I, uh . . ."

"Well, never mind just now. Get to it and don't interrupt us again."

Self-consciousness roaring through him, Wesley went to the other science monitor and tried to fake work, though he couldn't keep from glancing at what the others were doing.

"On with you, Commander," Picard said sharply.

Data glanced at him and picked up where he'd left off. "*Gorshkov* was carrying a special device, an electromagnetic pulsor which could deflect incoming rocketry and aircraft. The science was new at the time, but the Soviets had pushed through the preliminary testing and gone straight to a fully mounted pulsor on a vessel."

"Fine," Picard barked, "but what *happened* to them?"

"Oh . . . yes. Apparently the ship was . . . pulverized. Unexplainably and utterly."

"My God," the captain breathed.

"There was very little left of the ship," Data said, pausing then, "and absolutely nothing of the crew."

Riker nudged forward. "Nothing? Not a single body anywhere?"

"That's correct. Relations between major powers had been steadily improving since the early nineteen-eighties, but when analysis of the flotsam indicated a cataclysm from outside the ship rather than some problem with the ship's reactors, for instance, the world nearly buckled with mutual accusations."

"I shouldn't wonder," Picard murmured.

"But there was no proof that any nation had blitzed the ship. Add to that the appearance of seven Soviet naval aircraft from the *Gorshkov* which requested landing clearance on a United States carrier a short time later—pardon me, sir, I did not mean to be unspecific. The U.S. ship was the *Roosevelt,* and was hanging out in a nearby sea when the Soviet planes arrived in their airspace some sixty-nine minutes after witnessing the demolition of their own ship. Those pilots swore no missile had come in to cream the *Gorshkov*. Historians had theorized that if it hadn't been for those pilots' testimony so soon after the incident, international relations might have dissolved and World War Three started on the spot. Adding, of course, the blessing that the pilots were Russians themselves and could appeal to the outraged Soviet government without the baggage of racial distrust. Had the witnesses been American or British, we might not be here today. As it was, the issue was a canker between major powers for decades and a real pain for diplomacy."

Picard frowned and murmured, "Mmm . . . thank you, Data." He took Riker by the arm and pulled him to one side, then leaned toward him. "Why's he talking like that?"

Riker blinked, but that blink cleared his eyes not on Picard, not on Data, but on Deanna Troi, who was in turn holding her breath and staring at the helm—at Lieutenant LaForge. Her face was frozen in astonishment as sensation flowed from LaForge to her.

Instinct rippling, Riker shot his glare to the helm.

LaForge was rising from his chair, slowly, like a sleepwalker, his hands pressed flat on his control board. He rose so slowly, in fact, that he was drawing attention to himself.

By the time Riker stepped away from the captain and came to the ramp, everyone else had noticed and was tensely watching, unable to look away. LaForge's mouth hung open and he bent like a man punched in the ribs. His hands remained flat on his console, his legs stiff and slightly bent. Of course the visor hid his eyes, but from the set of his body, his face and lips, Riker could imagine what a seeing man's eyes would show. Shock.

Wesley stepped toward the ramp, his reedy young body all knots. "Geordi?"

Riker snapped his fingers and pointed. "Wesley, stay where you are."

But Wesley's movement had nudged Riker into taking over that movement toward the helm.

LaForge breathed in short gasps. He didn't respond, but stared—or seemed to stare—forward and slightly starboard of his position. He turned his head further

64

in that direction, then twisted partially around to look across the entire starboard side of the bridge.

Riker came around in front of the helm. "Geordi?"

"Sir . . ." LaForge continued turning, resembling more than anything a music-box doll on a spindle.

Before him, all around the starboard curve of the bridge, human forms were milling. Far different from the warm mannequins of the regular crew, these forms were flat, glowing, staticky yellow, striated with jagged impulse lines—but unmistakably human. Not humanoid—*human.* There was something in the way they moved, the way they turned and walked and gestured, that made him certain of it.

"Sir . . . somebody's here . . ."

Riker moved a step closer, his shoulders drawing slightly inward as a shiver assaulted his spine. "But there's no one there."

"They *are* here, sir!"

Riker held out one hand in a calming gesture that didn't work. "All right . . . tell me what wavelengths you're tuned in to right now. Help me, Geordi. I want to see them too."

Geordi moved choppily backward, bumping Riker, bumping his own chair, trying to avoid the unseen entities as he moved toward the science station on the upper bridge, but he never even got close. He bumped the bridge rail with one shoulder and couldn't move anymore, but stayed there trying to convince himself he wasn't going out of his mind.

"Geordi, just describe it," Riker said, glancing at Picard for reassurance. "What are you seeing?"

LaForge trembled. "I don't know . . ."

"Lieutenant," Picard snapped from above him, "give me a report. Analyze what you're seeing and report on it."

65

"Uh . . . they're . . . narrow-band . . . low-resolution pixels at several wavelengths . . . toward the blue in the invisible spectrum . . . but some acoustical waves are giving me a visual of animated pulses—"

Picard's voice was laced with impatience, but also with awe. "Are you telling me you can see what they *sound* like?"

"Yes, sir—more or less. God, they're everywhere!"

"Data," Picard urged.

"I have it, sir. One moment," Data said as he worked furiously on the computer sensory adjustment, then struck a final pressure point and looked up at the viewscreen.

The visual of the bridge was chilling. Each saw himself, in place, as each was now. All appeared normal, all things right. Their bridge monitors were flicking the usual status displays, the beige carpeting, the bands of color on Wesley's gray shirt, and the officers' red and black, gold and black, or azure and black uniforms showing that the colors were right and the picture crisp—not very reassuring at the moment.

On the starboard bridge, specters walked. Over a dozen humanoid shapes glowed yellowish white, flat as X-ray diffraction images. Form, movement, shape, without definition, without depth, glassy human shapes moving behind a curtain of spectral impulses, outlined by a sizzling blue thread. Some were moving catatonically, milling back and forth on the ramp and in front of the big viewscreen and in the command arena. Some stood still, as though looking back at Riker as he dared approach the monitor, absorbing what he saw. He was looking into a mirror and there were images staring back at him that were beside him in the room.

He spun, scanning a starboard bridge that looked

empty. His throat tightened and held back his one effort to speak. All he could do was watch as Captain Picard turned away from the monitor and also scanned what could not be seen by the naked human eye. Unlike everyone else, who had sidled away from that side of the bridge, Picard now moved toward it, his face a granite challenge.

"Open all frequencies. Tie in translator." He waited only an instant for the *click-beep* that told him Tasha had shaken from her chill and complied. He raised his voice. "This is Captain Jean-Luc Picard of the United Federation of Planets. You are invading my ship without invitation. What is your purpose here?"

There was nothing. Riker kept his eyes on the shapes in the monitor, no matter that the hairs rose on the back of his neck because he knew they were right behind him.

"We request that you communicate with us," Picard said forcefully. "State your intentions immediately."

Riker watched the monitor, unable to look at the vacant deck, and his skin crawled. Two of the X-ray images began to move toward Picard, one from the side, one from behind.

Riker bolted. "Captain!"

He got the captain's arm between both hands and pulled him aside, the urgent dance putting Riker between the captain and the approaching specters. Within a second, Worf dropped onto the command deck beside him, and above them Yar had drawn her phaser. In a purely human manner, Riker swiveled his head around, looking for what couldn't be seen, and his stomach contracted as he waited for blows from invisible hands.

Then—

"They're gone . . ."

LaForge spoke up clearly enough to make everyone *really* nervous.

Riker didn't believe it. Gut feeling told him otherwise.

But the captain trusted the wavelength-sensitive monitor that now showed only himself and his own crew occupying the bridge. Yet even he couldn't avoid a surreptitious glance about the deck.

"All right, Mr. Riker," he murmured then, "at ease."

But no one was at ease. No one at all.

Wesley Crusher tightened his young eyes and whispered, "The ship is haunted . . ."

Chapter Four

"HAUNTED," CAPTAIN PICARD snorted. "Superstitious claptrap. Belay that attitude, ensign."

He moved to the command center, not quite ready to sit down, plagued by the sensation that those entities were still walking around him. He cast an intolerant glance at Wesley Crusher, communicating that all they needed now was the wisdom of a teenager to gum up the works. As he caught Wesley's whipped-puppy expression, Picard felt once again the sting of his decision to make Wesley an ensign, a decision no good parent would make, yet one that he, as a man who had never had children, had made without realizing the consequences. He should have known better, for as commanding officer he was indeed the father of all his crew and complement. Wesley's face was the face of a child; no seasoned officer would take the reprimand so personally. And having given it, Picard could not take it back.

There were many things which could not be taken back. Such an error and a disservice, promoting the boy to the bridge so early, without the earning. *Not so much a disservice to the bridge, but to the boy.*

Picard watched the viewscreen, turning away from the young face that occupied his mind now.

Yes, promoting Wesley to the bridge had aroused the resentment of Starfleet officers who might not be as brilliant but might be more deserving. Wesley Crusher had become the supreme knick-knack—a pretty display of talent, but not really functional. Anything he did on the bridge had to be monitored, no matter that he could calculate things inside his head sometimes before the computer made its reports. That was just how it was.

And why did I do that to him? Picard wondered, letting the familiar thought roll through his mind all in that one glance. *Do I feel so responsible for his father's death? Do I owe Jack Crusher so much for the mistake that killed him . . . that I would make another mistake with his son? Am I so anxious to gain the gratitude of this boy's mother that I would use his brilliance to showcase my good will? And now I risk destroying his distorted image of himself if I withdraw his status as acting ensign and put him back where he belongs . . . Ah, Picard, tu t'es fait avoir.*

He sighed, and turned to his command crew. "All right. Ensign Crusher says ghosts. It's as good a starting point as any."

Worf's Klingon brow puckered. "But, sir, ghosts are fables!"

"Perhaps so, from a metaphysical perspective," Picard said evenly and without a pause. "But we're not going to address that. We're going to approach them from a wholly scientific vantage. Disband all thoughts of wraiths and think in terms of alternate life-forms and mind forms. Mr. Data, what can you give me on that?"

Caught off guard by having so folklorish a subject

cast at him, Data blinked and appeared suddenly helpless.

Riker stepped in, knowing better, but still not fast enough to stop himself. "An android wouldn't know anything about life, sir, much less the occult."

The captain's eyes struck him like blades. "I'm talking about spectral apparitions, Riker, and you are out of line with that remark. Aren't you?"

Bruised, Riker nodded smartly. "Yes, sir, I guess I am."

"I asked Data a question."

Data may or may not have appreciated the dressing-down on his behalf, but the fact was he found himself floundering on such a subject. To a being for whom knowledge had always meant plain facts, this mystical concept was quicksand. Very conscious of the attention he was getting, Data glanced at Riker, straightened a little, and spoke.

"Sir," he began, "I would postulate that, since the life-forms were picked up by Geordi's visor and then by the recalibrated bridge sensors, they are not foibles of Earth thaumaturgy, but indeed of a substantive hylozoic constituence."

Picard's mouth crumpled. "What?"

"They're real."

"Oh. You might've said so."

"Sorry, sir."

"What you mean," Picard continued, "is that something incorporeal need not be unalive. Traditionally, ghosts are unalive. These beings aren't."

Data cocked his head. "Difficult to say, sir. That transgresses into the realm of semantics. We would have to isolate what it means . . . to be alive."

The android's sudden discomfort with those words drew Picard's attention once again to his eyes, to the boyish innocence of a being who had gone all the way through Starfleet Academy, spent a dozen years on Starfleet vessels, yet somehow remained the quintessence of ignorance. Data would have to have that word applied to him . . . but no book learning, regardless of its extent, could replace the priceless pleasures and brutalities of living interaction.

"Do we have an analysis from the science labs yet?" the captain asked.

Data played with the computer board nearest him and accessed the information as it was fed back to him through the computer's sophisticated comparative-analysis system, then said, "They seem to be some sort of phased energy, sir."

"What does that mean?"

"Apparently they exist here in pulses. Here and not here. They don't always exist in one place. It's not energy as we commonly define it. It is more like a proto-energy. It has some of the properties of energy and matter, yet sometimes none of those. It seems unfamiliar to our science." Data looked up. "Apparently stability is not their forte."

"That's an interesting nonanalysis, Mr. Data. Seems to me the computer is turning backflips to avoid admitting that it doesn't know."

"At the moment, I cannot blame it, sir."

Picard gave him an acid glare, but was pleasantly distracted when Troi came to him, deliberately holding her hands clasped before her, evidence of her effort to keep control. "Sir . . ."

"Go on, Counselor, nothing's too outlandish at this point."

"If they are . . . ghosts—that is, the remaining mental matter of deceased physical forms," she said, "can they be destroyed?"

"Destroyed." Picard tasted the word. "You mean killed, don't you? To be able to be killed is one of the signs of life."

Moved by his blunt response to the problem, Troi forced herself to push the point. "And if they can be killed, does that mean they're alive?"

"No one has talked about punitive action yet, Counselor," the captain said. "But these images of destruction you're receiving," he added. "I can't dismiss those."

From her expression they could see she wasn't trying to split hairs; the question was very urgent to her, a true matter of life and death. "Yes, sir, I know. But I'm desperate that my perceptions not be misread. I don't trust myself to analyze them yet. I wouldn't want you to take punitive action before it's warranted, just because of me."

"Are you saying you *do* sense a danger to us?"

Frustrated, she tilted her head and sighed. "I'm trying not to say it, but I'm also afraid not to. If you understand me . . ."

"Oh, I think I understand. These entities exist on a plane so different from our own that their very existence may endanger us. We've run into that sort of thing before in Federation expansion."

"Yes, sir, that's what I mean," Troi said anxiously. "Even if they pose a danger to us, do they deserve to be killed when all they've done is trespass onto the ship?"

"Mmmm," Picard murmured. "And will they be as generous when discussing us, I wonder." He paced around her, contemplating the carpet. "I'll keep all that in mind. Whatever the case, I will not allow my crew to succumb to superstition. We will find the answers, and they will be scientifically based."

Troi straightened her spine. "Yes, sir."

"Yes, sir," Data said, turning to his console.

"I agree, sir," Riker said. "Whoever these beings are, we have to assume they're sentient, and that they have intentions that we'll have to figure out before we can act."

"Yes," Picard murmured. "And the question remains," he added softly, scanning the bridge, now as eerie and silent as a graveyard at dawn, "what are they doing *here?*"

The words put a pool of ice water around all their feet. The captain didn't wait for it to warm.

"Mr. Riker, my ready room. I'll have a word with you."

Riker forced himself to follow the captain's retreating form into the private room off the bridge. No sooner had the door brushed shut behind him than the captain froze him in place with a lofty glare.

"You undermined my authority, Mr. Riker."

Trying to replay the past moments in his mind without the jitters that still ran the deck on the other side of that door, Riker asked, "Did I, sir?"

The captain stood with his compact frame backdropped by the viewport's starscape, appearing quite the nobleman among the peerage. "You did."

Inclining his head, Riker offered, "But I saw those forms closing in on you. I didn't know what they intended."

"You needn't have done your Olympic pole vault on my account," the captain said. "A simple word of warning would have been sufficient."

Squaring his shoulders—but not too much—Riker proclaimed, "It's my job to protect you, sir."

"Yes, I know that's the official story," Picard said. "When you've come back alive as many times as I

74

have, you'll earn the right to have someone look after you as well. I'll thank you to allow me the dignity of taking my own punches from now on. Dismissed."

"Geordi, look at this. Geordi, look at that. Geordi, tell us what this is made of. Geordi, look through walls like Superman. Sure, no problem, I'll look. All I am is what I look through."

"Take it easy," Beverly Crusher murmured as she adjusted the tiny filter on the miniaturized low-power sensory compensator in LaForge's visor. "You know, you should have a medical engineer doing this."

"No thanks," the young man grumbled, blinking his flat gray unseeing eyes at her, trying to imagine what she really looked like—*really*.

"And you should have rested after what happened on the bridge," she told him evenly. "You can't ask your body to power this sensor system to that level without letting yourself rest. That's why it hurts you so much, Geordi. You're unremitting."

He nodded his cocoa-dark head in her general direction and said, "I don't mind the hurt. I can't just leave my post. But somehow I expected a little more appreciation from people who were stationed on *Enterprise*. I just assumed anybody who could get assigned to this ship would be a little more up to date than the run-of-the-mill ship's crew." He closed his eyes tight against the pounding headache and rubbed his hand across them, waiting for the medication to work. "Riker just expected me to *tell him*. It's not that easy. I can't just glance at things like you can. I can't just pop out with words for the sensory impulses that make my brain act like a computer interpreter. Do you know that at close range a computer with a sensory readout can't match me? It'll miss or misinterpret things, because a machine doesn't understand things like I do."

"That's because it doesn't have the intuitive sense for interpreting what it sees," Crusher told him placidly. "You should be proud of that."

"I am," he insisted. "But I didn't know what those forms on the bridge were any more than anybody else did, including Mr. Riker. When people look at me, they don't see me. They just see that thing." He cast his hand in her direction, encompassing all of her and the item she held.

"They don't understand," the doctor said, "and you can't expect them to. They aren't going to understand how much it takes out of you to make this visor work."

"I know!" he shot back with a frustrated slap of his hand on his knee. "I know . . . but it's hard to be reasonable sometimes, specially when everybody's kicking off a Geordi-what-do-you-see. They don't know what it took to learn to interpret all the information I get out of every square inch I see. I'm not a machine, doc, you know? My brain wasn't made to do this. It's not like I look at a thing and a dozen little labels appear to tell me what it's made of. I had to learn what every impulse meant, every vibration, every flicker, every filter, every layer of spectral matter . . . people don't know what it takes out of me to say, 'I don't know what it is.'"

Crusher stopped her adjusting and paused to gaze at him, suddenly moved by her ability to simply do that. Because he was blind now, without his prosthetic, he didn't see her pause. He didn't—couldn't—see anything. And she was glad of it.

"It's not easy, you know," he went on. "It took years of retraining—painful retraining—to make my brain do this. A human brain is never meant by nature to do what mine's doing. And every time I have to say, 'I don't know' or 'I've never seen anything like this before,' it goes through me like a steel bolt. It means I'm truly blind."

"Oh, Geordi . . ." Crusher murmured.

"Sometimes," he said, "I go through twenty or thirty levels of analysis and every one takes a piece out of me. When I can't tell what it is I'm seeing, it's not like a sighted person looking at a box and not being able to see what's inside. It's like holding your breath and diving deeper and deeper, no matter how much it hurts . . . and when you can't touch bottom, you still have to plow back to the surface before your lungs explode . . . oh, I can't explain it; I can't make you *see.*"

He reached out in his blindness and by instinct alone he found the visor she held as she stood nearby—a blind man's instinct that told him where her hands were—and with his artificial eyes back in his own hand he slid from the table and somehow found the door. As it opened for him he went flawlessly through it, homing in on the sound and the faint gush of air from the corridor, as though to show her he could be a whole person without the burden of his high-tech crutch.

"Geordi," Crusher called after him, but she did so only halfheartedly, for she had no words to help him. She winced as Riker appeared out of nowhere and Geordi bumped into him. It would've been such a smooth exit otherwise. . . .

"Lieutenant—" Riker started to greet, then simply gaped as LaForge plowed past him without even a "sorry, sir." After Geordi rounded the arch of the corridor and disappeared, Riker crooked a thumb in that direction as he came into the sickbay. "What's eating him?"

"You are." Crusher folded her arms and sighed.

"*I* am? How'd I get into this?"

"Funny you should ask." She grasped his arm and drew him into the sickbay, then planted him in the nearest chair and assumed her lecture position—any parent knows it. Sliding her narrow thigh up onto an exam table, she broached the subject with a practiced look of sternness. "He's a little bothered by that episode on the bridge."

"He told you about that . . . okay, I'll bite," Riker said. "Why's it bothering him?"

Beverly Crusher's lovely art deco features were marred by the situation. "You sure you want to know?"

Frustrated, Riker held his hands out. "When did I start looking so aloof to everybody? I want to know."

"That's not what you came down here for."

"No," he admitted. "I came down because I knew LaForge was here and I wanted an analysis of physical composition of those life images. I figure he's the best man to do it."

"I think you'd better get Data to do it."

"Why? All of a sudden, everybody's functioning at half power. Isn't Geordi LaForge the expert on spectroscopy?"

"Only by necessity," she said, "not by choice."

Riker looked at her; just looked at her. Then he shook his head. "You're mad at me. Been conniving with the captain?"

Suddenly a common thread looped around them and Crusher's lips curved into an understanding grin. "Oh . . . I see. No, I'm not mad at you. But let me give you a bit of advice."

"Please!"

"Listen to Lieutenant LaForge. Just listen."

"I do listen."

"You don't. You hear what he has to say, but you don't appreciate it. You think all he does is 'see.'"

Riker tried to interpret what she was saying by looking into her deep-set eyes and reading them, but after a few seconds of that he floundered and admitted, "I don't know what you mean."

She settled her long hands in her lap. "My God, Will. Do you think he just puts that thing on and sees? Okay, not fair . . . I'll explain. Of course that's what it looks like to everybody. I tried to tell him that just now, but from his perspective—well, Geordi LaForge is one of only four blind people successfully fitted with the optic prosthetic. I mean, four who've successfully learned to operate it. Four. That's all in the whole Federation."

"Really . . ." Riker muttered, rapt. "Keep talking."

Crusher drew in a long breath, trying to find the words to explain something she herself had never experienced. "When he looks at an apple, he has to interpret between twenty and two hundred separate sensory impulses just to get shape, color, and temperature. After that, he has to recalibrate to get molecular composition, density, and everything else he gets. Trust me—it's mind-boggling. Which is what it does to Geordi. You're talking some thousand and a half impulses just to look at an apple. Do you know that he gets exhausted if he doesn't take the device off several times a day?"

"No . . . I didn't. But he doesn't take it off."

"He refuses to give in to his handicap. And because of his dedication, he gets depleted and has to deal with some considerable pain."

Riker grasped the edge of the chair and crushed the cushion tight. "Pain? Are you telling me that thing hurts him?"

"He never shows it."

"I had no idea. . . ."

Dr. Crusher slid off the table and said, "That's the kind of crewman you've got, Mr. Riker. Now you know."

The first officer slumped back in the chair, his blue eyes slightly creased as he tried to imagine something his own brain simply wasn't made to visualize. But he understood pain, and he understood the resistance of it. And the dogged recurrence of it. Suddenly he was aware of how little time he and these special people had spent together. Special talents, yes, but also special handicaps. Data and his mechanical self; Yar and her explosive temper and overprotectiveness; the constant tug and pull between himself and the captain with the undefined split of authority on a starship with civilians on board as regular complement; Troi and what she was going through on all fronts; and now this with Geordi LaForge—blind, but not—a man who could see phenomenally or not at all, no easy middle ground.

This was hard. It was a strain. Since day one there had been troubles, troubles that made them put aside those all-important moments when people got to know each other. They had been through much together, yet they were still strangers. What did he really know about Geordi? How did Geordi feel about other things than sight and that helm he worked? What was Yar's favorite pastime other than polishing her martial prowess? Certainly such a woman, so young and so vital, would think about something more fun. What music did she like? Did her shoes hurt sometimes? And surely there must be something more to Wesley than just a typical sixteen-year-old invulnerability. And Worf—was he lonely? As lonely as Troi seemed to be sometimes? What kept him in Starfleet when he could easily go back to his Klinzhai tribes and be completely accepted? It wasn't a Klingon trait to reject one of their own blood, no matter the circumstances of his separation. Why didn't he go?

Somehow each had become nothing to the others but a name and one particular eccentricity. Data was the Android, Geordi was his visor, Worf was the Klingon, Crusher was the Doctor, Wesley was the Kid, Troi was the Empath, Picard was the Marquis—

I guess that makes me the gentry. Or the rabble, Riker thought, not caring what all this did to his expression as Crusher watched silently. *I don't know them. I don't know any of them yet, and all this time we've been depending on each other for life and limb. And Captain Picard . . . I know him least of all. But then, I haven't shown him much of Will Riker, either— have I?*

"Damn it," he whispered.

Crusher pressed her lips inward and tried to avoid a softhearted nod, for she saw the changes in his face and especially noticed when he started absently picking at a nail and looking guilty.

"What?" she prodded, very careful of her tone.

"Nothing." He stood up abruptly, committing the very crime he was hanging himself for. Even as he began to turn toward the door he realized what he was doing, and he paused, balanced on one foot. He tipped his shoulder back toward her and thought about turning. "We aren't . . . we aren't showing—"

81

"Commander Riker, to the bridge immediately. Yellow alert, all hands, yellow alert. Commander Riker, report to the bridge—"

"Something on the edge of sensor range, sir."

Tasha Yar's voice gained a sudden rock-steadiness as she raised her volume over the yellow alert noise.

Picard stood resolute at bridge center, glaring at the viewscreen, very aware of Counselor Troi beside him. "Scan it."

"Scanning."

"On your toes, everyone. And where the devil is—"

"Riker reporting, sir. Sorry for the delay."

Picard turned toward the turbolift and said, "I want you one hundred percent available the next twenty-four hours, Number One. We don't know what we've stumbled upon and I don't like riddles. Until we discover what's going on—"

"At your service, sir, no problem." Riker landed in his place between the captain and Troi with a faint thud on the carpeted deck. Troi caught his eyes for just an instant, and each had to work hard to keep from speaking out-of-place reassurances to each other. Forcing himself to look away from her, he noticed Yar working more furiously than usual at her tactical station and demanded, "Fill me in, Lieutenant."

Her pale brow furrowed. "Scanning something on the periphery of sensor range, Mr. Riker, but I can't get a fix—wait a minute—that . . . that can't be right. I'm not getting anything back. No, that can't be right."

Picard spun. "Nothing at all? No reaction to the scan at all?"

"No, sir," Yar complained, "not even readings of surrounding space debris or bodies—" She broke off and slapped her control board like an errant child. She straightened decisively, absolutely sure of what she was seeing on her instruments. "Sir, far's I can tell, it's absorbing the sensor scan."

Picard's face took on an arrogant disbelief. "That's the most curious damned thing I've ever heard of. Corroborate it with the space sciences lab immediately."

"They're already tied in, sir," she said, her eyes sparkling. "Same report."

He swung about and bumped his fist against his thigh. "Well, damn that." With an imperious stride, he approached the starfield before them, his eyes going to slits. "Boost the sensors."

Yar looked up again. "Sorry?"

"Yes. Put out a high-energy sensor burst over the nominal sensors."

Yar's hand leaned ineffectually on her board, and she looked with helplessness to Riker. Her mouth formed her silent question: *Boost them?*

Riker felt the weight slam onto his shoulders. At least a foot shorter now, he approached Picard. "Sir, could you refresh us on that procedure?"

To everyone's surprise—relief—Picard merely glanced at him and said, "Of course." He stepped to the Ops station, where Data had been sitting in silent vigilance all this time, and put one hand to the small tactical access panel on the Ops console, pecking the controls carefully. "It's more or less an unofficial skill, not something Starfleet engineers approve of . . . somewhat radical. If it's done too often it can cause quite a burnout. We'll have to key in the computer sensors, readjust the energy output for tight-gain/high-energy bolt, ask for a momentary scan so all the

83

energy is contained, and tell the computer to fire when it's ready. There you are."

His hand fell gracefully away from the instruments, leaving them with a surprising clue to his rogue side. Within seconds, sure enough, there was a flush of energy from the bridge sensory systems, and the scanning burst was off, crossing the distances of space with the unfettered speed of pure energy.

"Sir!" Yar jolted at her station. "Definitely reading something now! God! It's heading directly at us out of interstellar space—it homed in on us! It'll be here in seventy-eight seconds!"

The captain snapped, "Visual!"

LaForge kept his voice laudibly calm as he reported, "Sir, for visual of these readings, the sensors'll have to be adjusted twelve points into the gamma-ray spectrum—"

"Just do it, Lieutenant!" Picard roared.

The young blind man grimaced behind his visor, punched in the code, and nailed the engage button, then held his breath as the ship's systems whined their strain back at him. But the readings began coming in.

"Sensors at maximum output—draining their sources, sir," LaForge reported over the energy shriek. "Almost got visual—there!"

The starfield blurred before them, sizzled, and reformed into a new pattern—and suddenly the bridge was walled with a gigantic glassy false-color image, undulating and fluxing as it raced at them through open space. Its aurora borealis colors were chaotic, its luster blinding, its electrical nature obvious as it crackled across the huge screen.

Geordi instantly brought a hand up to shield his visor. "Chrrrrist—"

The fireworks blazed across their faces and ran amuck on their fears. It was a thing utterly alien, and struck panic in all their hearts—it looked like fire, like electricity. Like the face of hell itself.

Suddenly Troi came to life behind Riker and the captain, her horrified expression even more horrifying as the fulmination from the screen glared on her skin and in her eyes.

"Stay away from it! Don't let it get near us!"

Picard was beside her as though appearing out of nothing. "Counselor?"

Her slim hands clamped on his arm like talons. "Captain! Do *not* let that thing come near us!"

"I can't just—"

"Do *not* let it!" she repeated. "Captain, what am I doing on this ship if you do not take my counsel? If I'm wrong, I'll resign my position! If I never do anything worthwhile in my life again, I'll have done this! Captain, please!"

The purplish veins of light played ugly patterns between them, glowing as though to hammer out Troi's words and the conviction in her eyes.

The captain held her by the arms and bored through her with eyes that were doing something other than questioning her veracity. At once he sucked in a breath and his voice gripped the bridge. "Raise shields! Go to red alert status."

"Red alert!" Riker echoed instantly, flashing the words toward Tasha. "Speed and ETA?"

"Warp six now! Sixty-one seconds ETA!" She flinched under the prismatic light from the screen. Her blond hair sparkled orange, then amethyst, then blue, then a cruel white. Her arms moved among the fireworks, and the ship whooped into alert. Lights of their own flashed now throughout the starship, and all around the vessel, high-energy defensive shielding buzzed to life around the great hulls and nacelles.

Picard pressed Deanna Troi behind him, back toward the three lounges that were their command places in better moments, and shouldered his way into the glaze of lights. "Lieutenant Yar, fire phasers across its bow. Make our intentions absolutely clear. Warn that thing off!"

Behind him he heard Troi whisper, "Weapons . . . no!"

But it was too late.

Without acknowledgment, Yar played her controls and before them long-range phasers lanced space, thin as needles, their power twisted into threads so slim that they could strike even at this distance and be felt like solid blades.

"Captain, it's accelerating!" she shrieked then. "It's put on a burst of speed—warp ten now . . . warp twelve! Warp fourteen-point-nine!"

"LaForge!"

The captain's roar bombarded the bridge.

LaForge smeared his palms over the controls, jamming the starship into emergency warp. The change of speed was so abrupt that even sophisticated Starfleet equipment couldn't compensate for the stomach-sucking effect.

The starship wheeled in space and bolted into a sudden warp five, but there was no warp fifteen in its vocabulary. Before the ship could maneuver more than one light-year's distance, the thing was upon them.

St. Elmo's fire blanketed the bridge as the new *Enterprise* was given the shakedown of the millennium. A billion tiny firecrackers erupted across the heavy-duty shielding. Electrokinetic jolts fanned through the ship, through every person's body, through every bone and nerve, every circuit, every conduit, every skin hair, and crackled through every inch of stuff, living or mechanical.

Troi felt a short scream squeeze out of her as she crumpled against an enemy she somehow recognized. All around her, jagged voltage profaned the bridge with ugly blue fingers and left sparks wherever it touched. She saw her crewmates falling, writhing, fighting. She heard the whine of the ship's gallant battle against this electrical storm, and knew the *Enterprise,* like her crew, was defying the attack.

The weight of a thousand minds crushed into her head and she forgot the ship, forgot everything but the pain of it. They were screaming at her, shrieking the reedy noises of zombies and wraiths, the graveyard shrill of things Picard had ordered she not consider. She struggled against the sharp piercing clarions and tried to cling to that order. Her fingers were electric blue as they clawed at the air before her, her eyes frozen open no matter how she tried to close them.

The effect squealed around her, and as it sought her brain and all the parts of her that reacted to her telepathic self, it released her muscles one by one and she sank to the deck, still staring, still wrapped in the blue lightning.

Riker saw her fall, and tried to reach for her. But he too was being beaten by the attack. The ship might as well have been impaled on a lightning rod. Fiery blue veins accosted every panel, and beneath them the deck itself tossed and bucked as energy crashed through it. As the seconds dragged past, the effect sank away from Troi and left her lying on the deck as it scouted the bridge for whatever it wanted and couldn't find.

Riker was trying to reach Troi when the chair beside him moved abruptly and Data was dragged out of it and thrown across the Ops console on his back, and mauled by the electrical pistolwhipping. The ship shuddered one more time before the silvery blitz dropped away from its attack on the whole bridge, converged to a single point from all over the bridge and settled on Data, wrapping around him and his Ops console and effervescing there.

"Data!" LaForge plunged toward the android, only to be knocked to one side by Riker's shoulder.

"Don't touch him!"

Chapter Five

RIKER SHOUTED OVER the crackle. "Nobody touch him!"

LaForge shoved against the first officer. "It's killing him!"

Riker had to twist around and grab him in order to hold him off. The navigator continued to push his way toward Data, his hands biting into Riker's arm, but Riker simply refused to let him through.

Quivering, Data lay across the Ops panel in a skein of light threads, and his mouth began to work as though by an invisible hand. "Ship . . . con . . . tact . . . con . . . kill . . ."

"Is he in communication with it?" Picard shouted over the awful electrical din. "Data! Are you in contact? Are you in contact! Data!"

The ship began to settle as the effect fell away, leaving only the snaps and fizzes of frenzied equipment. Data was the last to be released. The iridescence had its fill of him and dropped off, seeping down into the Ops panel and leaving only a confused flicker behind on the board. Data slipped down the console and flopped to the floor, catching hold of the console's edge and managing to land on his knees. His face had a very human glaze of panic, and he was trembling.

Geordi shoved his way past Riker and skidded to one knee, giving Data his arm to lean on. Riker let him go, and they crossed by each other as Riker dropped to Troi's limp form on the deck, lifting her with one arm and using the other hand to tap his comlink. "Sickbay, emergency!"

"Shut down all systems!" the captain said at the same moment. "Passive sensors only. Do *not* hit it with active sensors!"

"Aye, sir, passive sensors," Yar confirmed, her voice cracking. Her features, spare as a porcelain doll's, worked as she fought for control.

"Where is it?" Picard demanded.

"Moved off, sir," Worf boomed. "Now hovering approximately two light-years distant. It's not doing anything but just roaming there snapping at us, working some kind of a pattern."

"It's moving?"

"Yes, sir. Random turns and coasts along a cube pattern. I think it's looking for us, Captain."

"Ship's status?" Picard scanned the bridge all the way around once, noticing the shimmying electrical quirks and vibrations that still flashed here and there.

"Shields drained seventy-nine percent, sir," Worf reported angrily. "Systems blown out all over the ship. Stardrive is down. Communications are out. Sensors are unstable. Most disabled are the shields, and they'll take the longest to recharge."

"Condition of the saucer section?"

"Intact, sir. They were shook up, but not as badly as the bridge and as the stardrive areas were. Looks to me like it focused on high-energy areas of the ship."

"What was that thing?"

Worf puckered his lips in a Klingon kind of shrug and glared at Tasha.

She fidgeted. "Evidently a bombardment of pure antimatter," she said, casting a nervous glance at Geordi and Data, still huddled on the floor. "Engineering reports the thing absorbed the energy from our shields and about half the systems on board, mostly the ones on the outer parts of the ship. The computer core itself is still intact, sir, but I doubt we could stand off another attack of that level."

"Seventy-nine percent drain? I should think not."

Now Riker looked up from where he knelt holding Troi and said, "I never saw such a burst of speed before. What happened? Why did it move off?"

"For the moment," Picard said steadily, "only it knows."

He stooped down and helped Riker lift Troi into her chair. Her eyes were crescents, and she was shaking even harder than Data. When two orderlies charged out of the turbolift, Picard directed them to her and stood to one side as they gave her a quick check.

"I'm sorry . . . I'm so sorry . . ." she quavered.

"Can't imagine why," Picard said gently. "If not for your warning, we wouldn't have had our shields up. I shudder to think what might've happened in that case. I want you checked out in sickbay. No, no arguments, Counselor."

Riker stood straight and said, "The antimatter would've ripped the ship apart."

"But the weapons," Troi choked, "I should've warned you . . . I didn't remember . . ."

"Remember what?" Picard prodded. "What are you talking about?"

"I knew . . . I knew the weapons would—Captain, I'm so sorry—"

91

"You knew the weapons would draw that thing's attention? Is that what you're saying?"

She fought to stay upright in the chair as her arms and legs shook, but she managed a very distinct nod.

"Get her to sickbay," Picard said, impatient to have her back to normal. "This subject is not closed."

"Yes, sir," she murmured, and let herself be led from the bridge by the two orderlies. She knew Riker was watching, knew he wanted to come with her, but there was so much cluttering her mind—so much. . . .

"Captain," Geordi interjected, and waited for this attention. "According to my spectrographic analysis, it was basically the same visual structure as those beings we saw walking around on the bridge."

Picard glowered at him. "Are you telling me it's a big ghost?"

"Sir?" Yar looked up from her readout screen.

"Go ahead," the captain said.

"I'm getting analysis from engineering now. The thing's peppered with antimatter, but it isn't made of antimatter alone. When it enveloped the ship, we became a million tiny explosions all over, wherever the bits of antimatter hit the shields. If it had broken through them, we'd—"

"Keep all systems shut down until further notice. Stabilize within that context." Picard tightened his fists and strode toward the Ops position. He tipped downward to get the attention of the floor brigade. "Data? You functional?"

Looking more like a threatened child than an android as he knelt shivering and holding on to Geordi, Data dragged back what little was left of his energy and looked up at Picard. "F-functional . . . sir . . ."

"Were you in contact with that thing out there?"

"With something . . . sir . . . conclude that must have been the case . . ."

"Anything to report?"

"Nothing clear, sir; there was no . . . no sense to the contact."

"On your feet, then. Can you?"

"Captain?" Lieutenant Yar seemed to really hate interrupting him again, and with more bad news, but she stiffened and pressed against the tactical station as Picard turned. "The thing's energy output is up thirty-one percent from before it hit us."

Riker shook his head. "Great. That's our energy it's got."

From below, Geordi was driven to comment, "And we sit here like a log on a pond while Irving the Entity out there digests three-quarters of our power."

Suddenly aware of Geordi again and feeling a renewed obligation, Riker said, "I'll bet a starship qualifies as extra spicy. I wonder how long till it's hungry again."

"Colorfully put, Number One, but not much help," Picard wryly said as he hauled Data to his feet. He held Data's twitching arm, and Geordi the other arm, while the android regained his equilibrium.

"No, sir," Riker admitted, "but if it zeroes in on energy outlay, we might be able to hide from it."

Picard looked impressed. "My thoughts exactly."

"Sir?"

The captain craned his neck around. "Now what, Yar?"

She braced herself, but plunged on with her report, because it was too bizarre to keep to herself. She bent over her readout screen and tried to disbelieve what

93

she saw. "Sir, I think our passive sensors might not be working properly. Or I'm not very good at reading them. . . ."

"Report. Now."

She tilted her head and frowned. "The thing's energy level appears to be slowly dropping. Definitely going down."

"In the thing itself?"

"Yes, *in* the thing."

"What's the matter with that?"

"Well, its mass isn't—Worf, can you corroborate this?"

"Checking," Worf rumbled.

"Lieutenant!"

"Yes, sir. The mass isn't changing. And there's no change in the antimatter, and it's not emanating enough energy to account for the drop."

"That's not possible," Picard said. "The energy can't go *no*where. That's a fundamental law of the universe. It has to go somewhere."

"I wish it would," she muttered. "Aye, sir, that's the strange part. It tends to phase as we're reading it. Its mass, its total energy—there's almost nothing about it that's constant."

"That's the clue, then. What's the conclusion? Hypotheses, anyone," he called sharply, doubling the pressure of the moment by putting the whole bridge on the hot seat for answers.

"Inter . . . inter . . ."

"Yes, Data? You have an idea? Data, you all there?"

"Inter . . . dimen . . . sionality . . ." The android leaned against Geordi unashamedly, but his expression was one of fierce concentration rather than the alarm of a moment ago.

"Keep trying, Data," Picard prodded, stepping closer to him but resisting the urge to help him straighten up.

"The only possibility," Data said, "is that it must exist . . . between dimensions if the energy . . . is dissipating without . . . emanation . . . sir." He steadied himself with a distinct effort, glanced in gratitude toward Geordi, and stood on his own. "That must be where the energy is going. It is the only way to account for the enormous energy drawn from our shields without our being able to detect it now."

Picard scowled, but the idea did make sense. It had better, since Data said it twice without realizing he was repeating himself.

On the upper deck, Yar shook her head. "Too weird for me," she grumbled.

"It is outlandish," Picard mused.

"But it's the only conclusion that makes sense," Riker said. "Hell, it makes our idea of ghosts seem sane."

"It does that," the captain agreed ruefully, "and it also means that anything we do from this moment on is pure guesswork. For all we know that thing could extend through a hundred solar systems on a hundred levels of existence."

Riker looked at the screen, at the image of the entity sizzling in the upper left of the starscape, two light-years off their port bow. "And any energy we use to defend ourselves is just its next meal. Maybe we should put some distance between us."

Picard bobbed his brows as though he'd very much like that idea. "We can't," he said. "At least not yet. That entity put on a burst of warp nearly warp fifteen. It'd be all over us in an instant. We've blinded it by shutting down our power. As we hang here, we're hidden. For the moment."

"How are you doing?" Riker asked privately, trying to make his approach to Wesley's side an inobvious one.

Wesley flinched. He hadn't thought anyone was paying attention to him, considering events. "Okay, sir. It's really a bother to just hang here in space, though."

Riker eyed the screen, and the distant false-color pattern that sought them. "It's all we can do until we get systems back on line and figure out a way to leave the area without attracting attention."

"Maybe a solar sail, sir? We could coast on the waves from the sun in that little solar system—"

"Too slow. It'll find us long before then. Look at it. It's working a search pattern that we can't escape on impulse power. A box pattern a couple of light-years across, and it's going at lightspeed. If we try to sneak through and it happens to pass that area while our shields are still down . . . well, you know."

Wesley's narrow shoulders tensed. "Guess I do. Sometimes I wish I didn't see things so clearly in my head. Then I wouldn't have to look at them. Mr. Riker, I never heard of passive sensors."

"Oh," Riker murmured. "Passive sensors can only analyze data that other entities and objects put out. Active sensors actually send out a beam, then wait for the information recoil to return. If that thing's looking for us, it'll be looking for an energy source. If we use active sensors, we'll be sending up a flare for it to home in on."

"Same with shields," LaForge added.

"And weapons." This cryptic bit from Yar, who

96

stood on the starboard ramp, keeping one eye on her tactical monitors and one on the false-color shape on the monitor as it roamed the area, hunting.

Riker waited until the impact of their words faded. He hadn't meant to be overheard. Leaning closer to Wesley, he lowered his voice even more, but it might as well have been going through a bullhorn on the eerily quiet bridge. With half the systems blown out and the other half shut down, the bridge noises were disturbingly low. "Without active sensors, we'll have to be very careful about plotting any course. We'll be as good as under sail again. Minor navigation will be very tricky."

Wesley nodded, and resigned himself to the undiluted truth; there would be no beautiful miracle of warp speed to carry them from the danger.

Standing at the foot of the port ramp, near the entrance to his ready room, Captain Picard clasped his hands behind his back and watched his crew work against their helplessness. He watched Riker and Wesley whispering to each other and felt a sudden jab of inadequacy. If only he could find it within himself to comfort them.

Suddenly he wished he was in the middle of a Romulan attack, outnumbered six to one. His only concern would be himself, his ship, and a band of fellow soldiers who knew what they were getting into when they signed on. He would have a free hand, then, free to be radical, without the anchor of concern for innocent spouses and children. Without having to worry about them if the ship took a hard lunge, much less charged into a hull-rattling battle. Every time the ship lurched, those innocent faces popped into his thoughts and ran under the flimsy umbrella of his protection, fully expecting to be safe there.

As he gazed at Riker, Picard indulged in a small feeling of envy. Each time he looked at his first officer, he saw Riker standing on the transporter platform with an away team, about to beam down, about to leave the captain behind to tend the ship. At those times, those interesting times, Riker was responsible only for himself and the away teams, while Picard must remain responsible for a shipful of families. Where was the old adventure of a ship with a lean, raw, trained crew? How had he suddenly become governor of a tiny overpopulated island?

At once he missed his days as first officer, and of captaincy in a vessel without children aboard. To be captain of a vessel whose calling is danger—it was the best of both. And now he was caught in the middle, governor of a group of spacegoing families. Neither captain nor first officer, answerable to the decisions of Riker, whose job it was—admittedly—to stand between Picard and that exhilarating peril that was any captain's right.

Trial by fire. Earn the right to be forever cushioned. And his first officer, who should be the trusted extension of himself, by circumstance became a resented obstacle.

In their few adventures together so far, Picard had told himself he could find a compromise. But there was no compromise in some situations, and that was the painful reality. Some situations required either forward movement or utter retreat, and this was one. Riker would always be a barrier. And that would always be the image in Picard's mind as he watched away team after away team beam off the ship without him. The feeling of being left behind would never subside.

Captain. Was that his true title? Or was he governor of *Enterprise?*

Here they were, these thousand-and-some, colonizing a ship instead of a planet. Colonizing space itself, citizens of the Federation at large. In generations to come, these children's children would come to see these kinds of ships as their country, their planet, their nationality. The answer to "Where are you from?" would be "I'm from *Enterprise.*"

Habitat. Environment. A place, not a thing, not a ship. A moving *place.* Instead of "I'm a citizen of this sector or that system, this planet, that outpost," the answer would be "I'm a citizen of the Federation."

Finally there would be total unity within the Federation, the first step toward people's being at home on any planet instead of only one. The principle from the old United States, basically; it didn't matter if you were raised in Vermont and lived in California. You were still home, still American. If your name was Baird or Yamamura or Kwame, you weren't necessarily loyal to Scotland, Japan, or Ghana, but to America. A few decades of space travel, and the statement became "I'm a citizen of Earth," and no matter the country. This ship was that kind of first step. Whether born on Earth or Epsillon Indii VI, you were a citizen of the Federation. The children on this colony *Enterprise* would visit the planets of the Federation and feel part of each, welcome upon all. This starship was the greatest, most visionary melting pot of all, this space-going colony. Unique. Hopeful.

Risky.

And it befell Jean-Luc Picard to make it work.

Why me? Has the prestige blinded me to my losses of freedom and adventure? Children. Imagine it.

"Mr. Riker," he spoke up then, breaking into his

99

own thoughts. "I want you, Data, and LaForge to go down to engineering and get me a thorough spectrometric and electronic analysis of the phenomenon's composition while we still have time. I want to know what'll happen if we fire our weapons directly into it, and what'll happen if we don't." He suddenly jabbed a finger at his first officer and firmly said, "Riker, *you're* in charge of figuring out how to deal with that thing."

It took every bit of Riker's control to keep from fidgeting. He felt his body stiffen. "Aye, sir." He nodded and wheeled toward the turbolift. "Data, LaForge—with me."

They filed off the bridge, and in a fluid bouquet of movement were replaced at the Conn and Ops positions by Worf and Tasha. Picard watched them leave and felt less alone against the coming hours' dark tunnel walls. He glanced around; the ship was still here, systems clicking and rerouting power in a million tiny alternative tracks, anything to get working again, stealing energy from each other, certain systems taking precedence over others as the giant computer core made the kinds of tiny decisions only machines could make. He felt the presence of the myriad engineers belowdecks, all scrambling to guide that delicate energy theft, felt them just as surely as Counselor Troi felt the presence of the beings who posed so plain a threat.

"I'll be in sickbay," he said, and started toward the turbolift.

"Confusion, sir."

Troi lay on the diagnostic bed in the artificial quiet of sickbay, trying to put words to that which had no letters, no punctuation. To her right, Captain Picard took charge, kept things in line, gave her fortitude. To

100

her left, Beverly Crusher provided another kind of anchor, watching her in a different way altogether. But now the captain wanted answers, suggestions, and none were presenting themselves without a fight.

"There seem to be thousands of separate emotional bands, if you will," Troi said. "Perhaps there are millions. I feel helpless to explain this to you clearly— doctor, may I get up, please?"

Crusher scolded her with a look, then said, "I suppose so. But only because I can't find anything wrong with you. That doesn't mean you're not injured in some way."

She swung the diagnostic shell away from Troi and stood back while the captain helped the counselor down from the table. Without a pause he led her to a nearby desk; evidently the conversation was far from over as far as he was concerned. He put Troi into a chair, motioned Crusher into another, and settled himself into a third, then clasped his hands and rested his arms on the cool black desk before him.

"Could it be that this thing is a vessel and you've been reading its crew?"

"That possibility has occurred to me," Troi said, determined not to say she didn't know, even if she didn't. "I haven't dismissed it. But if we can label those humanoid images as ghosts, I suppose there's no more harm in labeling these impressions as their . . . souls. No, please—let me continue. I realize that's imprecise, sir. I regret having to speak so. 'Soul' is a subjective term, but I believe that's the image these entities have of themselves."

"You're receiving a perception of self?" Crusher asked. The long copper fan of her hair moved against her shoulders as she leaned forward.

Troi's nymphic eyes widened. "Oh, yes! That's why

I've been doubtful of my perceptions. Some of the visions are startlingly clear. The image of Vasska, for instance, and the memory of giving him orders as that entity struck the *Gorshkov.*"

"You didn't say that before," the captain pointed out. His tone rang with annoyance, as though he did indeed expect her to give a clearer report on these unclear things.

"No, sir. I wasn't very sure of it before. I only remembered it when I was attacked on the bridge. I wish I could explain."

"You're empathizing with Captain Reykov, then?" Picard surmised.

"At times," she answered. "His is the strongest personality. But, sir . . . there are many others. Many others. Those sharp visions are clouded over by uncountable life forces around the phenomenon. Not *in* it, but existing in a halo all around it, as though drawn through space wherever it goes."

"Are they prisoners?"

As Picard shot those blunt words at her, Troi flinched. She settled back in her chair, almost as though to remove herself, and dropped all emotion from her Mediterranean features and those inkdrop Betazoid eyes. "Are you asking me to theorize, sir?"

"I'm asking you to help me formulate a plan of action," he said, "or at least a plan of approach."

"Yes," she murmured. "Rather than helping, I've put you in a difficult position this time."

"It's not your fault, Deanna," Crusher said.

"Not at all," Picard echoed.

Troi searched her telepathic self for more from him, but the captain was not a man whose feelings gave up their shields easily. She sensed his resistance of her probe, a resistance as refined as he himself was, and respectfully drew back within herself.

"If these life essences are prisoners, as you suggest, and we destroy the prison," she continued, "will we be committing murder?"

With that question, she cut to the core of Picard's problem. He studied her. She was graceful, thoughtful, exotic—yes, that was the word for her—and so concerned, yet as helpless as the rest of them.

"You do have an artistic curve to your clinical self, don't you, Counselor?" he observed softly. "I realize your task is a strain. But mine is too. If our only chance of survival is to destroy those thousands or millions of minds you sense, what do I do? Save or sacrifice? Whose lives are forfeit?"

"That's the one flaw in the Prime Directive, Jean-Luc," Crusher said. "When interfering with another culture is the only way to save the lives you've been entrusted with—I don't know what I'd do either. Count heads and see who has more lives to save?"

The captain leaned back and ran his knuckle along his lower lip. "From what the counselor says, that puts us in a rather noticeable minority." He tapped the nearest intercom on the desktop and said, "Picard to bridge. What's the status up there?"

"Unchanged on the thing, sir," Yar reported. *"Ship's condition is improving, but we're having to task many systems to reestablish power to the shields. Everything's strained, including warp power."*

"Charming," Picard responded. "They're going to have to work faster."

"Yes, sir, I'd like to see that myself."

"Picard out. Counselor, do you have anything, *anything* more concrete to say?"

Troi sighed. "I've been trying to isolate the impressions, to see if they're only memories of life-forms or actual life essences, but so far I have no specifics to offer."

"It's you I'm worried about," Crusher told her.

Troi's mouth bowed. "You're kind. But if I can't use my abilities to the good of the ship—"

"You know what I'm talking about," the doctor interrupted. "The inherent danger of telepathy. If other telepaths are more overbearing than you are, the force of their minds could damage you, Deanna. And I can't put a bandage on your mind."

"I've tried to close my mind, but they batter through my barriers—"

"Are you telling me these things could present an actual danger to you?" Picard suddenly roared.

Startled, Troi clamped her mouth shut and stared at the whole prospect. She hadn't yet heard it put into words, and it didn't sound very good.

"This whole business worries me," Crusher said. "After what Wesley described to me, I'd have suggested a mass delusion if it hadn't come over the computer screen. That element adds a frightening scientific reality to all this. Oh . . . Captain, Wesley asked that I apologize to you on his behalf."

Picard puzzled this for a moment, then asked, "Whatever for?"

Crusher blinked. "I don't know. I thought you did."

After a moment he shook his head. "Don't recall anything particular, doctor."

She shrugged, embarrassed. "I see. Then the apology is mine. Wesley's at that age where he thinks all adults are prejudiced against children."

Picard cocked his hand toward her and mused, "Of course we are. They're children. They have to grow out of it. No one expects any more, or any less. When they're adults, they won't be children anymore. And there'll be new prejudices for them to ford."

"You mean like those against superior officers?"

"Yes." He chuckled, his mouth lengthening into a melancholy grin. The change in mood cleared his head, and he found the difficult situation a little easier to accept.

Troi turned to gaze out the viewport, waiting for the moment to end. *And those against telepaths. To offer unclarity in place of another unclarity—to replace ignorance with ambiguity—is this my only service?*

"If these beings are prisoners," Picard mused, "then they become my responsibility as well. I wonder if I have the right to decide on their behalf. We're going to have to increase our efforts to communicate with them somehow."

Troi looked at him, her fears returning. "But that requires power, sir. The entity could focus on it and destroy us."

Crusher spoke up. "And there's something else."

The captain tried not to sound weary. "Yes, doctor?"

She dropped her gaze to the desktop for a moment. When she looked up again, she met Jean-Luc Picard's eyes squarely. "What do we do if they simply will not negotiate with us?" she asked. "You know what they say about the road to hell."

"Curious that Counselor Troi would have been focused upon by an electromagnetic disturbance."

"Keep your mind on your work," Riker grumbled at the android's comment. Irritation skittered through him as his hand hovered an inch from the intercom, an inch from calling sickbay. There was Data, a few steps away. Still walking around after that attack. Just

105

shook it off. And Deanna was in sickbay, fighting for control of her mind.

Data looked up from the readout screen. "My mind is always on my work, Commander. You see, I have a multiphase memory core which allows me to—"

"I don't care," Riker heard himself bite back. "I'm really not interested."

Data's brows poked up over his nose. "Perhaps if I explained on a simpler level—"

His back cramping, Riker straightened and glared into Data's yellow eyes. "Would you mind?"

"Not at all, sir," the android responded amicably. "The concept behind my special multiphase brain capacity is—"

"That's not what I meant!"

"Isn't it, sir? It *is* what you said."

Geordi reached over and tugged on the android's sleeve. "Don't push the issue, Data. Mr. Riker wants reports exclusively on the disturbance and its source."

With a childish blink, Data said, "Oh. No sweat." He pivoted and bent once again over the screen. "The phenomenon's physical makeup is confusing to the passive sensors. There is little for the sensors to focus upon because the entity is out of phase as often as in. Entity or mechanism, I cannot define it."

Standing between Riker and Geordi as they each bent over different computer access panels, Data indulged in an all-too-human frown at the graphics that danced at him there.

To his right, Riker furiously went on hammering the pressure points of the molecular microelectronics board. "Let's start by using the most obvious criterion of life," he suggested. "Are there any signs of organism? Skin? Bones? Cells? Anything?"

"Organism neither suggests nor precludes life, sir. I am partly organic, but also mechanical—"

"Don't take everything so literally, Data," Riker snapped. "I want a starting point. I'm not saying all life-forms are organic. This is just a process of elimination. I know perfectly well that life isn't physical components alone. We can keep a body alive indefinitely, but that's not life. Not human life, anyway. Get back on those instruments and interpret what you read."

He tightened his left hand into a ball and felt the sweat squish in his palm. A tangible enemy was one thing; he could deal with that. But all this business of life and nonlife, this wrestling to grab a definition so they could know whether or not they were killing something when they fought to save their own skins . . . *I hate this. And I hate the position I'm in. Advise the captain? How? Help him fight this thing? How?*

His hands might as well be strapped to his sides. As first officer, he might as well be nothing. First officer was the supreme go-fer of all time. Not a scientist, not a tactical expert, not a psychologist—nothing specific, and yet a little of everything, anything the captain needed him to be at the moment. What would it be the next time? Would he be ready? Frustration gnawed at him.

Picard . . . damn him. Figure out a way to fight the phenomenon. That's all. Easy. Yes, sir, right away, sir.

"These readings defy interpretation."

Data's voice grated across Riker's nerves. That tone of his, that take-it-or-leave-it tone . . .

"But if I must verbalize, I would say the phenomenon is behaving in a pseudo-mechanical manner."

107

"Try to be specific, will you?" Riker barked, his tolerance straining.

"Always. It's made up of individual energy components, but it acts like neither a machine nor a being. It seems to be a living tool—something fabricated at so high a level of engineering that it's virtually a life-form."

"Sounds familiar," Geordi grumbled.

Data glanced at him, his mouth open, but he still stung from Riker's demand and continued on that tack. "I'm reading high-potency disruptive energies. As soon as it finds us, it could rub us out."

Riker straightened sharply. "Stop doing that."

Data's eyes flickered as he raised his head. "Sir?"

"You're annoying the hell out of me. You're distracting everyone with that kind of speech. Cut it out."

"Slang, sir. Colloquial terminol—"

"It's insulting."

"I . . . beg your pardon? I am trying to be more human."

Data backed up against the panel as Riker closed in on him, and he could see that somehow he had infuriated the first officer.

"You're never going to be human," Riker ground out. "You're not human. You don't seem to get the difference between being human and mimicking humans. You can't be creative because you only see the affectation and none of the substance. You're missing life. Until you learn the difference, you'll always be a puppet."

"Sir—" Geordi appeared beside them. "He's only trying to—"

"I know what he's trying to do," Riker snapped.

They were all silent for a moment.

108

A look of deep injury crossed Data's face and he glanced at Geordi, then back to Riker. "I . . . I am only attempting to improve myself . . . to serve in the best—"

"Then serve," Riker blurted. "Put yourself to use in your true capacity. You're an android. Use that to its best advantage and quit trying to be something you're not. Give us something to work with if you can. Provide something for me to take back to the captain that'll help us out of this." He took a step even closer, an intimidating step that backed Data tighter against the panel. "If that entity attacks again, I want you to give in to it. See if you can interface with it."

Data's pale brows drew tight over his nose, raised slightly in a delicate expression, proof—at least to Geordi—that somewhere under the voltage were feelings that could be hurt. In a near whisper, he responded, "I promise to try, sir." Unable to meet Riker's eyes anymore, he slipped past Geordi and strode quickly toward the spectrometry lab. A breath of the door, and he was gone.

Riker watched him go, saw the tension in synthetic shoulders and the kind of stride a human walks when he's trying to keep from running. Burned into his memory were Data's android eyes tightened in that expression of humility and distress, an expression that said he hadn't meant to offend anyone. Riker leaned after the android as if drawn by sudden obligation. He might have taken a step.

Had Geordi not drawn his attention.

"If he gives into that kind of attack," the navigator said, "he'll be risking his life, Mr. Riker."

Gaining control over his voice, Riker quietly said, "I'm afraid that may be our best chance to save ourselves." He turned toward the monitors again, only to find himself blocked off as Geordi shouldered in front of him.

"So that's okay, then? Sacrifice Data because he's not alive?"

"Look, Geordi, I don't—"

"Are you telling me it isn't true that you always choose him for away missions because he's more expendable?"

Riker glared into the thin metallic visor and imagined the tension around LaForge's blind eyes. "As you were, Lieutenant."

"Would you try as hard to save his life as you tried to save mine on the bridge?"

"Man your post, mister!"

LaForge hesitated a telling moment, then stepped back, the muscles in his neck twitching, his arms like tree limbs at his sides. "Aye, sir. Anything you say."

Chapter Six

THE GREAT WARRIOR prowled his technology's ramparts, slowly gaining a foothold. He smelled battle. He tasted the raw meat of challenge upon his tongue like blood and ripped flesh. He heard the howl in his mind, the song of warriors shrieking through his instincts, and he couldn't abide the price of peace. He knew, deep in his soul, that there would be trouble long before there was peace, and every fiber of his being prepared for it now, lest he be surprised later.

"Worf."

Only great effort blocked the growl of response and replaced it with a civilized word. "Yes?"

"The captain'll want a report when he gets back up here."

Worf turned to the supple feminine body and the storybook face over it. She looked like a girl who was dressed as a boy. A girl from the stories his adoptive human parents once told him, stories that never satisfied his hunger for adventure. Very young was he when his Starfleet parents gave up telling him stories of girls who dressed as boys to fool the churchgoers and replaced them with meatier tales by Bram Stoker,

Melville, Dumas, Stervasney, and Kryo to satisfy their rare son. Those he could chew. Those made him howl.

"He will not be happy with what we have to say, Tasha," he told her, quieting his thunderous voice as they stood together on the upper deck, buffered from the bridge by the tactical station a few steps forward.

"I know," she agreed. Beneath the lemon cuff of her hair, clear gray eyes kinked at the prospect of facing Picard. "I've been doing a study and you're right. That thing's working a pattern all right, but the pattern does have some random movements in it. It must be designed to be unpredictable."

"Yes, I've seen it," was his husky bass agreement. "It's working out a search that's deliberately hard to evade. It gives us less than a fifty percent chance of escape."

"That's a more-than-fifty percent chance of getting caught." Tasha bit her lip and took the whole problem personally. "And that's only our certainty level. The actual odds could be a lot drearier. Have you been getting the same results? Is it doing what I think it's doing?"

"If you mean do I see the pattern closing in," Worf said with ominous certainty, "yes. Our odds are dropping with every minute we wait to take action. They won't get better. They'll just get worse. The cage is tightening."

Tasha struck off a few steps of useless pacing, a pitiful echo of the huge cage that was closing around the ship. "What if that thing gets an adrenaline surge or something and bites down harder than it did before? Even if we get shields up to power, we might not be able to take it. At least, not like we are now. Not with shields taxed to protect the whole ship, I mean."

Worf's large brown face pivoted up from the small monitor he'd been glaring at. From beneath his Klinzhai skull and the two downturned lances of his eyebrows, his eyes bored through her. "You're not going to suggest—"

She chewed her lip for a few beats, but her eyes showed none of the vacillation she felt. She shifted from one foot to the other, then, as if braced, to both feet. At her sides, small fists knotted.

"Yes, I am," she said. "Oh, yes I am."

"Do you have the slightest perception of the danger of your proposal, Lieutenant Yar?"

Tasha took refuge in standing at attention as Picard paced around her. Around them the glockenspiel of bridge noise provided little respite. She drew in a long breath and tried not to feel too small as she stood beside Worf. It took all her restraint to keep from snatching a fortifying glance at the Klingon before she could begin.

"Yes, sir. I do. But I feel it's—" She stopped, gulping back her voice, as Picard suddenly turned and coiled his lariat of dare around her. She couldn't talk while he was glowering at her like that.

"Let's hear it," he snapped, as though he didn't know what her problem was at all.

She refused to flinch, but her stomach shrank anyway. "Yes, sir. We've—that is, I've been calculating—"

"Never mind the blasted calculations and give me the bottom line."

"As the ship is, I put our odds for escape at less than fifty percent and shrinking. I've made an analysis of the last attack and it looks like the thing attacked only the high-energy portions of the ship. The warp engine

113

chambers, the high-gain condensers on the weaponry, the sensors, and the shields."

"Your point, please?"

"Um . . . is that the saucer section by itself may not attract the thing's attention."

Picard's glare was molasses, but somewhere in it Tasha was sure she saw a tiny flicker of hope that she could walk away with her head and at least one arm.

"Separate the ship's hulls?" he murmured.

"That's . . . my suggestion, Captain."

"Realizing, of course, that would leave the saucer section with only rudimentary shielding and no appreciable weaponry if the stardrive section were to be destroyed. You *do* add that into your equation, do you not, Lieutenant?"

Tasha actually broke attention and turned toward him. "The saucer section's chances of sneaking away on very low impulse power go up to almost ninety percent, sir, especially if we run some power through the stardrive section and distract the thing."

"Not counting any unknown variables."

She backed into attention again and focused her eyes on the bulkhead over the main viewer. "Correct, sir. But also, if stardrive doesn't have to put out a shield envelope around the entire saucer section too, we'll be able to pump more power into our shields and maybe withstand another attack. Long enough to fight it, I mean, sir."

Picard also turned, but to eye the glowing, pulsing, fuming, flat wall of electrokinetic power that searched for them in the upper range of the screen. "And stardrive's chances of escape in your scenario?"

Tasha now took that glance from Worf, and held it like a lifeline. "Less . . . than eighteen percent, sir."

Jean-Luc Picard circled his two personal hotheads,

came around behind them, saw their shoulders twitch, one set narrow and braced by the gold tabard, the other set broad and tall, making a field of black-over-red. He came around starboard of them again and stopped in front of Worf, with Tasha blocked from his view. Before them the great wide viewscreen spread, holding in its starfield the glaring enemy. The silence mutilated their nerves, the ticking clock of the entity's encroachment, and yet there was strength in the captain's voice when at last he spoke.

"I'll take those odds. Get Riker up here."

"Report, Mr. Data."

Picard hadn't told them his plans yet. Riker now stood near him as Data and Geordi LaForge squared off before them on the bridge.

Riker hovered nearby, acutely aware of Deanna Troi's absence. Was he just being too sensitive or was Data making a point of not looking at him?

Am I imagining it?

"From its actions and its capabilities—lightspeed, for instance," Data began, "I shall risk concluding that it was indeed constructed and couldn't possibly have evolved naturally. It possesses a rudimentary intelligence, reacting to everything on a basic, simple set of instructions, rather like an insect. When a praying mantis eats its own mate, for example, sir, it is simply doing what instinct tells it to do, without any concept of rightness or wrongness."

Picard rubbed his palms against his thighs and resisted the urge to pace. "You're telling me it's the galaxy's biggest bug."

Data cocked his head in a semblance of nodding, but he wasn't ready to commit to that. "Essentially."

"Which leaves out reasoning with it," Riker offered.

115

"Correct, sir," Data said, "but if we can interface with it somehow on its own level, I may be able to effect changes in that simple programming enough to fake it out—" He caught it fast, and glanced at Riker. "Enough to alter its actions."

Data's self-consciousness disappeared as the turbolift opened and emitted Troi, with Dr. Crusher hovering after her, obviously unwilling to let the counselor out of her sight.

"Captain!" Troi blurted. Immediately she drew back, collected herself, and plainly announced, "Sir, they want something from us."

Picard looked at her dubiously. "I beg your pardon? Have you been in contact with it again?"

"You could say that," Crusher said, eyeing Troi. "For a minute there, thought we were going to lose her."

"Indeed. Are you all right, Counselor?"

"Captain, they want something," Troi pushed on, "something we can provide for them, or at least something they think we can provide."

At the center of a brewing storm, Picard turned to accuse Data. "Well, Data? That's certainly not the wrinkle we expected to develop, given your assessment."

Data's finely wrought lips slid open on nothing for a moment. "Sir, that cannot be accurate. All evidence suggests that the hostile is not capable of consciously wanting something from us. It has the intelligence of an insect on all response levels. It responds automatically to stimuli. Its reactions do not involve thought as we know it, but only stimulus and response."

Picard wagged a finger toward Troi and said, "But the counselor tells us otherwise, while you"—the finger swung full about—"tell us it's not attacking out

116

of malice. Something in its very simple programming triggers its actions."

"Yes, sir," Data was glad to agree. "Our weapons attracted and agitated it."

"We do have to realize that there may be a difference between the hostile and the minds I am sensing, sir," Troi pointed out.

"But in any case," Riker pointed out, "we have to deal with it. We can't reason with it or frighten it, and there's only a low chance of deceiving it. But the advantage is that we may be able to figure out its programming, as Data suggested."

"But not," Picard pressed, "if it's rational." He placed his hands upon the bridge horseshoe rail and gazed up meaningfully at Deanna Troi. "If it's rational, we may find ourselves impaled on the horns of Mr. Data's logic."

Data stepped down to the main deck and stood beside his chair at the Ops station as though to draw strength from a companion. "I cannot decipher its program by its actions alone, sir. There would have to be some form of communication or interface. In deference to Counselor Troi, I suggest that though it is programmed, it is also fundamentally alive. It does sustain itself with a basic survival drive."

"If we can figure out that programming," Picard followed, "we can thwart it much as we would draw a moth into a trap with a bright light."

Geordi chose this moment to step past him and take his post at Conn, muttering, "We're gonna need one sucker of a butterfly net."

"There is a danger, sir," Data went on, "in attracting its attention. We might inadvertently get its Irish up and lay an egg."

Picard had already started to comment, but instead

he glowered at the android for a moment. "Yes, I'd already surmised that. Thank you. Mr. Riker—"

"Sir?"

"Prepare to separate the modules."

Riker jolted around. "Sir?"

"You heard me, didn't you?"

"Yes, sir, but . . ."

"Do you have a question?"

Riker straightened and changed his tone. "Yes, I do, sir. Saucer separation is ideally only for situations when we'll be going into battle and can leave the saucer far behind, well out of the danger zone. If we separate in this situation, they'll be completely helpless!"

"Interesting way to put a question." Picard eyed him foxily. "This isn't the time to get cold feet about this ship's capabilities. Lieutenant Yar, recount your statistics for the first officer."

Yar stood straight behind tactical, her cheeks flushed. "Aye, sir. We calculate only a fifty-fifty chance for the whole ship to escape, but if we separate and the battle hull distracts the thing, the saucer section may have as high as ninety percent chance of escape."

"And the battle hull?"

She fidgeted. "About seventeen percent."

A vertical crease appeared over the bridge of Riker's nose; he felt the tightness of his expression as he glared at her, saw a film of sweat break out on her face, though she withstood the force of his glare. He felt the tickle of a single lock of his dark brown hair, like an irritating thread over his left eye. His mind echoed Yar's words, the spectacle they would bring. With them, he felt again all the implications, all the reasoning, all the trouble of having a ship that could do what this ship could do. All the problems of a battle-ready vessel that was also supposed to serve as home and hearth for families, and how awkwardly the two really went together. A battleship is supposed to plunge forward into adversity, a colony vessel to run from it. Both were honorable answers, but what happens when both are the same ship? And when one of them isn't fast enough to run away?

This *Enterprise* had only been separated once before, and that wasn't even a shakedown test. And he himself hadn't even been on board when it happened. He'd heard about it. An insane move, at full warp speed, only the captain's prerogative. Not one Riker felt he would have chosen, but he wasn't Jean-Luc Picard, either. In his mind he suddenly envisioned the starship breaking into two parts at lightspeed, imagined the stardrive section shooting on by as the saucer section abruptly fell out of the warp envelope and crammed down to sublight, an effect that must have thrown every one of its passengers to the deck.

Passengers . . . damn this straddling.

The captain's words rang out. "All hands, prepare to transfer command to the battle bridge."

Picard evidently wasn't interested in opinions on the subject. There would be no group decision this time, Riker saw. If he were captain, there never would be. Not even about whether or not the captain should participate in dangerous away missions. Not even that. But, as he told himself again, again, again—he wasn't Jean-Luc Picard, wasn't the man who now scanned the bridge crew and diplomatically said, "I'll need a volunteer to command the saucer section in this crisis."

Riker wasn't about to speak up. He clamped his lips and waited for someone else to volunteer. Tasha opened her mouth, then closed it, and seemed to hope

119

the captain didn't see. Worf never so much as considered the offer, that much was clear on his swarthy face. Data started to turn from his position at Ops, but thought again and swallowed his unspoken response. Geordi slunk down in his chair to the point of invisibility.

On the upper deck, Beverly Crusher and Deanna Troi stood like mannequins, not daring to rupture the captain's carefully phrased offer or the reactions it would bring. Troi stood especially still. She felt the quandary of each person here as the captain's request flowed into each mind, stirred their consciences, and flowed out again.

Picard turned in place, touching each of them with his gaze. He took this unlikely moment to shake his head almost sentimentally. "I'm very proud of every one of you," he said.

At bridge center, William Riker beamed at them, proud of the stock he had behind him.

Picard touched the intercom on his command chair. "Engineering, this is Picard. Chief Engineer Argyle, report to the bridge to take command of the saucer module."

"Argyle here. Did I hear you right, Captain?"

"You did. Get up here, and bring an adjunct bridge crew with you. We're going to take some action."

"Yes, sir. I'll be right there, sir."

The captain turned forward now without the slightest pause. "Mr. Riker, you may begin."

His stomach churning so hard that he actually bent forward—he knew that Deanna saw the change if no one else did—Riker faced the helm and forced out words that bothered him. A lot.

"Mr. Data, activate the battle bridge power junctions so it's ready when we get there. All hands,

120

prepare to adjourn to the battle bridge. Go to yellow alert. Secure for saucer separation."

The mandolin jangles of starship noise jumped to life on the compact and utilitarian battle bridge. This was a darker place, in some ways a more private place, a place with its mind on its work. The viewscreen here was markedly smaller, as though to demand more focused attention.

Enterprise's command crew bolted from the turbo-lift and settled into their respective places. Tasha and Worf to the tactical and science stations, LaForge to the helm, Data to Ops, the captain to the command center, Riker to the place of all first officers—to the right and slightly behind the captain's shoulder. There was something about that place. Even when a first officer was somewhere else, he was still always right here. And above them, far above, the vast saucer section would soon break away from its sustaining power source, leaving the stardrive section to its little seventeen percent chance of survival and the gratification of knowing what only self-sacrifice can provide to the human soul.

Everyone was aware of LaForge's fingers moving across his panel. Beside him, Data slid into his seat and fed in the corresponding internal adjustments—thrust to get the two modules away from each other as they hung here at full stop, careful limitation of energy surge, just in case the entity could pick up on their move, and myriad other tiny calculations required in what the naked eye saw as a simple maneuver. But this wasn't like pulling apart a child's toy. A million circuitry signals would have to be rerouted, and the energy to feed them would have to be ready. All the while, the creature outside moved along their starfield, glowing and snapping, hot on the trail of what it had so recently tasted.

"On my mark," Riker said, knowing perfectly well they could do it without him. In the corner of his eye he saw the cool back of Data's neck, the muscles working there as Data pegged down to calculating this tricky maneuver, saw the efficiency of android fingers, and felt suddenly crude. "All systems at nominal. Energy feed at fifteen percent, allowing for a twenty percent surge on separation. Flight shields only, star-drive aft thrust at point-zero five sublight. All sections comply clearance of turbolifts and maintenance shafts."

The bridge lift opened. Riker's concentration shattered.

"Deanna, what are you doing here?" He actually stepped away from the captain toward the lift, so driven was he to ask this, to ask why she would expose herself to so puny a chance of living beyond today. But he saw it in her almond eyes as she met his scolding tone unyieldingly, and he felt it in the emotions she flung at him in the next few seconds. He drew up short, canceling what he was about to say—whatever it was.

Even if he had spoken, the words would have been battered aside as Picard jammed his way in front of Riker. "Counselor Troi, damn it, you were ordered to remain with the saucer section. Explain yourself."

She had been completely ready for this, it seemed, for she remained the quintessence of poise. "Sir, I'm needed here. If there's any chance of communication with those beings, I am the only person who can provide it. I'd like to volunteer to remain here."

"Yes," Picard rasped. "And I notice you waited until the lifts were shut down rather than volunteering while we were still topside." He pointed at her and ferociously said, "I'll discuss this with you later. Providing there is a later for us."

Troi let her shoulders settle, and breathed, "Yes, sir." Her legs ached with the tension and now the relief of knowing she would stay and bear this out.

Perhaps she could evade the captain, but not Riker. Her gaze caught his, and he had that look on his face, that look with all the levels going back through it, back and back to the core of his being, and she could see all the levels as though looking into an infinity mirror.

"Mr. Riker, we don't have all day."

"No, sir, I know that. Mr. LaForge, Mr. Data. Effect saucer separation—now."

Every breath held. Every spine stiffened. A subtle hum of power came up from beneath them, up from the caverns of *Enterprise*'s gigantic power factory to the interlocking mechanisms in her neck. With a dissonant grind, the ship pulled herself apart. No level of mechanical perfection would ever diminish the power of that dividing moment, no matter how faint, no matter how insulated. They either heard it or thought they heard it—a husky *clunk-chunk* as couplings released, grippers let go like great claws, their pads sucking back from the ship's yoke with a rubbery reluctance, pins and bolts, lashes and hasps came loose from their harnesses, and all the little pins, which had moments ago held the intricate circuitry that ran the ship, retracted. As though severed by the ax of a great woodsman, the ship became two. The saucer section, with all its families, was suddenly cut adrift.

On the battle bridge, Picard and his command crew watched the stardrive section back slowly away. They seldom got this view of their starship—or even part of her. The saucer section was a wide plate with tapered edges, her frosty whiteness everywhere reflecting the rings of light from rectangular windows and energy-release points. Lights everywhere, like a glittering foil Christmas tree. A kind of pain cut through Captain Picard. He watched as the saucer's impulse engines suddenly came to life and glowed a bright silvery blue. Starship captains were supposed to be decisive. Yet their decisions were like raw surgery to him. Why must there be such things in the universe? Why must there be snakes in the water?

Riker watched the saucer section drift away, mesmerized. *Hmm. Wasn't so bad. Let's hope everything else goes that well.* When he could pull his attention away from the sheer beauty of the saucer, he looked at the captain.

If he'd ever seen Jean-Luc Picard vacillate, now was that time. The captain looked as though he might suddenly call that disk back into place, gather all his charges beneath his robe. For several seconds Riker expected to have to give that order, even figured out what words he would use to keep the captain from looking too foolish.

But Picard said nothing. In silence he bore out the courage of his conviction.

"All secure," LaForge reported. "Free to maneuver, sir."

"Acknowledged," Picard murmured. The taste of commitment. "Maintain status. Send a low-band communiqué to Mr. Argyle. Tell him to maneuver behind that small asteroid belt on the other side of the gas giant. It may mask their escape."

"Aye, sir," Worf said. "Dispatching."

They watched in silence as the saucer section's impulse drive flared for those few moments, then

124

faded back, providing the huge disk with just enough thrust to coast toward the dangerous parameters of the entity's shrinking cage. For Riker especially, this terrible moment had its profundities. There were many kinds of civilizations that would never have provided him the chance to die here today, at least in a place of his own choice. The beauty of technology awed him. It was the freedom to build what floated outward before them, the freedom to strike toward greater goals and more profitable accomplishments, to have the resources to use the wealth of their healthy society to create marvels like the one he'd just seen, and it was the freedom to die in space if that was the turn of the day.

He glanced once again at Captain Picard, and yes, it was there too. Awe. The captain didn't seem afraid. More than anything, he looked a bit miffed at the entity for making him break his ship in two.

Or is it something else? Riker wondered. *I know him so little.*

Their trance was broken as Picard turned to Troi and bluntly asked, "Getting anything at all?"

The black curls of her hair made her face seem pale, the dark eyes set there like onyx chunks. "Nothing yet, sir."

"Worf, any changes in its energy pattern?"

Worf's guttural response carried a distinct impatience. "Only the same flux and shift it's been doing all this time, sir."

"Lieutenant Yar, you keep an eye on the locations of the saucer and that thing. I want to know if they're about to run afoul of each other, and I want to know ahead of time."

"Yes, sir," she said, and instantly bent over her glossy board.

"On second thought, best we not wait. Mr. Riker, let's make a noise in the darkness."

Riker nodded, never mind that it was a silly gesture. His throat was dry and he didn't want to speak up until he'd swallowed a few times. Then he tapped the command intercom and said, "Riker to engineering. Do we have warp power?"

Engineer MacDougal spoke up so quickly she might as well have been on the battle bridge with him. *"Stardrive is still down, sir, but we should have it back on line soon. It was an electrical burnout and not a matter of power generation."*

"I'm not asking for warp drive yet," Riker said, watching Picard to see if this was what the captain had in mind. "I just need a flush of power through the tubes. Say, ten percent. Enough to keep its attention off the saucer until they're out of the area. Be ready to shut down immediately so we can hide again too."

"I understand what you need, Mr. Riker, but warp power isn't that easy to control. There has to be a grace period on either side of the flush."

Riker glanced self-consciously at Picard, who was watching him, and acknowledged, "Whatever works. And whenever you're ready. Riker out."

Now they would make a noise. They would flip a coin in the dark warehouse and hope its tiny ring could be heard but not found.

Up from the bowels of the engineering section, deep within the core matter/antimatter reactors that made a starship what it was, came a surge of raw power. Even that tiny surge, that ten percent, could be felt.

Then there was a change on the screen. The crackling infrared diffraction image of their pursuer suddenly paused in its search across the bottom of the

126

viewscreen, and made a deliberate turn in their direction.

"It's coming after us," Yar reported. She gripped the edge of her panel, refusing to look up at the screen. Instead she watched the two target points, starship and hostile, close toward one another. Her voice quavered. "Direct line."

"Point-three-zero sublight, helm," Riker said, gripping the headrest of LaForge's chair, "heading, two-two-four mark one-five."

"Aye, sir."

"Faster, LaForge."

"Aye, sir, executing."

"Lieutenant, is it following?" the captain asked, not turning.

Yar nodded, even though he wasn't watching her. "Aye, sir. It is."

"Speed?"

"Point-four sublight."

"All right . . ." Picard didn't sit down in the command chair despite his movement toward it. "Let's cast the pearls and see if the swine follows. Lieutenant LaForge, increase to fifty percent sublight."

"Point-five, aye."

The beheaded stardrive section, its energy-rimmed nacelles now its most prominent feature, slid around on an imaginary rail and cut diametrically across the entity's search pattern, exactly opposite to the heading of the saucer section, away from the swirling gas giant, away from the tiny belt of asteroids that would someday pull together into a new planet and circle the proud little sun of this system.

"Captain," Worf said, breaking the concentration, "MacDougal reports we now have sufficient power for shields, but not stardrive and not much for weapons. She estimates just a few minutes for those."

Picard nodded without looking.

"I think it's working, sir," Riker told him, his voice so low that it hurt his throat. He mentally ticked off the distance between stardrive and the saucer, and the time needed until the saucer section could be considered safe. "Good thinking, Captain."

"Sir!" Tasha rasped, sudden horror in her voice. "It's—"

"I see it. Full about. Power up the shields! Get that damned thing's attention!"

"Powering up," Tasha said instantly. "Battle shields at full."

No matter how careful the plan, no matter the amount of hardware, the high-tech physics, the level of mathematics and detailed analysis—no matter any of that, mankind had never been able to second-guess, sideswipe, or overcome plain old bad luck. Who could know how long the thing had been roaming the galaxy, doing what it was doing today? There was no way to know what habits it had developed, what preferences, what impulses it had learned to follow. And who could know what it spotted?

A glint of light off the saucer's hull . . . a tiny leak of subatomic particles from the impulse fusion reactor . . . a high-frequency output from maintenance? These were things that would be completely ignored in the daily running of a starship. But somehow, something told the menace that this was the likeliest source of dinner. Its bug brain got stuck on the idea of *that* target instead of *this* one, and so it turned on the saucer.

Picard spun to Worf. "Anything?"

"No change, sir," the Klingon said clearly and

fiercely. "We're putting out twenty times the energy being emitted from the saucer section right now, but it doesn't seem impressed."

"Make a tight pass. We've got to draw it off."

Geordi LaForge fought to keep his hands from shaking on the controls at the idea of sweeping by that mass of ugly. What he saw with his enhanced vision was so vicious a knot of power that he avoided looking at the screen. He would fly on instruments; he would do as ordered. He would push the ship past that nightmare and swing around it on the end of an invisible rope.

Too bad this ship didn't have a chicken switch.

The ship swung through space, doubling back toward the crackling energy field of its enemy. Now the saucer section was dominant in the viewscreen, and between them and it. A wall of blinding, snapping electrical tongues, a terrible prism to look through.

LaForge increased speed without being told. He knew what he had to do. Give that firecracker a taste of raw antimatter.

For one self-indulgent moment, he looked toward Data. The android was deceptively impassive, a human form wrapped in infrared, a man-figure of hot and cool places, all moving inside a glow. As nothing mechanical could, Data felt the gaze and returned it. He responded only with a significant lifting of his straight brows. Together, at least. Like soldiers should die if they must die at all.

Behind them, Riker held the helm chair more tightly than he meant to. Now the screen before them was ablaze with the closeness. If luck went with them, they'd be in big trouble damned soon. A spear of anger pierced him when he saw the saucer section's impulse drive come back on. Argyle knew it was following them now, and that they were too hopelessly slow to get away. Even so, like a turtle trying to get off a road in the middle of traffic, the big disk kept surging forward on full sublight. Frustration bent its ugly face over him. He wished Picard had insisted one of them stay. All at once the saucer section needed a real command and not just engineers.

The entity stepped up speed to follow, and stardrive did the same, even faster. The ship tipped as LaForge swung it around in front of the enemy's electrical body. As they passed it they saw that it was indeed more flat than round, a gigantic field of computer fakery, yet somehow completely animated, somehow walking around in space without the screen it was supposed to be displayed on. Its electrokinetic bands sparked and erupted as the stardrive section plowed past it and swished off in the other direction.

Picard came up between Data and LaForge. "What the devil! Nothing?"

"No response," LaForge said, and somehow he was disappointed.

"Worf!"

"No explanation, sir," Worf boomed. "It's unrelenting on the saucer."

Data looked up and said, "Perhaps it is something more than an insect, Captain." And as he said it, he looked across the small bridge at Deanna Troi, who stood now beside Tasha, ominously silent, leaving herself open to assault by mind weapon.

"Shark," Riker muttered.

"Number One?"

Riker turned to the captain. "It's a shark focusing on one fish in a school. It ignores tastier morsels for the one it focuses on."

"Sir." Troi spoke up suddenly. Her voice was a

130

shock on the compact bridge. "We must draw it off. The saucer—"

"Won't stand the attack, I know, Counselor, I know. Shields to full power. Engineering, this is the captain. Have we got warp speed?"

"MacDougal, sir, and barely. I can give you up to warp three."

"Do so! And I want an emergency antimatter dump on my mark—"

Riker spun around. "Sir?"

"We're going to make damned sure it can't ignore us again. We're going to crash the gate, and right now. That thing is *not* going to—"

"Sir!" Yar choked. "It's closing on the saucer! Burst of speed at point-seven-five—"

"Set course dead center on it, warp three and engage!"

Both LaForge and Data actually cocked their heads toward each other as though to see if they'd both heard the same thing, and that the captain saw it.

"I said engage!" he thundered. Then his voice lowered to a whisper, like a gathering volcano. "We're going right through that pretty bastard."

Chapter Seven

PICARD STOOD HIS battle bridge as though it were a chariot. In his hands he held the reins of chargers, in his eyes the image of the enemy.

Even to Riker, who himself was a tree trunk of a man, Picard suddenly seemed larger than life. Every ship had its no-win scenario; this was theirs. Despite the primitive programming of that thing out there, it was very efficient and it had them cold. They were going to have to deal with it; there was no getting away.

It filled the screen now, leaving no black edges, a wall of fulmination and color, just the kind of thing a mother tells her children never to touch, never even to think of touching. The stardrive section aimed its great cobra's head for that wall and jammed forward at all the speed she could muster. And even warp three—warp anything—was impressive and terrifying enough for anyone in his right mind.

In the last few seconds, Riker closed his eyes. He had to, to accept the fact that he was about to die to save the others. That was his unspoken duty, he knew;

it was why the ship separated at all—when push came to shove, the stardrive section was expendable. They were supposed to sacrifice themselves, to step in front of the bullet. This was the whole idea.

His thick body tightened. He'd tasted the metallic flavor of the thing's attack before and now—

Enterprise crashed into the electrical wall at dead center, and erupted into pyrotechnics with a deafening *crack*. Voltage snapped throughout the ship, accosting every panel, every living body, a terrible concussion after concussion. Spasms racked through, each one accompanied by a blitz of senseless lights. Riker heard Deanna shriek as it focused on her, but he couldn't even turn around, couldn't even look.

Crack . . . CRAAAAAACK . . .

And the ship burst out the other side—a shaken vessel, filled with shaken people, sucking a tail of spectral fire after it.

"LaForge, veer into the asteroids! Engineering, this is Picard—"

How could he talk? How could he still be getting sound up out of his throat?

Riker tried to turn again, this time toward the captain, and this time he managed it. Picard was crouching against his command chair, one elbow locked over the chair's arm, shouting into the intercom. "Engineering! Emergency antimatter dump on my mark—do you copy!"

"Engineering . . . uh, we copy . . . ready when—"

"LaForge, are we in those asteroids yet?"

Trying to push his hands through a snapping electrical field that still swirled around his panel, LaForge pecked the course into the helm. Each time he pecked, his fingers were assaulted by the churning voltage, but he kept on until the ship was driving itself into the dirty trail of preplanetary garbage between the gas giant and the star.

Through a glittering cloud that filled the bridge from bulkhead to bulkhead and ceiling to floor, Riker strained to see Picard and beyond him, Deanna.

She was crouching too, both hands holding on to the bridge rail, her face turned toward one arm as though to shield her eyes and perhaps much more of herself.

But an instant later it was the viewscreen that snatched his attention, in time for him to see the thing drop the bone it was carrying and try to get the one it saw reflected in the stream. Its colors flared and it shot toward them, now huge on the screen, filling it, racing toward them at unimaginable speed. They'd done it—they'd attracted its attention. Too well. "Captain, it's after us!" he shouted over the electrical lightning all around them.

"Full speed!" Picard thundered. He too turned, looked, saw.

"Entering asteroids now, sir," LaForge called, his special sight barely able to stand the dance of lights around him.

Picard's voice rang through the ship. "MacDougal, dump the antimatter tank—now!"

When the exhaust was triggered, it sounded for all the world like a giant toilet flushing. There was a swirl of sound, then a shudder crashed through the lower sections, and in a radical maneuver that was reserved for unexpected containment leaks, the ship regurgitated and dumped all the contents of her antimatter tank. Antimatter washed out from the nacelles and spewed into the asteroid belt. Wherever it struck matter in the vacuum of space, there was an

134

explosion—a huge one. An explosion that whipped its tendrils of fire this way and that for thousands of miles, some hundreds of thousands. Each blow and its corresponding halo of smaller blows sent matter/antimatter shock waves plunging across space, rocking the starship forward each time as she raced to get away.

The ship coursed through the asteroids and out the other side, but as soon as the antimatter was flushed the warp speed fell away and they dropped to an impulse crawl. Everyone on the bridge was thrown forward as the ship whined to compensate for the shocking drop in speed. Riker raised an arm to shield his eyes from the pyrotechnics still running amuck on the bridge, and found the viewscreen in time to see a string of bright yellow explosions, large, small, blinding.

"Keep the shields a priority," Picard gasped. "They'll be weak on impulse power alone, and you may need to tap phaser energy to maintain them. Engineering, do you copy?" He was still hanging on to his chair somehow and funneling orders this way and that while he watched the thing settle into the asteroid belt and sit there eating explosions.

Then one last splatter of color and voltage ignited on the bridge and shocked each of them like a jolt from an exposed circuit. But it wasted no more time. Now it whistled around the bridge with a kind of finality, drew its vortex into a knot, and latched onto Data as though sucked there. It hit him with a stiff hand, knocking him right out of his chair. For every volt of electricity the others were now suddenly spared, Data had to take up the slack. He was dragged sideways and driven backward against the bridge rail until the force could push him no farther. A red-orange envelope formed around him, sparks flashing inside it, and shook him. Within it he shuddered and gasped, the bellows that served as lungs being squeezed along with the rest of him.

"No!" Geordi shouted. This time the menace was familiar, and neither it nor Geordi's reaction was unexpected—by Riker or by Data.

As Geordi bolted from his own chair, Riker caught him at the end of a good old boardinghouse reach, his hand clamping around Geordi's arm like a vise. In the same instant Data used one of those awful squeezes to gasp out, "Stay away! Geordi—"

The static sizzled across Geordi's hand as he reached out, but Data's command made him draw back again. Through his visor he stared at the devilish infrared sheath, and it spat back at him with a strangely comprehensible warning.

"LaForge, as you were!" Picard maneuvered between them. He examined the white field of static as it snapped around Data.

If Data could feel pain, he was feeling it now. If they had any doubt that he could, for this moment they had none.

Riker came around forward of Data, keeping just clear of the static envelope. Only once did he look away from it, only long enough to check on Troi. She was on the upper deck, gripping the rail, staring over it at them, her face lined with concern and anticipation. But she looked okay for now, considering.

"Captain," Riker began, holding out a hand as though to steady the situation, "if we can talk to it now—"

LaForge pushed forward, stopped only by the presence of Picard. "No! We've got to get him out of it!"

"This might be our only chance," Riker insisted.

"He doesn't deserve to be on your sucker list, Mr. Riker," LaForge said bitterly, just short of snarling.

"I know," Riker told him. "I know. Move back. That's an order. Captain . . ."

Picard made a half-circle around the android and the force that held him. "Yes . . . yes . . . steady, everyone." He moved in so closely that the static field ran down his arms and legs and caused ripples on his skin. "Data, can you hear me?"

The crackling settled down suddenly. It was as though a balloon popped and shrank to its natural shape, ugly transparent colors wrapping Data and schooling around him. His breathing lost some of its gaspiness, though he still panted and strained against what was obviously still an attack. His eyes were fixed on the dimly lit battle bridge ceiling, but working as though there were words up there to read. He blinked and squinted, fighting for meaning in what he saw. His arms were flared at his sides, his hands spread, long fingers twitching.

Riker moved to the captain's side very slowly, and spoke in low tones barely above whispers. "There's some kind of harmonic sympathy going on. Like radio waves causing a crystal to vibrate. Somehow, he's compatible with it."

Picard nodded, once.

"Data?" he began again. "Can you hear me? Do you understand me?"

For a time there was nothing.

Then, the tiniest "Yes . . ."

The response went through them all like a knife.

"Data, speak to me," the captain prodded, using his resonant voice for the effective tool it was.

"I . . ."

"Go on. Try harder. I'm listening. Go on."

"Sub . . . circuit . . . com . . . com . . ."

"Communication?"

"Yes . . ."

"That's what I was hoping to hear. Can you talk to it?"

Data's brushstroke features contorted with frustration. "I can't . . . can't transmit . . ."

"Keep trying. Stay calm, everyone. No one move. Worf, report."

Even the Klingon was driven to lower his voice in the presence of the vortex's assault on Data. "Still chewing the antimatter reactions in the asteroid belt, sir. No sign of changing course."

"Speaking to you . . ."

Her voice was soft, but this time it had an inflection they didn't recognize, one that made them turn to her now in spite of Data's entrapment as Deanna Troi stepped stiffly down to the main deck. Riker reached out for her and she took the hand he offered, but her expression was that of one who was looking into a blinding light. The same as Data's now—seeing something that wasn't there.

"Your language," she murmured. "I speak in."

Riker was holding her hand, and now he began a hesitant step that would draw him right up close.

"No," Picard said sharply then, gesturing him back. With an extra push he nudged Riker away and came between them, quite aware of Troi's hand, suddenly empty, reaching for Riker's as it fell away. So part of her was here, at least.

"Who are you?" Picard began carefully.

Troi's eyes began to tear with the strain.

"All . . . you end . . ."

"We don't understand. We don't know what you are," the captain clearly said.

138

Troi began to tremble, a bone-deep trembling that came as much from her own effort as from the effect of whatever was happening to her. Despite Picard's renouncement of folklore and ghost stories, the battle bridge took on the hazy elemental aura of a seance. Troi herself was like a specter now, a thing of dark times, of times when ignorance made indelible marks upon the imaginations of all men for all time. She was a whisper of legend somehow transferred into the present. Her hair glowed, ebony beneath the flashings, and in spite of all the lights from Data's assailant, her eyes were their usual pumice black. Yet in the midst of enchantment there was also the conscious work of a scientist. And never once were they allowed to forget that Data was also involved; the snapping brightness from the vortex around him slithered across Troi's face in a constant and patternless reminder.

Riker stepped tentatively toward her, and was grateful that Picard didn't try to stop him. "Deanna . . ." he began. Then he had nothing to say afterward.

Troi forced herself to speak. Somehow they could see and understand that the insistence was hers and no one else's. "You . . . can end . . . it."

The captain squinted as though he could see the words. Something about the way she said it made him motion the bridge to silence.

Her voice—still soft. A raspy whisper only. But it held a power, a decisiveness Picard hadn't expected to hear at such a moment. And when the statement was over, it was completely over. Her effort slid off, she was allowed a deep breath, and the light patterns reflecting on her face began to fade.

Riker and Picard spun about, and sure enough Data was looking more like Data and less like a Fourth of July sparkler.

"No one move!" Picard warned. "Wait till it's completely gone."

In spite of the order, Riker sidled toward Troi, keeping his eye on her while Data glittered in his periphery, and when she suddenly collapsed, he was almost beside her.

The color fled from her face, and Troi dropped so sharply that Riker almost missed her completely. He was able to catch her upper arm and keep her head from striking the bridge rail, but she turned in his grip like a dangling fish until he could rearrange himself and lay her down on the deck. He knelt beside her, brushed the trailing black curls from her forehead, and looked up in time to see the same thing happen to Data.

The android's denser body struck the deck with a loud thud, and both Geordi and Worf were there to turn him over. In the dimness that suddenly reestablished itself on the bridge, he looked baffled and confused, but unlike Troi he was conscious.

Picard glanced once around the bridge to be sure the electrical effect had truly gone away. Then: "Yar, condition of that creature?"

"Still involved with the asteroids, sir," she reported, "though going after the antimatter explosions very deliberately. It doesn't seem to understand what the disturbances are. Seems unclear about what it should do."

Picard huffed. "Aren't we all. LaForge? Leave Data to Worf and get us away from here quickly."

"Yes, sir—heading?"

"Back toward the saucer. While we still have the chance."

With that he knelt beside Riker, who was hovering rather helplessly over Troi. "She alive?"

"Her pulse is like a bass drum," Riker told him. "Under these circumstances, who knows what that means?"

"I'll take it for the good," Picard said ruefully, "since it's all we've got."

"Are we going to reestablish contact with the saucer, Captain?" Riker asked, though he knew the answer. This time reestablishment wouldn't mean the trouble was over. Quite the opposite. It would mean they'd utterly failed.

Picard eyed the screen. "Looks like we crowed before we were out of the woods. Tasha, contact Engineer Argyle and inform him we're picking them up."

"Aye, sir; right away."

"Make that low band, as frugal a message as possible."

"Aye, sir."

Now the captain lowered his voice as he turned back to Riker, and clasped Troi's wrist to find her pulse for himself. "What do you make of all this? Those words she spoke . . . and is she in contact with the same thing that's contacting Data?"

Riker shook his head. "It's pretty boggy right now. Whatever it is, it doesn't seem to be affecting them both in the same way. She keeps talking about these— well, these *people* as though she knows them, and it doesn't glitter around her like it does on Data. And it didn't grab her. Did you notice she could still move around? It's like the electrical field of the entity is focusing on him, but speaking through her."

"Yes, but these messages she's perceiving. How accurate is her telepathy? I've never seen anything like this from Troi before. You know as well as I do that Betazoid telepathy is subfrequency and seems super-

natural, but that it's perfectly explainable scientifically. This business of behaving like a spiritual medium,
though . . . I don't buy into that."

"If it's any help," Riker told him, "I don't think she
does either, sir."

"What was it she said? We can end it? End what?"
He tilted a little closer and lowered his voice. "Have
you any idea at all?"

Riker licked his lips. So this was what a first officer
was for. To come up with hypotheses about things he
knew nothing about. To fudge answers out of nothing.
Then again, sometimes that was the best way to get
the answers: plow on through until you hit wall or
water. "End it. *We* can. I wonder if that even means us
specifically. Could it have been talking to the life
essences Troi was sensing?"

"Or rather, were they talking to it? Tell you what,"
Picard said with sudden conviction, "soon as these
two can sit straight again, we're going to put them
down side by side and get some answers. We've got the
messages right in our hands, and we simply aren't
interpreting them correctly. It's time we did."

"How is she, Mr. Riker?" Tasha Yar kept her voice
low. Afraid to attract attention to herself, possibly
because she had stepped away from her post at this
critical, touchy moment, she knelt beside Troi and
leaned over her, nearly whispering.

"I'm no doctor," Riker said simply, venting his
frustration. If he had time to step away from his own
post, Troi would be on the way to auxiliary sickbay,
but there simply weren't those extra seconds to spare.
So she would remain here, beneath his hands, within
his sight, under what little care he could offer.

"Sir, are we going to reconnect with the saucer

section?" Yar asked. She looked at him with eyes that wanted everything to be all right, and she seemed as innocent and hopeful as a Disney drawing.

"I don't think we have much choice," he told her. "It just didn't work. We get used to situations that work out, and it's hard to get hit with one that doesn't. Fortunes of risk, that's all, Lieutenant." He gave her a dismissing toss of his head, silently ordering her back to tactical, but she didn't go.

"Mr. Riker?"

"Yes, what is it?"

"Sir . . . it was my idea to separate the sections." Tasha paused, waiting to catch his attention again. When she did, she tightened her thin narrow lips and asked, "Should I apologize to the captain?"

Riker dropped himself into the wishing well of those eyes, just for a moment. Her eyes were enhanced with a simple stroke of eyeliner and a touch of mascara; not very much, as though she were unsure and self-conscious about her femininity. Riker found himself fascinated by those thin brown lines, now slightly smudged and a tad uneven. Tasha Yar was all good intentions in one package. Had Riker not reviewed the personnel files of the bridge officers when he got this assignment, he'd have taken one look into those eyes and at the supple, slim body under them and reassigned her to teaching kindergarten to all the children on *Enterprise* who would brighten to see her face each day.

He felt that way right now—like she was the child and he was the teacher. There was nothing in her face, in her eyes, to remind him of her upbringing on a pathetic excuse for a colony, yet he thought of it. A colony that had actually seceded from the Federation. Its economy crashed within three decades of that

143

secession. That distant colony where gangs became the ruling bodies, a place that resembled nothing and nowhere as much as it resembled the aftermath of the French Revolution, a place where a bad system was torn down in the name of the people and replaced by something entirely worse. A place whose day-to-day life made the Reign of Terror look organized. Mobs, gangs, indulgence of some, starvation of others, parents teaching their children to be alone because self-sufficiency meant survival. Children functioning like rats in the rubbish. And among them, Tasha. Surviving. Running. Fighting when she had to, eating when she could. Developing the single-mindedness that would allow her to move in record time to chief of security on a mainline starship. Didn't happen every day.

A wicked way to grow up. Too quick, too hard, and too unforgiving. She'd missed all those girl things, all the giggling and the ducking behind each other and the moon-eyed crushes and the wondrous ignorance that lets a girl believe what she sees on first glance. For Tasha there had been no mirrors or fussing, and if there had been mirrors, wouldn't she have shrunk away from the gaunt teenager whose hair was cropped to make her look like a boy—less likely to attract the attention of those who took their low-class habits out in casual rape? From the day her mother first took out a knife and sawed off her four-year-old daughter's knee-length braid, Tasha had learned to deal.

Yet she could still look at him now with this absolute cleanness, this complete faith in him and in everything she saw when she looked at a senior officer, everything Starfleet meant for someone who had grown up under mob rule. As he looked at her now, a half ton of responsibility fell on him. What could he say to her that wouldn't wrinkle that antiseptic faith? She was stronger with it than without it, a better officer in her purity than the woman she might have become if she gave in to the callousness to which she had every right.

Reaching over the stirring form of Troi, Riker cupped Tasha's elbow. "Whatever you do," he said, "don't apologize."

Chapter Eight

BEHIND THEM, ANTIMATTER explosions were still lighting up the solar system in all directions. Amazing that so little antimatter connecting with so little matter could result in such conflagration.

Getting away from the immediate vicinity was easy enough—the creature wasn't watching for the moment, busy devouring the pure energy of matter/antimatter reactions among the asteroids, and therefore stardrive had a few extra seconds to ride the detonation shock waves and get back toward the saucer section. Easy, considering what had gone on so far today.

Reuniting the ships was something else.

Riker stood beside the science station where Deanna Troi was now sitting. She appeared disturbed, fatigued, aching, somber, like someone who had just heard bad news, but she seemed aware of the circumstances, perhaps too acutely aware.

Watching the disconnected saucer section loom toward them in the viewscreen, Riker felt a shiver of anticipation. This was the tricky part, the difference between pulling an ocean liner out of a dock and pulling back into one. Or maybe like docking one of those aircraft carriers the screen had shown them. Angle had to be right. Every linkage, hasp, and junctor had to line up exactly to its sleeve. Luckily *Enterprise* had computers made to do that. There was really no such thing as doing it manually, although that was the term they used for less-than-fully automated hookup. *Really* doing it manually would take all day and half the night. But for the moment Riker was glad Picard watched so carefully as the big ships approached each other, saucer at full stop, stardrive moving forward on inertia so as not to attract the entity's attention. At no other time would they be more helpless than during those last five feet before hookup.

At the last moment a shock wave from the antimatter explosions in the asteroid belt washed across the two ships and pushed between them like a wedge.

"Reverse!" Picard sharply ordered, and beneath him the ship moved to comply. "Stabilize. Smartly now. We may not get another chance. Approach on tight-frequency tractor beams. Get us in there."

"Aye, sir," LaForge mumbled, sweating.

"Worf, assist."

"Yes, sir," the Klingon acknowledged. He left Data sitting on the deck steps and slid in behind Ops.

Data blinked and watched, but made no attempt to regain his position; in fact, Riker noticed a thick preoccupation on the android's part.

Now what? he thought. *Look at him. He looks as though a straight answer would do him as much good as it'd do me. Maybe he tried too hard. Maybe he took me too seriously and let that thing get inside and poach him. Next time I'll keep my mouth shut.*

147

Maybe.

The deck rocked beneath him. He grabbed for the bridge rail and looked at the viewscreen barely in time to see an artificially lighted view of the saucer section's docking sleeve. Then the viewer went black and disengaged automatically.

"Docking complete, Captain," LaForge reported. "All sections, all junctions show green. Docking chief reports all secure."

"Signal acknowledgment. All stop. Well," Picard said with a sigh, "that was a blasted fiasco if ever I saw one. Evidently there's not going to be an easy way out of this one."

"Orders, sir?" Riker asked.

"Captain!" Yar blurted. "It's gone!"

The bridge might as well have whirled under them like a giant lazy Susan, they all turned so fast.

"Gone?" Picard repeated. "Just like that?"

"Even faster." Yar glowered over her equipment as though angrier at the phenomenon's disappearance than she had been about its attacks. It was allowed to go away, but not without checking with the security chief first. "No trail, no residual energy, nothing. Popped out of existence."

"Charming. It's playing some bloody game with us. Well, I'd say this confirms Data's hypothesis about interdimensionality with rather alarming panache."

"Maybe we should get out of the area while we can, sir," Riker suggested.

"Oh, no, not on your life, Number One," the captain responded, "and I mean that quite literally."

"But if—"

"Can't you see? It's demonstrated quite clearly that it's no insect and it's no shark. It's a trapdoor spider.

We move—it springs. All it has to do is wait. Wait until we make a move. And we're not going to." He turned to the waiting faces of the tactical bridge crew and authoritatively said, "All stop. Shut down all systems including internal with the exception of basic life support. Turn off everything that can conceivably be turned off. Suspend experimentation and testing of any kind unless I specifically order it, all food processors, all extraneous utensils, terminals, holographs, intraship communication, generators, plumbing, everything. Reduce ship's heating and lighting to bare minimum. Keep sound levels down. Tell people to get where they're going, then stay there. We're going to shut down the turbolifts within ten minutes and use only maintenance ladders. Have you got that?"

Riker tilted his head dubiously. "I don't know how long we can hold out like that."

Picard's dark eyes thinned. "Cities have endured blackouts before, Mr. Riker," he said, "and so shall we. Ever since submarine warfare and the blitz, groups of people have had to endure periods of excruciating silence."

"Those were trained military personnel, sir. It's going to be harder on—"

The captain silenced him with a toss of his head and unexpectedly lowered his voice. "Don't be insulting."

"Right. Sorry, sir." Riker cast an appropriate gesture at Worf and said, "Shipwide systems comply. I'll check everything personally."

The captain nodded. "As soon as we get back to the main bridge, I want a complete systems check in preparation to feed antimatter from the reserves into the main tank to make up for our loss just now. I want it to go smoothly, Riker. That's a lot of energy

149

changing places, and we don't want it detected. Notify engineering. They'll have their hands full with the exchange and the charge up to warp power."

"Aye, sir, I'll see to it."

"All hands, prepare to transfer command—"

"Captain—" Troi came to life abruptly and pushed herself unsteadily from the seat. Had she not caught herself on the command chair, she might have fallen, but there was something more than physical stamina keeping her on her feet.

The captain caught her arm. "Counselor, you stay where you are. I want to have Dr. Crusher look at you again."

"Later, sir, please. Captain, may I speak with you privately?" she asked, with a small glance at Riker. "This is . . . feels very personal to me, sir."

The captain indulged in a long study of her eyes, her expression, the degree of strength with which she clamped her hand on his arm—something she didn't seem to realize she was doing—and he measured her veracity like a lie detector. His gauges were his experience, hard-earned abilities to judge what he heard by the expression of those who were saying it, the tone of voice and the slight quavers in it, the flickering of eyes, and the slight tightness of lashes. He believed her, believed this wasn't just a whim, that she had something critical to say and was still rational enough to know the difference.

He sensed Riker approaching, knew the first officer was looking over his shoulder, taking advantage of his height to look at Deanna Troi and silently ask if perhaps he could also be involved in her secrets. Only that made the captain's decision tricky.

"Very well," Picard said. He took Troi's arm and

steered her toward the turbolift. "All hands, transfer command back to the main bridge immediately. Riker, you square off with Data. Get some answers. We're going to hit this problem from both fronts. Counselor, my ready room. The rest of you . . . stations."

Riker watched perhaps too longingly as the captain escorted Troi from the dim battle bridge. He could live without her; perhaps he would have to. He'd called a halt to all relationships when he accepted this post, staring at twenty years of single-mindedness, and he'd kept that promise to himself well enough. Until he stepped onto the ship itself. Until *she* floated out of nowhere toward him. Suddenly the years ahead appeared more a test than an assignment. Was it unwise for long-term commanders to commit themselves to relationships? This whole business about having families aboard ship . . . it was so new. Did anyone know if ship's commanders reacted differently when their loved ones were on board than they did if they could divorce themselves from everything but the dangers at hand?

Deanna would know. And she's the only person I can't ask.

He was jolted from his thoughts as two forms stepped by him toward the turbolift, and he shook himself. Before him, Yar and Worf were on the lift with the captain and Troi. Brushing his left arm, Geordi had just stepped by with Data in tow.

Catching Data's arm, Riker stopped him. "Data, you stay here."

LaForge started to turn, protectiveness roaring up in the set of his jaw and shoulders, and only a bark from the captain caused him to leave Data behind in

151

the hands of a less-than-compassionate superior. "Coming, sir," he said, his tone low, as though to warn Riker.

Perhaps it wasn't insolence, and perhaps it wasn't a warning. But Riker couldn't blame him if it were.

The turbolift doors shut with a vacuumlike *cussshhh.*

Data remained facing the lift for a wishful few seconds. Actually it was longer than a few. Enough longer that the pause was obvious. When finally he began to turn, he was at full attention—a stance recognized by both of himself and Riker as painfully unnecessary.

"How do you feel?" the first officer asked.

"Functional," Data said, "though weak."

"Want to sit down?"

"No, thank you, sir. I shall stand."

The better to walk away from you, my dear. Come on, Will, make your case and be done with it. "Do you have a report on what happened to you?"

That wasn't exactly what he hoped would come out when he opened his mouth, but Riker faced Data squarely with the question and told himself he'd find a way to bring up the other subject sooner or later.

"I have some new information, sir," Data said, "though not all clear."

"I'm listening. Make it concise."

Data nodded once, then thought about the right words.

"The phenomenon," he began slowly, "is like me."

"Like you? Some form of—" Riker stopped himself and was embarrassed when Data filled in the blank.

"A mechanism," the android said. "Crafted by someone else. A living tool, fabricated at so high a

152

level of engineering that it may or may not be a life-form."

"Were you speaking to it, then?"

"I was in contact. I dare not say there was a conversation, however. It took from me what it pleased and gave me only what it chose. I was receiving, but I was unable to transmit. Perhaps I was too far away from the source. Or perhaps I was simply not built to be a transmitter . . . as I hoped I would be."

"Data, we don't expect you—"

"Perhaps if I go out alone in a shuttlecraft, I could gain more intimate contact."

"Don't be crazy," Riker blurted. "Nobody's going out in anything, not even you."

Until it came out, Riker didn't think about the callous implication of that sentence, but now he held his breath and hoped Data bleeped over it.

"This mechanism is dangerous to us, sir. I am no longer in doubt of that," the android went on. The dim lighting of the battle bridge caught the starkness of his coloring as he stood there on the upper deck. "It must only be a matter of limited time before it learns to differentiate between general matter in this area of space or that nearby solar system and the construction of the *Enterprise.* It will demolish the ship, just as it demolished the *Gorshkov* three centuries ago."

"Now wait a minute," Riker said, holding up his hand. "We aren't sure that's what happened to the *Gorshkov.*"

"*I* am sure. It will destroy us in a singularly violent manner as soon as it can. It intends to destroy us as soon as it can find us again."

And he was absolutely sure, if that could be gleaned from his expression. He was even more impassive than usual, and Riker had to look hard to see any flickers of emotion. Data might be an android, but his face was usually pleasantly animated, and the blankness bothered Riker. Data's habitual demeanor would have reassured him a little.

Slowly he asked, "Did you get any clues as to its nature?"

"It was built eons ago, and it contains the destructive power of several starships," Data said flatly. "Most disturbingly, though, sir, it is encoded with what it believes is permission to use that power at its own discretion."

"Oh, great," Riker moaned. "I've seen bulldozers with more discretion than that thing."

Data paused, and if he could be in a mood, he wasn't in one for chitchat. The pause was long enough to make Riker uncomfortable, enough to make him look up.

"Go on," Riker said with a touch of weariness.

"As I said, it may be a level of machine evolution so high that it is virtually alive."

An ugly prospect, Riker thought, but luckily he didn't say that. "And?"

"And . . . it destroys mechanical vessels which contain energies it recognizes, while preserving the life forces of the living beings involved."

"But why? Why would it roam the galaxy sucking up life essences? Who would build a machine to destroy ships but preserve the stuff of living consciousness? That doesn't make sense."

"Unknown, sir. But it does make sense from a defensive point of view. We do not as yet know if it has the same reaction to whole planets as it does to vessels. If so, it may be a weapon of defense that turned on its own creators."

"Is that a real possibility?"

"No, sir, it is only a guess."

"But it unconditionally preserves the life—what? —life forces? Of the beings it absorbs?"

"Not only that, sir, but the entire consciousness. Memories, desires, everything. They are, in effect, still alive in there."

Folding his arms, Riker leaned forward on the bridge rail and pondered the idea. "Imagine not being enslaved by time. Mankind's been looking for that kind of Utopia for eons. Absence of want, hunger, fear, pain, death . . . I wonder what it looks like from inside." For several seconds he simply gazed at the idea. It sounded idyllic, even Biblical. How many people looked up toward space when they thought of heaven? He pushed himself off the rail and held up a finger. "There are two things going on here," he postulated. "Correct me if I'm wrong—"

"I will, sir."

"Uh . . . yes. Are we witnessing two kinds of contact here? You with the mechanism or whatever it is, and Troi with the life essences trapped by it?"

Data's birdlike eyes darted sideways for a moment in a disturbingly computerish look of calculation. He stood completely still for a few seconds, then canted his brows and said, "That does seem to describe the evidence, sir. Counselor Troi seems to be the path of least resistance for the life essences in their attempt to contact us. They do seem to be separate from the entity which buoys them. I should have thought of it myself."

"You're doing enough," Riker said, trying to ease the stiffness he sensed under Data's tone even now.

Then the android said, "No, sir . . . not enough. I may have technologies within myself that even I do

155

not know about and do not know how to use yet. Somehow, the mechanism and I have congruous responses to each other. I believe—" And he paused again, this time even more movingly. He didn't look at Riker, but rather fixed his eyes on the forward screen, now a grainy gray wall. "On impulse-idle with only flight shields up, the mechanism did not home in on us. I believe it fixed on me and was then able to focus on the ship—"

"Don't flatter yourself," Riker interrupted. "It found Troi first and me next. You're third on its taste test, so don't start blaming yourself. It's too . . . human."

The proffered lightness didn't come off. Rather the contrary. Data's sudden silence was ponderous.

Riker rubbed his hands together and made a second attempt. "Look, Data, about before . . ."

"If I may say, sir," Data said quickly, "your sense regarding my nature is correct. It seems I . . . have been deluding myself. I am . . . apparently more mechanical than living."

Riker moved across the small space between them and tried not to look like a superior officer circling an underling. When it did start to look like that, he stopped and simply faced Data. "Now, listen. I want us to understand each other."

"Yes, sir," the android said clearly. "It is not your fault that . . . while I cannot be alive, I am apparently programmed to be self-deluding about it."

The statement rang in the empty battle bridge. Several seconds ticked by, accentuating the fact that there was no real answer.

Data straightened then, as though to slough off the discomfort of those seconds. "Whoever built the entity out there knew what it is to be alive. It knew life

156

and knew how to preserve life even when the body is gone. And it clearly recognizes machines for what they are."

Shaking his head, Riker sighed. "You're not making this easy on either of us."

All at once Data fidgeted, actually changed the position of his feet.

Riker held out a palm and said, "At ease, will you?"

Data glanced at him. After a beat he crossed his wrists behind his back and looked at the floor. "It seems that I too am a mechanism," he said introspectively. "A utensil. Not a creature. Not only may I not be human, but I may not even qualify as a life-form. I may be less alive than the first protozoan that murmured through Earth's primordial muck."

With a sympathetic frown, Riker fought to digest the concept as Data perceived it. He felt suddenly crushed by his own mistake, and by his own inadequacy to ford this crossing.

"I am a versatile device," Data went on, still gazing at the floor. His voice was completely without the emotional rasp that would have entered a human voice by now, and yet there was a heaviness in his tone that lent meaning to his confession. The harsh but meager lighting on the battle bridge played poorly upon the soft and pale contours of his brows and jawline. "I am an instrument. No real human can do the things I can do. That alone should have been proof to me long before this."

"Part of being human," Riker attempted, latching on to a tiny hope, "is accepting your talents as well as your faults. That's one equation no machine can compute."

"Please, sir," the android said, looking up now, a move that went through Riker like a wooden stake. "If

157

indeed I am nothing but a machine, then I cannot have a sense of self and consciousness, but only programming that includes an illusion of self. Those are facts I may have to accept. I have been soundly reminded by my contact with the alien mechanism that I am . . . a fake."

Riker winced. This was a sample of what Captain Picard must already know. Riker had noticed the captain holding back from comments that might have been bold, rude, or comforting on several occasions, and he'd often wondered about the captain's choice of silence in those moments. But perhaps Picard had learned the hard way: keep your outbursts in check. A senior officer gets listened to, and everything he says gets remembered. Nothing can be casual, nothing can be emotional without the risk of hurt. It was the price of high rank. And it wasn't going to go away. When it came right down to it, he didn't know if Data was alive or not and he shouldn't have opened his big mouth. He never really thought Data would take his comments so much to heart—but perhaps that was the android in him too.

He saw in Data's eyes, in his expression, an intense need to define himself and discover his true nature. *And here I am, at the heart of his struggle. Part of that struggle may be to admit a truth that isn't very pleasant.*

"I don't know what you are, I admit that," he told Data with a vocal shrug. "I'm not qualified to say. But Starfleet checked you out and you tested out alive. That's good enough for—"

"By machines, sir," Data reminded painfully. "Machines will report whatever they are told to report. No human looks at me and thinks I am human too. And you, more than anyone, still treat me like a machine."

158

Until his chest started hurting, Riker didn't even inhale. What had he been thinking about, admitting the truth? *What happens when it slams you across the face and insists you look?*

"Sir," Data began, solemn again, "if I may go now . . ."

Sadly Riker leaned on the command chair and nodded.

"Dismissed."

From behind him—he didn't watch—he heard the hiss of the turbolift door and the soft sucking noise behind the wall as the lift shot away through the ship. Riker found himself staring at the spot where Data's boots had left a faint impression on the carpet. Now he breathed deeply, though it gave him no comfort, and listened to the thickness of his own voice.

"The tin man wants a heart."

"You wanted privacy. You have it. All I ask is that you make good use of it, Counselor."

Her delicate white hands were trembling, and nothing, nothing would make them stop. She didn't blame herself for the lack of control—in fact she didn't even do much to stop it. Burying what she was feeling and experiencing would only do her damage. But the captain was here and he was ready to listen to a confession, a confession that would take a single trouble and multiply it. She had thought having the answers would help her, ease her burden, but no. She knew many more things than she had an hour ago, and nothing was easier. Clarity in this case was more painful than obscurity.

Her head and neck ached as though someone had been sitting on her shoulders and twisting her skull.

"I've never experienced anything like this before,

159

Captain," she said, easing into it. "I've had to block thoughts before, but these simply crash through my barriers. These people are so desperate that they're forcing their way into my mind, no matter how I try to close them off. I don't understand the science, but there are definitely living, conscious life essences inside the phenomenon. Not memories, not residues, but the actual living essences of individuals. Somehow this thing preserves the consciousness and discards the physical body. And they do have a clear sense of self, Captain."

"All humans?"

"I'm not sure, sir. I receive impressions of others, but it may be that only the humans can empathize closely enough with me to communicate. But . . . I know who they are now."

Picard sat behind his glossy black desk and nodded. He tried, tried hard, not to appear impatient, and though there was no fooling her, at least she might appreciate the effort. But there was a definite "I'm waiting" in his posture. "Arkady Reykov and the members of his crew," he said, quite flatly and with a touch of anticlimax.

Troi blinked. "How did you know?"

Picard flopped his hand on the desktop and casually said, "One needn't be telepathic."

She faltered, frowning into the black shine of his desk, and said, "Yes, I suppose it is obvious. But there's more, sir. Or shall I say, there *are* more. Many more. Millions more, in fact. Their level of communication is much higher than anything verbal, as though they've forgotten over the years how to use simple words and pictures. We may be the first outside contact they've had—"

"Since 1995," she supplied steadily.

160

"Yes," she murmured. "For a while, what they wanted was very confusing. There were so many minds shouting at me, some rational, some not . . . only the strongest of those can still maintain a single self-image, but only for limited amounts of time."

"Like the appearance Riker witnessed in the corridor."

"I believe so," she told him, not ready to commit herself to that with a blind yes.

"And now it's clearer?" Picard prompted. "What they want? You have some idea?"

Troi bent her elegant head, lashes like black whisk brooms dropping to shade her eyes. Then she looked up. "Captain, I haven't told you everything."

Jean-Luc Picard leaned forward, his elbows rubbing across the desk's smooth surface and reflected that she of all people was not one whom he counted on for courteous lies. Courteous silence, perhaps. But deception, no. The first reaction was anger, but that flared and died more quickly than a match in wind. Yet such confessions on a starship could cost lives, and always provoked him.

But something had driven her to this, and Picard's curiosity was plenty bigger than his ego at this point.

"Then tell me everything now," he said.

Troi raised her chin as though to walk into the word. "About the confusion. It's true that there are millions of minds pressing upon me, but there is . . . an absolute unanimity in what they want—"

The door buzzed.

"Yes, who is it?" Picard barked impatiently.

"Riker reporting, Captain."

Picard started to admit him, but Troi grasped the rim of his desk and pulled forward in her chair. "No, sir, please don't. Don't let him in."

The curiosity burned. "Not even Riker?" Picard said.

"Please, sir . . ."

He gazed at her for a moment, then spoke aloud to the intercom. "Just a few more minutes, Mr. Riker."

There was a thunderous pause. Picard could imagine the glances running the main bridge.

"Yes, sir . . . I'll be out here."

Picard indulged in a little grunt and muttered, "Sounds a bit wounded, doesn't he? Now, what's this all about, Counselor? These people want us to do something for them?"

"You have a decision to make that no single person should have to make. I thought you shouldn't also have to live with the opinions of the entire crew. That's why I'm speaking to you privately."

"I appreciate that, but please—"

"Most religions describe a kind of hell, Captain," she said carefully. Her shoulders shuddered with the effort. "Now . . . I know what that is."

"No doubt, but what's that got to do with these beings?"

Troi's lovely eyes took on a bitter anger. "I can't make it clear enough, sir, that these people are still alive. They're not supernatural. They're living creatures, many of whom are—or were—human as much as you are human. They have truly achieved immortality. They are still conscious and self-aware."

"All right," Picard told her, "I understand that. What do they want?"

She clamped her hands into two tight balls, the skin thinning over her knuckles and turning icy white. "They want you to help them die."

* * *

"Quit saying that. You're not a machine. I can tell that by just looking at you."

Geordi LaForge gave Data a playful push as they entered the dark corridor that led to the warp reserve. It took clearance through three doors, each marked AUTHORIZED PERSONNEL ONLY before they were admitted to the especially heavy door marked

RESTRICTED AREA
ANTIMATTER RESERVE CONTAINMENT CENTER
NO ENTRY WITHOUT LEVEL 5 CLEARANCE

The room was very dark, lit only by two tiny pink utility lights on either side. Data's flashlight cut a clean white path before them. Though the darkness still pressed around them, Geordi could see quite well by that small brightness, and he led the way through stacked storage crates and high-clearance mechanical and computer panels.

"I expected a lot of problems to come my way on space duty," Geordi said, "but I didn't expect one of them to be trying to find a definition for life itself."

"That is indeed the captain's dilemma now," Data said, "because of me."

"It's not because of you. Cut it out. Boy, after all this trying to act human, you sure found an annoying way to actually do it."

Data looked up into the darkness, quickly, hopefully. "What am I doing?"

"Pitying yourself, that's what. Knock it off."

Since he hadn't been aware of doing it, Data wasn't quite sure what to knock off. By the time he found *knock it off* in his memory banks, the subject had passed and Geordi was leading the way into an anteroom that held most of the computer monitors for the actual antimatter containment. On the dim

163

panels, a few lights and patterns were flicking and flashing away happily in their mechanical ignorance, as if trying to say that all was well, all was as it should be.

"It's got to be here somewhere," Geordi muttered. "You try the antimatter injector and I'll—"

As the doors came together behind them, there was a corresponding clatter on the starboard side of the room that made them both look, just in time to see a dark form duck behind a panel.

"Who's there?" Geordi demanded.

Data stepped in front of him and sharply ordered, "This is Commander Data. You are in a restricted area. Identify yourself."

An innocent face peeked up in the corner, suddenly looking very guilty.

"Wesley!" Geordi exclaimed. "What are you doing in here? Come out of there."

Wesley's lanky form, still trying to grow into its own long bones, slowly sprouted from behind the panel. His hands gripped the hem of his sweater, a dark and thickly knit sweater that under these circumstances looked like reconnaissance gear. He'd known he was going to be in a cool area of the ship, evidently. "What're you two doing here?" he echoed. "I mean, it's sort of the middle of a crisis, isn't it?"

"Right in the middle," Geordi said. "The captain's ordered an energy blackout—"

"I know."

"And we picked up a power drain in the reserve tank. We've got to find it before the creature picks it up." Through his visor Geordi saw Wesley's face suddenly erupt with infrared.

"It can't be much of a drain, can it?" the boy asked. "If you haven't picked it up before . . . right?"

164

"That's right, but it doesn't make a bit—Wesley, what do you know about this?"

Data approached them and said, "Wesley, if you know about the power drain, you had better tell us. The antimatter from the tank has been emergency-dumped, and we cannot restock from the reserves until we discover the nature of the leak and lock it down."

Wesley's young eyes flashed in the dimness. "Well . . . I only . . . I was . . ."

Geordi fanned his flashlight's beam angrily. "This area's off limits, for Christ's sake, Wes!"

"I know, but that's just a technicality and it would've taken weeks, maybe months, to get the power authorization if I'd gone through channels—"

"Channels exist for a reason. So do rules like off limits. You know what off limits means? What're you up to?"

"Nothing, really."

"Report, Ensign," Data said, cutting through the familiarity and putting juniors where juniors belong.

"It's really nothing. Someday it might be, though," Wesley said, intimidation forgotten in enthusiasm. "Just wait. I'm doing an experiment on an idea I had to increase phaser power without pulling any more energy. I've got a little mock-up over here—"

He led them to a table that held a shapeless contraption. It looked like so much scrap, except that a light beam was glowing straight through the middle of it.

"What the hell—" Geordi stepped up to the model and pointed at it. "What's this hooked up to?"

Wesley's sheepishness returned. "I was . . . tapping the antimatter reserve."

"Goddamn, Wes! You have an acting rank. Don't you know that means you could be court-martialed?"

"But it's never used! They don't use it once in twenty years! How was I supposed to know they'd need it?"

"You do know this area's off limits to anyone but authorized personnel," Data said.

Geordi barely let him finish the sentence. "You start screwing around with the antimatter reserve and get a short or something, and suddenly there's another sun around! It's dangerous to tap the reserve directly. Don't you know that?"

"Oh, come on, Geordi, it's not that bad," Wesley complained. "Under normal operation, nobody'd notice. It'd be like plugging in one extra lamp in a hotel. But with all the power shut down—"

"You know better than this." Geordi shook his head, then said, "Then again, maybe you don't. How long have you had this thing hooked up to the AR?"

"Well, only about four . . . or five . . ."

"Days?"

"Weeks."

"Oh, my God. You gotta be kidding me. What were you trying to do?"

"I didn't mean any trouble."

"Well, you've got trouble, mister."

Wesley pulled out a professional whipped-puppy look. "You'd turn me in?"

Geordi looked at the little contraption again and scanned it for invisible leakage. "This is a starship, not a playground, Wes." The device was working, somehow, doing something, though Geordi couldn't tell what.

Now what? Report the boy? Wesley was genius material, sure, but not experienced. Had he not been living on a major starship, with all its labs and state-of-the-art technology, where experts in actual applied science, applied engineering, applied mechanics were readily available, some even teaching classes to the kids, he'd be just another smart sixteen-year-old. Living on Earth or such, he'd be bright and showered with opportunities, but not like this. Not to the point of getting his hands on a starship any old day. Geordi knew Wes Crusher had a natural ability to conceptualize the way the universe works, but the only way he could learn to apply it was through all the redundant practice a sixteen-year-old hated even to think about. On the bridge a week ago, Geordi had let Wesley try the helm controls because the boy had so quickly picked up the theories and principles of navigation, only to find that he had plenty of difficulty actually working the controls. Only time, only experience could teach that.

But this—this kind of game-playing was dangerous, and Wesley couldn't see the danger. Hadn't had his hands burned yet.

"Shut it down," Geordi ordered.

"Okay," Wes mumbled. "That's what I was doing anyway."

"Ah—so you knew we'd pick it up. This is wrong and you knew it. What's the matter?"

"Well . . ." Wesley hesitated, then said, "I'm not sure how to break the flow without rupturing the magnatomics. Besides, this could never pull enough power to cause a problem. That's why I went ahead and did it."

"Wes, even senior engineers don't tamper with antimatter. Data, look this over. We've got to disconnect it."

The android moved in, and Wesley stepped aside. "What is the principle behind this device?"

Using his hands to illustrate every little twist and

167

turn of his idea, Wesley explained. "Basically, it breaks down the phaser in its initial cycle, into its increment frequencies and energies until the final cycle, when you recombine the phases all at once."

"What is the problem with it?"

"It . . . doesn't work."

"I see."

"But if it did, this model would have almost four times the power of a hand phaser, and draw from a reaction chamber only half the size of standard."

"This little toy?" Geordi blurted.

Data looked at Wesley briefly. "Did you remember that with the splitting, you'd have to increase the power by the same magnitude as the split?"

Wesley looked from him to Geordi and back again. "Uh . . . no."

"Otherwise it would not be strong enough to cycle," Data postulated. "I'm concerned that the splitting would cause a loss of harmonics in the crystal focusing system. The crystal might break down and result in—"

"Heat. I already know that."

"Listen, you two," Geordi said, nudging Wesley even farther back, "Riker's gonna split our harmonics if we don't lock down this leak and get back topside. The creature could pop out of innerspace at us any second and I don't want to be down here when it happens. Wesley, you get out of here, pronto. If the senior engineers find you, you're going to know the meaning of reprimand."

"But what about—"

"Data and I can shut it down. I'm going to have it disposed of. You're on probation. If I hear about any more of these unauthorized experiments of yours, I'm reporting you to the chief engineer."

168

Wesley dropped his eyes and grumbled. "Yes, sir."

"Out. And I mean a straight line out of this area and back to the saucer where you belong."

The infrared glow increased on Wesley's cheeks, and without a word he pivoted and strode out.

"Kids," Geordi said, looking back at the glowing bundle of parts. "Can you unhook it without a backflush?"

"I believe so," Data told him, carefully picking at the octopus of wires attached to one end of a long rod. "It actually is a remarkable idea. It may not have been tried before."

"Yeah, Wesley thinks ideas are cheap. He doesn't understand that implementation isn't. Everything's shortcuts when you're a kid."

"Is it?"

Geordi paused. "Oh . . . sorry."

"No cause to apologize, my friend. I may be forced to accept what I am."

"Now, what is that supposed to mean?"

The android's slim form glowed within its filmy sheath, and perhaps the glow increased very, very slightly. "I am on a . . . quest."

"Oh, no—what quest?"

"I must discover my true nature."

"That's what I was afraid of. Why do you worry about it so much? Maybe you're just special. Maybe you don't have a true nature that you can compare to anything else because there's never been anything like you. Ever think of that?"

"No, I hadn't," Data admitted. He paused, then plucked an inset from part of Wesley's monster, and the whole thing suddenly shut down with a clean *buzz-sigh*. The beam of light snapped out an instant later.

169

Geordi repressed a shiver. "That's a relief. I get the willies thinking he's had this hooked up to the reserves all this time."

"There wouldn't necessarily have been a rupture," Data said, "but that's problematical now."

"I wouldn't want to test it, thanks. Let me check the stabilization . . . looks clear now. Concur?"

"I do."

Geordi tapped his insignia and said, "LaForge to Riker."

"*Riker. What was it?*"

"Just a malfunction in the seals."

"*I don't like the sound of that. Are we clear to restock the main tank?*"

"I think so, sir. You might want to have it checked by a containment engineer."

"*We don't have the time. Counselor Troi insists that entity's still in the vicinity and even though it doesn't show up on any of our monitors, I've got to assume she's right. How's Data?*"

Geordi glanced at the android as Data looked up. "He's . . . fine, sir."

"*All right . . . we're going to flush the antimatter reserves into the mains right away so we can power up for warp speed if we have to. You stay there and monitor it. Yell if there's so much as a ripple.*"

"Yes, sir. LaForge out." He shrugged. "I don't think he hates you as much as you think."

Data gathered the remains of Wesley's experiment and stuffed it into a reconditioning chute, piece by piece. "Mr. Riker may be right about me. I have had to accept it."

"You're starting again."

"Perhaps so," the android said, straightening and facing him. "But it is important for me to discover

170

where I fit into the range of humanness. The question of whether or not the entity is a life-form or what it is to be human—body, spirit, pulse, compassion—all these are things which will show where there is a place for me." He paced toward Geordi, and finally past him to the big main schematics that showed a faintly lit diagram of the ship's entire warp engine system, and in a gesture almost gentle, he placed his hand on the lines and lights. "I may be part of the scheme of evolution for the future. Man lives . . . man develops machines, learns to use them, to improve them, to create machines that are smarter and faster than himself, more efficient . . . and he uses those to better himself, even to make them part of himself." He paused, turned, looked at Geordi's visor, and knew that even in the faintly lit darkness Geordi could see him with astonishing clarity. "Like you, my friend. You are part of the scheme too. Eventually, perhaps man achieves symbiosis with machines, perhaps even creates life?" He gazed at the board again. "Is that my place? Machines that live?

"And now Captain Picard must decide what to do. Because I know . . . I *know* that thing means to destroy this ship when it finds us again. It believes that is its purpose. Yet I have received impressions inconsistent with that goal."

"Like what?"

"Like fear. Am I right? That isn't consistent."

Geordi shrugged lamely. "I dunno. It could be. You mean it's afraid of us?"

"No. It is afraid *for* us."

"Sorry, but you'll have to explain that one. I just see well, remember? I'm no psychologist."

"The aliens who created it actually knew what life is made of. They knew the moment when consciousness

171

and sense of self begin in a mass of cells. Somehow they encoded the entity with the belief that it must absorb us in order to protect us from this very ship."

"That's great," Geordi grumbled, "just great. Doesn't it have the brains to know the ship is what's protecting us from the environment of space?"

"It is a tool, Geordi. A mechanism that decides for itself according to its best judgment." Data spoke softly, as though entreating him to understand what it could be like to rely only on memory and not on intuition, on programming rather than insight. He paused, and flattened his hand even more intimately on the display board. "It is my greatest fear," he said, "that I may find I am nothing more than a tool."

Aching with empathy, Geordi felt the sting of his own helplessness. He could mutter some useless reassurances, but he had no answers. None that would satisfy or comfort Data as there might be comfort for a human being. Data's relentlessly analytical mind wouldn't allow him to accept simple answers, and he had stumbled onto a question that defied answers, and would defy them until time ground to a tired halt. Then everything would start up again and the question would resurface, slippery as ever.

"Data . . ." he said finally, "if it's any consolation, I don't think I could be friends with a machine."

The android's eyes lost their focus for a moment. The kind words ran through his body, and actually warmed him. Geordi could see the change.

Then Data looked at him askance, and his mouth lengthened into that crooked little grin. "Thank you, Geordi. I will never forget that. No matter what happens."

Still soft, still sentimental. No slang, no trappings.

172

That was the real Data. Except for the hint of fore-knowledge in his tone, which Geordi didn't digest for several seconds.

Perhaps it was that Data didn't look away, but that he kept gazing with that curious look, a look that said he had something else cooking in his idea kitchen, and after a moment Geordi took a suspicious step toward him.

"What do you mean, no matter what happens? Hey!"

The deck dropped out from under him. His arms and legs flared out with the initial shock of being lifted, and he realized that he too had committed the crime of forgetting where human ability stopped and android ability took over.

"Data, put me down! What are you—"

The room spun, and he was deposited neatly on his feet at the *top* of a stack of heavy-stress storage units. As he got his balance he noticed the flash of metallic skin as Data plucked the insignia-com from Geordi's own chest and stepped down from the crates.

Geordi waved his arms and complained, "What're you doing?"

It took him several seconds to climb down, but that was enough for Data to step back and press the closure circuit for the transparent contamination wall. Two clear wall panels slid out from sockets in the opposite walls and closed in the middle just as Geordi reached them. He was forced to watch helplessly as Data shorted out the lock and fused it. A flare of sparks, and Geordi was trapped.

"Data! What's this for? Why are you doing this?"

"I'm sorry, Geordi," the android said, and truly he sounded sorry. "This may be the only time when I am not expected to be on the bridge."

Geordi's voice was muffled now behind the clear wall. "I don't get it. Let me out."

"I will be taking a shuttlecraft. Please inform the captain and Mr. Riker that I will attempt to get closer to the creature in hopes of communicating more clearly with it."

Geordi pressed his hands on the transparency. "Data, come on, don't. Don't! That's insane. Come on, open up. Don't do this. Don't risk your life."

"Some would say I have no life to risk."

"Oh, don't be a wart! Open the door. How'm I supposed to inform the captain of anything if I'm stuck in here."

"That is an excellent point. But I must take advantage of the opportunity." He started to turn away, only to stop, pause, turn back. He gazed at the floor for a moment, then looked up once again at the only person who'd ever treated him completely like a human being.

"Thank you for the past, my friend," he said, his face astonishingly animate. Now he grinned sentimentally and added, "You've been a pal."

174

Chapter Nine

THE CAPTAIN STRODE back into his ready room after being gone for nearly forty-five minutes. Deanna Troi still sat where he'd last seen her, her hands still folded in her lap, and she blinked as though coming out of a trance.

Picard came around his desk into her line of sight, though she already knew he was here, and waited until she looked at him.

"They're waiting outside. They've been fully briefed. Are you sure you're up to this?"

Troi sighed and nodded. "Believe me, sir," she said, "I'm just as worried about my own sanity as I am about those beings out there. I'd like an end to this. And I need help finding it."

"Dr. Crusher has been reviewing up-to-date medical policy and debate on the rights of the terminally ill and all current hospice psychology and the thoughts of terminal patients in every sentient species—"

"That's my profession, Captain," Troi said, a twinge of defensiveness creeping into her voice.

"I didn't think it wise for you to be doing research right now. However, I'll need your expertise to collate the information the doctor is bringing in with her. Fair enough?"

She managed a thin smile, but one that conveyed genuine gratitude, and she said, "You're very gracious, sir. I didn't think of that myself. I might indeed be inaccurate at the moment."

Picard slid into his chair and said, "I'm not worried that you will be. You seem perfectly in charge of yourself, at least for the moment. I haven't noticed any aberrations in your personality, Counselor."

"But it may come, sir," she admitted softly. "I'm fighting even now to maintain my individuality. I don't know how long I can deal with the pressure from them. It's beginning to affect me physically. I feel weak and nervous, as you might feel after exerting too much energy."

At her solemn tone, even Picard had to stifle a wave of concern. His doubt began to stir. This made him uncomfortable, this inconcrete business, and he steeled himself to accept what she had said and what she would be saying over the next few minutes. He'd had to do that before—depend on those whose talents were other than his own. He would tug the cord of instinct and insight if he had to, but as he looked at her and saw her effort to remain in control, he knew guesswork would be only a last resort. Starfleet had surrounded him with people of various abilities, and it was his duty to make use of them.

"Yes," he murmured. "I'm depending upon you to hold your ground against them. It'll be up to you to tell me, as nearly as you can estimate, what those entities want."

"I have told you."

"And we're going to examine that." He pressed the intercom and said, "Come in, plea—"

The door opened.

Picard leaned back in his chair. "Well, that was subtle, you two," he said as Beverly Crusher and Will Riker strode in. "Sit down. I've explained the situation to both of you. According to Counselor Troi, the life essences inside that phenomenon have asked unconditionally that we destroy them. They want their existence to end. Death is their choice rather than formless life, apparently. When I leave this room, I want as clear a picture as the four of us can provide of what exact action this ship is going to take. I tell you now that I would much rather face an enemy with eyes I can look into and whose intents I can read. If I'd wanted to be faced with these pale ethical problems, I'd have become a priest. I don't like this. You know what these entities have asked of us, according to Counselor Troi's translation of their wishes. It's up to you to help me decide if this is euthanasia," he said, "or butchery."

An unwanted silence blanketed the ready room, broken only by Will Riker, who had finally had enough of it. He slid one thigh up onto the captain's desk and settled there, the toe of the other boot still planted on the floor, and folded his arms. "We'll do our best, sir."

"I know. Dr. Crusher, you've reviewed all the material on current medical ethics."

"Well, *all* is an inappropriate term for a half hour's study, sir," the doctor said, "but I've done my best. As a matter of fact, I had to refamiliarize myself with the subject upon accepting the post as chief surgeon."

"Luckily," the captain commented. "On with it."

"Just remember you asked for this," she warned, and adjusted her narrow hips against the back of her chair. She looked like she was settling in for a long time, which made both Riker and Picard wonder what they were getting into. "The word *euthanasia* doesn't mean what most people think it means. It's an intransitive concept, for one thing. It's something you get, not something someone does to you. Its true meaning is simply a gentle, quiet, good death, usually just a matter of luck. Society has come to take it as ending life painlessly so as to end suffering. What we're really dealing with, however, is the point at which the only chance left for a person to have euthanasia is for someone else to kill him. That's the closest to what we're facing."

Troi gripped her hands tightly together and said, "This is not a case of our deciding to terminate their lives. They've decided it for themselves. I don't think that can be minimized."

"I'm getting to that," Crusher patiently said, and she started ticking things off on her long fingers. "There are complications, believe me. We get into the questions of suffering or not suffering, rationality or not, direct or indirect killing, killing by providing pain relief, the difference between personhood and potential personhood, capability of expressing a rational desire to die, death of biological organisms as opposed to persons, the distinction between ordinary versus extraordinary means of keeping a person alive, that ever-elusive phrase *quality of life,* failure to supply help versus active harm with kind intent, sanctity of life, obligation to live, freedom of choice versus deific property, being and not being the cause of a death other than one's own, avoidance of giving euthanasia for selfish reasons—keeping one's conscience clear, for instance—"

Picard rubbed a hand over his eyes and wearily groaned, "Cut my losses, will you, doctor? If you've already run the process of elimination, might you just give me the upshot of it?"

She dropped her busy hands and said, "It's not a simple subject, Jean-Luc."

He leaned forward. "No one's asking for simplicity, doctor. Just brevity."

"Well, there's the medical definition of death. Will that help?"

Before the captain could say anything, though he started to, Riker said, quietly, "It'd help *me*."

"Okay," Crusher said with a toss of her hair. "Unless you're into horror stories, we all basically know what death is. We start with dying—as a recognizable physiological process, one that medical science can pretty easily recognize. We know the difference between a living body and one that's being kept alive. Any intern worth his salt can spend ten minutes with the readouts and tell which is which. But the clincher has always been brain activity—the flat electroencephalogram. As far as current medical consensus goes, the only absolute criterion for death is its irreversibility. That's not the only criterion, mind you, I didn't say that. Death is a cluster concept and requires several criteria in a lump, but irreversibility is the only absolute one."

"Dying is irreversible in my estimation," Picard said. "At least I thought so until now."

"They're not dead," Troi said. Her steadiness was wearing thin. She felt it pull and strain against the crushing pressure of a million identities. She heard it in the sudden flatness in her voice, and knew it showed in the immobility of her body. She tried to force her legs into a more social position, but they remained tightly knee to knee, and soon she gave up trying. This discussion was time wasted, chewing at

179

her, frustrating her. She knew what the decision had to be. Over and over in her mind echoed her own words: *They're not dead. They're not dead.*

"I accept that," the captain said. "They have yet to experience their deaths. I may be old-fashioned, but to me death is final. Death doesn't have degrees. Suffering does, but not death. This isn't a matter of betting one way or the other. It's a matter of deciding to intervene."

"Or deciding not to," Riker plowed in.

They all looked at him, and discomfort entered the room.

"Yes . . ." Dr. Crusher murmured, eyeing him. It took her a moment to return her full attention to the captain. "Well, there's also an additional problem; over about the past century and a half, medical doctrine has had to include some very strange life-forms and all their habits, customs, physiologies, and abilities."

"I can't decide for the whole galaxy, doctor," the captain said. "Let's stay with humans, shall we?"

"I thought you'd say that, so I did. And I agree with you on that point."

"That's heartening, but could you give me a bit more?"

"Oh . . . a bit."

"Oh, God . . ."

"You did ask, sir."

"Yes, I did. Go on."

"Where was I? Oh, yes. There are the mythological and religious concepts of death, which involve the soul leaving the body—"

Picard's finger shot forward. "Now, we're not going to get into defining the soul, are we? I unconditionally refuse."

Crusher looked surprised. "Well, *I'm* certainly not. What you'll have to do before this is over, I can't predict. Anyway, there's that concept, and there's the medical concept, which is a process. It's the difference between a door being closed and the whole building disintegrating. Medical science believes there's nothing to come back to. And there's also a veritable blur of platitudes from the religious sector, which I'll bet you don't even want to hear."

"I'd be so grateful," Picard said with a fatigued nod. "I've been trying to demythologize this from the start. I intend to stay with policy regarding the terminally ill and use that for a fulcrum."

"But these people aren't terminally ill," Riker interrupted, somehow feeling he'd have to be holding the rudder on this conversation. "For all we know, they could go on like this indefinitely."

Silently Troi nodded, not looking up. When she spoke it was with absolute conviction in those voices she heard in her mind. "That," she said, "is their biggest fear."

"Counselor," the captain addressed her, since she had drawn attention back to herself, "you say you feel a unanimous opinion. Can you guarantee you're picking up on all the feelings, all the life essences?"

Cool sweat broke out on her palms. She felt her control begin to slip. "No, I can't. The opinion is unanimous among all those who still retain a solid consciousness."

"Hold it right there," Riker said. "That qualification bothers me."

Troi shot him a glare. "Yes, it's true that I'm perceiving massive insanity among the minds who've lost control of their personhood. That is also what the others are afraid of. Do you blame them? They've

181

made a decision for themselves and the others who aren't able."

"What do you mean by 'aren't able'?"

Troi took a deep, cold breath between clenched teeth and forced herself to be clinical, no matter her tattered emotions. "I would classify it as dementia praecox."

"What's that?"

She gave him an intolerant look and said, "Dementia is irreversible deterioration of mental faculties with correspondent degenerative emotional instability. Praecox is simply prematurity."

"Which brings up the question of next of kin."

Troi gripped the arm of her chair and continued glaring at Riker. "Don't you think they're better able to judge their companions' wishes than we are?"

Riker had to nod a reluctant agreement. "I suppose if you and I had been sharing eternity, we would qualify as each others' next of kin."

He suddenly found himself held tight in Picard's gaze. He hadn't meant to say anything profound, yet they *were* sharing eternity. The two of them, perhaps more than any other pair on this ship, were most likely to make that decision for each other, that life or death choice. As first officer, Riker's first responsibility was Jean-Luc Picard's well-being. As captain, Picard's most valuable and needed commodity was his right-hand man. Together they had to be guardian angel for each other and the whole ship. They were—or should ideally be—each other's family . . . next of kin. Ironic that on a ship full of families, the bridge had somehow gotten itself stocked with people who had nothing, no one, but each other.

"And the others are like accident victims," Picard

182

said to him as they shared the moment. "Completely dependent upon a machine for sustenance."

"Yes," Dr. Crusher agreed. "They're mentally competent and nonterminal, but they want to die. Modern medical history since the twentieth century has had to deal with that, and it hasn't gotten any easier. Medicine took a tremendous leap forward during that period and has improved exponentially since then. The only constant is the idea that each euthanasia case has its own variables and should be considered individually. Then there's the problem of active versus passive euthanasia. Do you cut off intravenous feeding, or do you just let it run out, and what's the difference, and what are the moral implications of each—"

"You're piling up questions," the captain observed. "I asked you for answers."

"There aren't any," she said broadly. "That's the problem. We regard it as inhumane to let animals suffer, but we've always had difficulty applying that to our own species."

"But historically," Riker said, "isn't it true that this whole problem has been one of deciding whether an organic body without a mind is still alive? What we have here is the other way around. Minds . . . no bodies."

Crusher cast him a glance. "No, you're wrong. There's nothing new about minds without bodies."

When Deanna Troi spoke up, though her voice was weak, all turned to listen to her. But this time she didn't speak of the entities who pressed upon her, but of the question they were actually wrestling with. "That's how physically crippled people see themselves. Minds without bodies. At least for a while. It's often not true at all and they often change their opinions about themselves with time and therapy."

For a few seconds, nobody said anything because they expected her to keep going. When she didn't, Dr. Crusher shifted uneasily, turned back to Riker, and added, "But there've also been plenty of cases of conscious, rational people wanting to decide for themselves, and *not* changing their minds, Mr. Riker. Some people don't want to live if they can't function independently. Some can commit suicide, which is its own problem, but for those who can't, the problem takes on the special complication of bringing in another person."

"Who also have rights," Riker argued. "The right not to commit murder, for one."

With an impatient huff, Picard gripped the edge of his desk. "Yes. We do have the right to consider our own consciences. Is there a definitive answer, doctor? Even one of general policy from the Federation Medical Standards Council? Or do you have a ruling that we could consider ship's policy?"

"Me?" She shook her head and blinked. "This is one subject I nearly failed at medical school. I never found a single case that fit into the grooves of any other case. There's just no grounds for comparison."

"And Federation policy? Doctor, I need a precedent and I need it now."

She paused, thought about it, her mouth twisting with contemplation, then shrugged. "A line was finally drawn, clinically speaking, between animals with memories and animals with memories who were also able to imagine a personal future and have desires for that future. Even that had its faults. Babies, for instance. They simply don't care about the future."

184

Now it was Picard's turn to sigh. He pressed his mouth into a line and groaned, "Beverly, you're making me tired."

She appeared sympathetic, but admitted, "There's just no streamlining this issue. Which is why there hasn't been any law passed regarding it. Some things should simply never be legislated."

Riker straightened his back and folded his arms tighter. "Leaving us on our own."

"Consider it a privilege," she shot back at him.

"But these people, these 'souls,' if we have to use that term," Riker continued, "are not dying. They could go on forever like this!"

"Yes"—the doctor nodded, not very patiently—"the real question is not one of someone who is dying choosing when the end should be and we as society forcing him to live until the last moment, but rather . . . what is it that makes life worth living?" For this, a thick and weighted question, she turned directly to Picard, and held out an empty hand to him as though expecting him to fill it.

The captain stared back at her, entranced neither by this woman's beauty nor by his own feelings toward her, but by this question she asked of him, this question that was poised on the threshold between life and death.

What makes life worth living?

Beside Crusher, Troi stirred. "A person who is dying does ask if his disease has taken away everything that makes life worth living, as you say. There will be no more moments that resemble life as he has known it. When pain takes away any enjoyment of sight, scent, sounds, touch—"

"But we're not discussing pain, Counselor," the

captain snapped, his voice growing rough. "These entities have communicated no pain whatsoever of a physical nature, is that not correct? If not, you'd better tell me now, because this is a damned precipice we're walking over here."

"I wish they had," Crusher said dryly. "The question would've been simpler. My realm of the physical is much simpler to manage than Deanna's realm of mental anguish and confusion." She turned to the counselor and said, "I don't envy you."

The captain got up and paced around the desk. "Doctor, I had hoped you'd be more help than this."

Beverly Crusher shifted her gaze for a moment, settled back, crossed her long straight legs, and looked up at him again. "I *can* be more help," she told him. "But you have to ask for my personal opinion."

"Oh, damn it. Of course. I'm sorry." He reached a requesting palm toward her. "Please."

She sighed and thought about it. "They've expressed a well thought-out, reasonable desire to die."

"And?"

"And I think that should be respected."

"Does that mean acted upon? Come on, doctor, don't make me grill you."

"You mean, would I do it? Captain, let me put it this way. I've found that suffering can be mental and that it does no one any good."

"Would you," he repeated, "do it?"

She straightened her shoulders. "Yes."

Data found his way through the barely lit starship with an android's faultless sense of direction. Ordinarily he'd have thought nothing of that ability, but today it had a stubborn presence in his mind. He was aware of himself today, where usually he was not, at least not when he was alone. But today each pink wedge of utility light along the floor as he passed it was a tiny reminder of his doubts. Each doubt needled his thoughts and made the process inaccurate, irritating. He wondered what thinking was like for humans. To think one thought at a time, some without figures, without context . . . it seemed almost dysfunctional. But humans often perceived things that he missed entirely until they were pointed out to him.

I seem to be on a cross pattern away from humanity rather than toward it. What they see as simple seems difficult and incongruous to me. What I can compute and perceive without effort, they consider arduous. As time goes by I catalog more and more information, yet I move further and further from humanness because of it. The more time I spend among them, the more complicated they appear to me. Perhaps now these conditions will change. Perhaps this is what they mean by destiny.

He felt his body come to a halt and readjusted his pilot mode, letting himself slide instantly out of autolocate, and indeed found himself right where he wanted to be. The hangar deck. He stood before the door, staring through the dimness at the lettering.

SHUTTLECRAFT HANGAR DECK

AUTHORIZED ENTRY ONLY

A.C.E. CLEARANCE REQUIRED
INQUIRE DECK 14
OR CONTACT SECOND OFFICER

He lost track of those few seconds during which he studied those letters and their significance. All his internal alarms were ringing, telling him to track

187

down the assistant chief engineer, but there was no time. And that would give him away. Of course, being the second officer got him off the hook fairly well too, even if his internal alarms couldn't be programmed to know that. Information like that was rational, a matter of thought. The formalized ranking of human beings, of life-forms of any kind, was difficult for machine thinking to absorb, and had to be handled by what Geordi liked to call Data's subdominant hemisphere—the part of his brain that was organic, the part of his personality that let him be subjective. The part of him that Geordi insisted was no machine.

Data looked down at his left hand. He opened the fist and saw the glint of gold and brush-buffed platinum in the stylized A-shape that he himself had earned the privilege of wearing. Yet this was not his. His own was still riding safely on his chest, proclaiming the honor of his past and the degree to which humanity had opened its arms to him. He could never look at his Starfleet insignia and think of humanity as inferior to any other species; few species would accept such as him. He had known the shunning glances of prejudice before. Geordi would chide him for not realizing that significance until now, that prejudice was in itself a kind of privilege life-forms kept among themselves.

The gold turned rosy-pink under the utility lights above the door. He felt a strange, unexpected pang in his chest as his synthetic heart pounded in reaction to the high-gear racing of his nervous system.

This insignia, this one in his palm—this was Geordi's.

Forgive me. I know I have never done anything resembling this to you before. I would have warned you, had I expected to behave this way. . . .

Illogical. Geordi wasn't here. Geordi was locked in the antimatter reserve center.

Data clutched his left hand tightly around the insignia. Also illogical. He should put it down, leave it behind. There was no purpose to carrying it. But rather than leaving the insignia behind, he dismissed the thought and kept his fist tight. With the other hand he quickly tapped in his authorized-entry code and the thick tunnel-shaped doors parted for him.

The hangar deck stored a few regulation shuttlecraft and several smaller, faster ships of various styles, all hidden neatly away in their stalls, ready to be elevated to the hangar bay, one deck up, when they were called for.

Very human impatience gnawed at him. He knew very well what impatience was. But there was no alternative to the time he must spend here before he could embark on his mission.

His hand twitched. Fail-safe programming sent quavers through his biomechanical nervous system, telling him that what he was doing he must not do.

As easily as ignoring a nagging ache, he rerouted his awareness away from the internal warnings and looked around for the mechanical stock he would need—yes, there it was. He had been concerned that in the midst of a crisis, supply engineering hadn't managed to deliver these small stock crates in time, but here they sat, stacked neatly before him. He gazed at them in the same manner as he had gazed at the letters on the door. On top of the stack was an authorization chip that simply said: *Request of Lt. Commander Data. Esn. F. Palmer—okay.*

Time was limited. Yet he was hesitating. Never before had he found himself literally at odds with himself, literally battling his own body to make it do

189

what his programming—his . . . conscience—had always considered wrong. Deception. Disobedience. It was not in his progr—in his *nature*.

His left hand twitched and opened. Geordi's insignia clattered to the deck with a metallic *ting*. Data looked down at it.

Impassively he stooped and picked it up. If he took it with him, the starship's mainframe would pick up on it and use it as a locator beacon, and would tell the bridge that Geordi was with him. Such a consequence . . . he would leave the insignia behind.

He would leave it.

He paced toward the exit and went to the nearest computer panel, still looking at the insignia in his hand.

"I *will* leave it," he insisted. His voice in the empty hangar deck was a loud sound. Why did this insignia whisper to him?

He put it down quickly. So quickly that it spun on its pin and ended up sideways. He paused.

Almost as quickly, he pulled off his own insignia. It too was gold, platinum—identical to the other. Except that this was his, what he had earned, and that was Geordi's. Each was encoded with the biopulse of the owner, including identity, and microsensors, and miniature communicator—Starfleet jargon called these insignia the "minimiracles" of recent science.

But today it was the shape and not the science that intrigued Data. Today his attention was held by the modern-day heraldry of the Starfleet emblem and what it meant to such as him.

His powerful heart pumped harder, a heavy muscular action, like the great machine that it was. He heard it thud clearly through his body, and felt the strain upon his systems as each struggled to push its own interests through his biomechanical nervous system, unsure which of the impulses to follow.

With a gesture of finality, he placed his own insignia on the panel beside Geordi's and turned away, leaving them there together.

When he knelt beside the crates the engineers had left here on his order, his body began to settle down as it recognized a task at hand. As the pumping of his heart subsided to its usual cadence, Data began opening the crates of specialized parts and mnemonic encoders and set about constructing a makeshift cloaking device small enough for a shuttlecraft.

"Now wait a minute!" Riker slid off the desk and fanned his hands before Troi. "We can't just interfere!"

"We must," Troi said, loudly this time. She felt the color rise in her cheeks and anger take over her heart. How dare he stand in her way!

"Now look," Picard angrily reminded, "I called this meeting for a clear reason and it's getting muddled. If I'm going to be forced into making a decision, I intend to have all the precedents behind me. Let's streamline this, and that's an order."

Before Riker had the chance to respond, Troi leaned toward Picard, the first time she had changed position since all this started. "Captain, humans are interventionists by nature. Since ancient times, and even before that, we've intervened in the course of evolution by selective marriage, all the way back to tribal beginnings when the chief got his choice of the fairest, youngest, strongest maidens, and they had children who grew up to be the decision makers for the whole tribe. It is our heritage!"

"That's nonsense," Riker accused.

"Not necessarily." Crusher pressed on. Her tone had a defensive sting and she turned a cold shoulder to him and spoke to the captain instead. "When we cured pneumonia and TB, we altered evolution forever. Countless millions who were weak and meant to die simply didn't anymore. When glasses were invented, all the millions of nearsighted people who would've been functionally blind in an earlier century suddenly were completely normal. They not only lived, but prospered, mated, had more nearsighted children. Mankind's been circumventing natural selection for so long that it's become immoral not to. There's your precedent, Captain. I don't believe the question is whether or not to interfere."

"What about science?" Riker interrupted, circling the desk to the captain's side. "Could technology eventually put these captive entities into bodies? Like Data's?"

Picard glared at him for a moment, then pivoted to Crusher. "Doctor, what about that?"

She shifted from one elbow to the other and dubiously said, "I'll just wave my magic wand. . . . In my opinion, it might be too late for them. If they've been in a virtual fugue state since 1995 and most even before that, they may have lost their ability to be embodied in humanoid form."

"You mean like a blind man suddenly getting complete sight?" Picard suggested. "Something like that?"

"I mean exactly that. There are plenty of circumstances that allow current medicine to replace or restore sight, but unless the patient is very young, there are usually grave complications. If I suddenly restored Geordi's sight with some kind of transplant or something, he'd have to completely retrain his senses. His whole body, his whole brain. His sense of visual depth would be all askew, for one. He'd be grabbing for things that were ten feet away, because he wouldn't be able to tell the difference. He probably couldn't walk with his eyes open either. Not without extensive therapy. His equilibrium would be completely thrown off. His balance would suddenly be affected by something that had never affected it before. There've been too many disastrous cases of restored sight. Some patients ultimately opted to have blindness reinflicted rather than continue with sight."

"My God . . . seriously?"

"Far too many for me to recommend trying to hook up these whatever-they-ares to android bodies." She lowered her voice and let empathy slip into her professional assessment. "It'd be a worse hell than they're already going through. And, Captain, I think the only rational, moral decision," she added, "is the one they've selected for themselves."

"We're not that sure of what they want," Riker insisted.

Troi twisted in her chair, her face a sculpture of pure melancholy and disappointment. Her face ached with the misery she felt inside and the insult she heard from without.

"Well, you're not," Riker said to her. "You're not, are you?"

"Bill . . ." she choked.

He circled the desk and confronted her. "You yourself have admitted that these people could be insane and incapable—"

"Some of them, but—"

Dr. Crusher put her slim hand on his arm and

actually pushed him back from where she and Troi were sitting side by side. "This life-sucking machine is violating the rights and needs of its captives."

Riker whirled and glared down at her. "Which rights?"

"The right to normal life as they see it and the dignity of self-decision. It's robbing them of a quality of life to such a degree that all they see left for themselves is death."

"So we provide it, all on Deanna's say-so?"

Troi lowered her eyelids now, and tears broke from them. "Oh, Bill," she whispered.

But he pressed on. "How do we know their decision is rational? It may be one of plain despair or temporary depression."

Crusher didn't back away from his challenge, but was ready with her own. "You call three hundred years temporary?"

"On that thing's time scale? It might be. And you don't know and I don't know otherwise. That thing could be a galactic utopia, for all we know. It could provide endless time to think about things and intermingle and share memories—who knows what else? Maybe Deanna's only picking up the wishes of a handful of new arrivals who don't know what they've got."

"I don't believe that," Troi said, her lips tight.

"All right—all right, say I don't either. Say you've convinced me. What happens once we do this? Once we've tasted this? If we open this door a crack, it may not close. Candles can start holocausts, Captain."

Crusher suddenly got to her feet and stepped toward him, using her height and her own grace to prove that he wasn't the only imposing one in the room. "We can keep control of ourselves, Mr. Riker. Medical science has had to live with self-control on a personal basis for centuries. Captain, I know you don't like to use the weapons, but that thing is a tyrant!"

Riker bent over the desk, his palms flat on its black top. "If we bend our rules," he insisted, "or even amend them, even at the request of the terminally ill, then we risk all of us. When we turn down the death requests of individuals, we protect us all." He looked at the captain and said, "We're playing ethical roulette, sir, and I'm not comfortable with it."

Troi didn't look at him, but there was a poignant lack of charity in her tone. "It's not your comfort we're talking about."

His eyes flashed. "No," he stabbed back, "but we're risking the ethical security of every sentient life we contact from now on. How long before this gets out of hand? We're at risk as a society if it does."

The captain frowned at him. "I'm not willing to take on the moral burden of all humanity, Number One," he said, "but I intend to take a stand here and now. I appreciate your playing devil's advocate, but—"

"I'm not," Riker told him. "I don't think it's our place to do this. And I don't think it's fair of those beings to ask this of us. We have the right not to become murderers."

"Captain," Crusher interjected, "we're past the point of no return. Our killing them may be hard on us, but their living is harder on them."

"That's your opinion, doctor," Riker clarified.

"Yes," she said. "The captain asked for my opinion. If you're captain someday, you don't have to ask me."

Bitterness swirled between them, and for several seconds, she let it have its way. Once the silence became oppressive, she inhaled deeply and addressed the captain with her final word. "Sir, in my judgment as chief surgeon of the *Enterprise*," she said, "we have what will go down in my report as acceptable prior consent."

The captain heard the ball drop cleanly into his court. Was his responsibility to the beings inside the entity, or to the entity, or to the ship, or to those life-forms whose essences would be absorbed by that thing in the future if he failed to act now?

"It's Federation mandate to avoid policing the galaxy, Captain." Riker's face reflected clearly in the viewport.

Picard nodded tightly. "Yes, we can't forget that. Federation policy will have to be my guide on this. The dirty reality is that we may not even be able to save ourselves. The better part of valor may be to get away and let the Federation decide how to deal with this thing."

Troi rocketed from her chair. "You don't understand! These people can't even communicate with each other! There are millions of them, all alone. Alone! It's not like a crippled body. Even then there can be sight, sound, interaction—these people have nothing!"

The captain started toward her. "Counselor—"

She backed away. "You don't know what it's like! You can't know. You can talk and discuss and argue, but you don't *know*. Captain, if that entity comes after us and there is no way to stop it from absorbing us, I promise you I will not go on like that! I will *not*! I'll kill myself first."

"Deanna," Crusher began, reaching for her.

But every one of them was affected by the utter conviction in her voice, her face, by the irrational promise from a person they knew to be supremely rational.

Riker felt especially responsible, and he stood a few paces away, unable to make himself go to her.

Dr. Crusher put an arm around Troi and steered her toward the door. "Come with me. I'll give you something to calm you down."

Troi started to go, but now she pushed away violently. "No! I don't dare let you sedate me! I can barely keep control now. Doesn't anyone understand?"

"Yes, yes," Crusher told her. "You know I do. Let's just go out to the bridge." She steered the other woman toward the door, and cast a scolding look back at Riker and Picard. "We'll just be a few minutes." Her words said one thing; her look said another.

Picard watched them leave without uttering a sound. When he and Riker were finally alone, he turned to the viewport and stared out into open space.

Before him was the panorama of distant stars and solar systems, the gas giant that had recently been their biggest problem and suddenly looked puny and insignificant as it whirled in bright green innocence at the very edge of his view. Two deep lines bracketed his mouth. He was a man with too many choices.

"That infernal thing is hiding out there, waiting for us to make a mistake," he said. His voice dropped to a near whisper. "How many more of this kind of thing are out there, Riker? How many more decisions like this? What do we do when we have no doubt about a person's—a community's—rational, reasonable desire to die?"

Standing beside him, Riker could offer no real solution—but he had his own personal answer. One as first officer—not captain—he could afford.

Without moving, he quietly asked, "Do we have that, sir?"

Picard continued to stare out the viewport, but a furrow appeared in his brow and his eyes drew tight. "I have to know, as closely as I can know, if this thing is a floating utopia," he mused, "or an interstellar hell."

Chapter Ten

"I DON'T LIKE THIS at all, Jean-Luc. I'm putting it on record that this is happening under my protest."

"That should make a lively record, doctor, if it ever reaches Starfleet."

Sickbay's isolation unit was buzzing, preparing itself for total zero-grav and the captain's exact body temperature. Picard watched with a guarded expression as Dr. Crusher prepared a hypo that would do for him what no sane person should allow. Perhaps it took a touch of insanity to drive a man to such measures, or perhaps it only took desperation. All dangers, all risks, all rationality must yield to the single-minded quest of him upon whom the decision fell. And that was Picard.

Beside him, Troi was showing signs of wear. The fine dark hairs around her forehead were moist and curling, her eyes were tense, and her posture slack. Everything that had always seemed so easy for her suddenly appeared an effort. In spite of her desire for him to know what her empathic contacts were experiencing, she found the presence of mind to say, "I must agree with the doctor, sir. I've never considered sensory deprivation a valid technique."

"It's out of a horror chamber, if you ask me," Crusher said, bobbing her head once with finality.

"All right," the captain told them, "then you two can conjure up a better way for me to know what it's like for those people and do so now, because I'm out to eliminate as many doubts as possible while we have the time."

The two women shared a long look, each hoping the other would conjure up an alternative.

Picard gave them the courtesy of waiting, which of course was its own form of pressure. "What can I expect?"

Crusher held up her hypo. "Well, the first effect will be—"

"Sir," Troi interrupted, "they didn't know what to expect when this happened to them."

Picard stared at her for a blank moment. For the first time, the prospect of what he was about to do frightened him. His gratitude that she would look after the accuracy of his experiment was tangled with annoyance that she had to do it quite so well. "Mmmm," he uttered, frowning. "I suppose. All right, let's get it going."

He stood stiffly as the doctor pressed the hypo to his carotid artery and it hissed against his skin.

"I'm limiting the time," Crusher called as the captain stepped into the isolation cubicle.

"Don't tell me how long," he said.

"Would I do that? You understand it's not like sleeping, don't you?"

"Actually, I know very little about this," the captain admitted, and he sounded proud of himself.

"Ready when you are, Captain."

"Go ahead."

The isolation unit closed itself off with a thick and solid wall of layered soundproofing, the kind of stuff that would muffle almost anything short of a major earthquake.

Troi watched it close with growing apprehension, and moved to the doctor's side as Crusher completed instructions for the isolation program. "What will it do to him?"

The doctor shrugged. "Physically, the narcotic will paralyze his body and deaden all external sensory impulses to his brain. It'll do nothing to his consciousness at all. Once I get this punched in, the chamber will provide zero-G with light tethering to keep him from floating into a wall, and it'll go completely dark in there."

Troi shivered. "He'll be just like them."

With a cryptic nod, the doctor said, "And just as helpless."

Captain Picard stood at the center of the small gray chamber, waiting for full isolation to kick in. His fingers had been tingling since the hypo came away from his neck, and he couldn't feel his toes anymore, but otherwise there was no effect yet. He glanced around the room, an exercise in flat paint. Thirty seconds and already this seemed interminable. Troi's descriptions sent a chill through him as he recalled the past few hours and how deeply she had been affected by what she was feeling. What she was being *forced* to feel.

"Well, get on with it," he muttered. How long did it take to program so simple a pattern? This wasn't the holodeck, after all.

He tried to tap his fingers against his thighs to vent

201

his impatience, and in his mind he indeed did that, but his hands wouldn't form into the shapes his mind thought of. He started to look down at them—but couldn't make his neck bend. His head swirled as he tried to move, but only his eyes could still shift in their sockets. His legs were putty, his back arched and began to ache as sensation quickly seeped away. After a few seconds the ache started to go away too, and suddenly he missed its reassuring throb. A little trickle of panic erupted and he had to fight it off as he stared at the blank gray wall.

Maybe we should cancel this.

He couldn't hear his voice. He'd heard it before; where was it now? His tongue moved slightly in the back of his throat, but that was all there was left to him.

When the zero-G kicked in and he saw the wall move very slightly before him, his involuntary systems yanked a breath into his lungs and he heard the gasp. At least something was still attached to his brain. Strange sensation, though—

The flat gray wall wavered. Or did it? Now the paint looked glossier—almost reflective. Yes . . . there was a face.

A face . . .

A man. Picard instantly dismissed the idea of reflection. It wasn't his face at all.

The eyes came into focus first, and very clearly. Without blinking they stared directly at Picard as a squared jawline and wide shoulders formed beneath. There was dark hair with a streak of white over one temple, and an expression of pure decisiveness. Even anger.

Picard heard his heart pound in his ears, a long

distorted sound, and not for an instant did he have any doubt about who shared his cubicle or the realness of what he saw. Riker had described exactly this and Picard entertained neither question nor guess. Paralyzed, he stared back.

Captain to captain, across the ages, the silent meeting became interminable. Picard's mind raged to be able to open his mouth and speak to Arkady Reykov, to ask him the question that would make everything much simpler, but his body was numb, gone. And the cubicle was getting dark.

Damn it! Why now? Give me ten more seconds!

Reykov lifted his hand, and the hand became a fist. He showed it to Picard—not a threat, but some kind of example. Picard tried to shake his head, to communicate that he didn't understand. That too failed him.

Reykov opened his fist and spread his fingers in a European exaggeration that Picard's French background allowed him to understand perfectly: *Well?*

Darkness closed around them. And darker still . . . and darker. *Not yet, damn it!*

Blackness. Blacker than a dead computer screen, blacker than space. Was Reykov still here?

Full panic struck. It was as though his heart snapped. Picard's mind suddenly flashed back to childhood, to those awful horror stories children can't get enough of, to what wasn't there and what pretended to be there—and what *was* there. He waited to be grabbed.

But he wouldn't even feel it if it happened. He might've been grabbed already. Was Beverly monitoring his heartbeat? His brainwaves? He hadn't discussed that with her. She would think of it, wouldn't she?

All right, get a grip on yourself. You've just seen a ghost, and there's nothing to be done about it. Be practical. Get concentrating on the task at hand. You're fine. You're in the isolation chamber, it's dark, and you can't move. It's exactly the correct conditions and you asked for it. You've needed a rest anyway. How bad can it be for a few hours?

Geordi paced the small area Data had trapped him in for about as long as he could stand it before he started tearing the facing off the wall to look for a circuit he could splice into to get that contamination shield to open up. Or maybe he could cut into the communication network and buzz for help. Just about anything would be better than stalking around here like a big chicken waiting for its feed while Data flew off into nowhere to get deep-fried. What a pair.

Data. He took everything so personally. If that didn't qualify him as a person, what did? Only persons can take things personally. Machines don't. How come Data listened to everyone *else* lately?

"Why don't you pay attention to *me* for a change?" Geordi howled. He glanced up from the close work of digging through all the exposed circuitry in the wall. "What'm I? I'm part machine too, y'know! Damn . . . where's the main link?"

Shuttlecraft. Great, just great. Data was probably gone by now and there was no way to change what was going on out there.

His hands started to sweat. The going got slower as his fingers began to tremble and slip. Only the microfilters in his visor kept him from making twice as many errors as he was already making. And only his dogged reliance on the occasional snide remark kept him from admitting that he was plain scared.

That thing, that light show out there . . . horrible. Geordi shuddered as he carefully weeded out the circuit chips he'd need to bypass the shorted-out lock. He'd had nightmares that looked like that thing. The times when his visor was malfunctioning, he'd see things wrong. Light would be distorted, heat would stretch things—like having a fever and no way to cool off.

The others didn't know what Data had been put through when it attacked him; they didn't see like Geordi did. They'd never understand, and they'd never quite believe him if they couldn't see it for themselves. *I don't blame them . . . exactly. It's not the kind of thing you believe until you see it for yourself. If I have to plug myself right into the computer core by the eyeballs, I'll make them see it. I'll make them get him back. That means you, Mr. Riker. Yes, sir. You.*

This is certainly strange. Enjoyable. I haven't thought of Laura for years. How many? An entire age, perhaps. And such beautiful memories to have set aside. There was a poem she liked. Which was it? She liked long poems and epics. She had such patience . . . who reads epics? She read them aloud sometimes, all in one sitting. And so well for an untrained voice. Or have the years made it sound better?

> *Absence, like dainty Clouds,*
> *On glorious-bright,*
> *Nature's weake senses shrowds,*
> *From harming light.*
> *Absence maintaines the treasure*
> *Of pleasure unto pleasure,*
> *Sparing with praise;*

Absence doth nurse the fire,
Which starves and feeds desire
With sweet delayes.

He'd heard it read once before. Once. And hadn't
thought of it since. Listened to and forgotten; his
brain caught up with the girl and her voice and not the
poem, yet now he remembered and reexperienced
every word, every syllable, every nuance. The meanings of the words together, their meanings separately,
even the music of the letters. The whole poem. Fulke
Greville, Lord Brooke—*Caelica*, wasn't it? When had
he picked up so much literary awareness? Certainly he
had paid little attention in that class he signed up for,
especially since he only signed up for it so he could
walk Laura there every other day. Ah, young men.
Young women.

This experience was enthralling too, this complete
freedom of his mind to explore and remember and
examine the things he'd seen in his life. Old experi-
ences that he thought had faded came charging back
in full light. Once again, and one at a time, he became
intimate with his own memories, all the pasts a man
his age could accrue. It wasn't a bad-looking past at
all, really, dismissing a few knocks, stumbles, and
burned fingers along the way.

After the past was enjoyed, something in it reminded him of quantum physics and away he went on
that fast ship through all the science and math he'd
ever been taught or figured out or even watched being
figured by someone else. It all seemed so simple now!
Equation after theory after hypothesis after
experiment—stunning and dazzling, all the compart-
ments his mind had closed and kept treasured all

these years. Dead relatives, missing comrades, absent friends, friends who also died, one after another they came to visit him in his silent place here and he reexperienced them, from pleasure to pain, and he felt himself cry. Or thought he did . . . Where were his eyes? Where were his tears? Why couldn't he feel the tears on his cheeks?

How long have I been here? In fact, where am I?

Oh, yes. The ship. I should have Riker try this. It's exhilarating, seductive . . . having no distractions, no clock to answer to, nothing to concern my mind other than its own thoughts, not even an itch to rupture my attention. Though it would be reassuring if I could just wiggle my toes. . . .

How will I know if the ship needs me? We could be blasted out of space and I'd never know. No . . . Riker would have me brought out if I was needed. What is this strange irrationality?

Were those birds? He'd heard that kind of birdsong once before . . . Canis IV? Yes, of course. The fluffy birds with the silly faces. They made a pretty song. Perhaps he'd just hang here and listen for a while.

Something about Canis IV—a long time ago.

No. No, I don't want to remember that. No . . .

Riker paced the bridge, eyeing the deceptive emptiness of space on the huge viewscreen. The bridge was reduced to nightclub dimness. The walls and carpet, usually the color of sand and camels, were dark now and Riker felt like he was walking around inside a cup of espresso. The shiny black computer panels and liquid crystal schematics of the ship's operating systems were reduced from their usual foam greens and blues to muddy and muted patterns. With the lights down and the displays subdued, the broad viewscreen jumped to shocking prominence. Suddenly they were players on a proscenium and everything they did was crucial. The level of their voices, the sheen of sweat on their skin, the sequence of their movements. Everything was magnified. And before them, space was their audience.

As empty as space was, and as cold as it was, it never quite looked that way. Thêre were always stars to twinkle their pastel lights and broad nebulas to shimmer in the distance, but it was hard for the human mind to accept the wholeness of that distance, so everything looked much fuller than it was. He often liked to watch space go by, but today it gave him no comfort. Today there was a rat behind the woodwork. Still out there. Hiding behind all that nothing. Riker knotted his fists and dared it to come out.

"Lieutenant Worf, anything further from life sciences or engineering on that thing?"

Worf's huge frame straightened from Science Station 2. "We're trying to lock down the individual components of its exostructure now, sir, using the postulation of interdimensionality as a guide. Don't worry, sir. We'll figure it out if I have to slice off a piece of it and beat it to death for an autopsy."

Riker nodded, but he couldn't manage the smile that would've shown his real gratitude. Nearly fourteen hours now, hanging here in silence and dimness. He'd never been much of a wait-around type, and this kind of tension was mutilating. How often had they told him at the Academy that battle was nine-tenths waiting? Waiting, planning, analyzing, waiting. Deadly. Sometimes deadlier than the battle itself. It made for recklessness.

He wished the captain was here. This business of isolation, sensory deprivation, sounded risky. Never mind time-consuming when time was one thing they might not have. *Then again, I'm the one pacing around with nothing to do. The captain's probably getting something accomplished while I wear a rut in the rug.*

He found he'd worked his way up to Worf's station. Riker leaned over the muted display, keeping his voice low. "No clues about some way to fight that thing off, Worf?"

"As a matter of fact, sir," Worf's deep voice returned clearly, "we've brought it down to a question of its tolerance level."

"Tolerance?"

"Yes, sir. How much energy it can take in at a given time. We think that's why it backed off us before." Worf's big brown fingers poked in a few commands, and the faint jade image of the *Enterprise* was enhanced. Specific areas on the display then quietly flashed. "These were the areas most affected by the drain. We're trying to narrow down its power consumption at the moment it backed off. If we can calculate the amount of energy drained from the ship up to the point when the entity backed off, we may be able to calculate its breaking point."

Riker straightened. "Boy, that sounds shaky. You're proposing we overfeed it to overload it."

"That's the conclusion so far, sir. We're keeping our minds open for alternatives, but it likes the taste of energy and the phasers—"

"I know. All right, keep going. I'd like a couple of choices to present to the captain when he comes out of his experiment, and exhausting all the ship's power trying to stuff that thing till it pops isn't my favorite. That leaves us with no second chance."

"Understood, sir." Worf made no ceremony about turning his fierce countenance back to his console once again, his dogged perseverance taking over completely. Riker watched him for a moment, taking refuge in the fact that Worf was ignoring him. He wished all his crew could be so unaffected by the presence of an officer at his shoulder. Even Data wasn't this imperturbable. *Not with me, anyway. But I guess I make him nervous.*

All at once he turned. "Where *is* Data? Still down in AR?"

Worf looked puzzled as he said, "Now that you mention it, sir, we haven't heard from either him or LaForge since they cleared us to refill the mains. They were monitoring from the source."

"Doesn't take this long. Get them back up here."

"Right away, sir."

"Worf, how do you feel about all this? What are your instincts telling you?"

"My instincts, sir?" The big man came to his full height and frowned in thought. "The captain never asks me about tactics, sir."

"Well, I'm asking."

"Klingons are warriors, sir. Our goal is to die in battle. Some Klingons have even made wars and feuds begin so they and their clans could go out and die right. But this thing," he said contemptuously, casting a glare at the wide viewscreen and its glitter, "this thing is a coward and a bully. There is no honor in fighting it."

210

"You wouldn't feel obliged to fight it if you could find a way to escape it?"

"No more than I would feel obliged to fight a thunderstorm, sir."

"I see," Riker murmured. "Thank you."

"My pleasure, sir."

His pleasure sounded like a threat. *What a voice. Glad it's on our side,* Riker thought as he strode away, trying to think like a Klingon. Coward and a bully. Yes, that was true. A big stupid phenomenon with more power than it knew how to handle and a propensity for stealing more. It probably thought preserving the life essences of its victims was the decent thing to do. If it thought at all, which it probably didn't. Or did it? Data had been in contact with *something,* and evidently not the same something Deanna was sensing. Maybe there was more intelligence at work than was apparent—

It didn't matter. Getting away mattered. Not falling into the trap mattered. Riker remembered too clearly the anguish in Arkady Reykov's eyes when the two had "met" in the corridor. Met—if only they could. Envy pierced him suddenly and he wished he could crawl into Deanna's mind and have a conversation with Reykov and Vasska. What would it be like? To contact men of that age? Such a fascinating part of history, that brink of the great plunge into the space age—what a time it must have been. They could build ships like that and float them on top of the water and put five *thousand* people inside. Wouldn't it be interesting to speak to Timofei Vasska and compare first-officer notes? What did Vasska have to know? Things about the sea and atmosphere that probably seldom occurred to captains and officers these days. And all the political tumults of a civilization like Earth's—

211

what an experience it would be to understand the thoughts of such people as they must have been. They'd have to be decisive and quick. Their opinions were probably right up front all the time, no disguises, no shady diplomacy. And here they were, within reach. Asking for help, in fact, according to Deanna. Part of the brotherhood of big ships.

All at once, guilt entered his thoughts. How sure could he be of his own convictions? What had Reykov tried to convey to him when they met in the corridor? What had that extended hand meant? Riker knew he'd hurt Deanna with his arguments. He remembered how her face had grown pale, her eyes sad as she looked at him during those moments. Arguing with Crusher was easy enough. Doctors were used to that, and Beverly was so low-key her heart only beat once a day. But Deanna had never really known what to do with confrontation. It wasn't part of her nature. He'd hit her when she was down.

He approached the command chair and touched the intercom. Quietly he asked, "Tell me where Counselor Troi is now."

The computer's response was immediate and conspicuous on the quiet bridge. *"Counselor Troi is in sickbay lab isolation area, unit four."*

"Still? How long are they going to let this go on?" he muttered, clasping his hands behind his back.

"More information is required to answer your inquiry, please."

"I didn't mean you. Cancel."

"Thank you."

"Pain in the ass," he grumbled back at its sugary female voice, and strode forward away from it.

Something had to work. So far, nothing had, but something would have to. Separating the ship had only gotten them into bigger trouble. Increasing power to the shields had only attracted and fed the creature. Phaser power would probably do the same, albeit with a different kind of energy. There had to be some weapon to devise, something, some idea in Starfleet's new technology that could get them out of this. It was here, that idea, Riker made himself believe. All they had to do was find it. Except . . . all the cards were in the deck. They didn't have enough information about the enemy.

He turned expectantly and looked at Worf's hunched shoulders as the Klingon bent resolutely over the science station.

Riker sighed, and paced.

Going to space on a ship like this . . . it was easy to get smug, to figure the deck was solid and the ship was impregnable. Easy to become imperious about mortality. And when the wisdom of the age put children on board—well . . . safe, right?

"Sir!"

He spun, dragged around both by the alarm and the accusation in the voice that stormed the bridge. On the upper deck, LaForge was charging out of the turbolift.

"Where've you been?" Riker demanded. Then LaForge's appearance registered—little electrical burns on his sleeves, his dark features glossy with sweat, and even behind the visor anger showing clearly in his face. Riker paused and redesigned his question. "What happened to you?"

"Data locked me in the AR decontamination stall and shorted out the safety shield. It took me this long to tear the wall apart and get out," LaForge panted. "Mr. Riker, he's gone."

"Gone?" Riker blurted. "Where?"

"He took a shuttlecraft and headed out to find the creature. And it's your fault, sir."

"He took—are you sure?"

"I was just down at the flight deck. The autolog in the deck control loft says he left over half an hour ago."

"Worf! Check that!"

"Won't do any good," LaForge said. "He bypassed all the relays that would've notified the bridge. He knows all the tricks, sir. You know he does."

"Worf, try to track him," Riker amended as he climbed the ramp in three long steps and confronted LaForge. "You got any idea what his thinking is on this?"

LaForge said, "He's hoping to be able to communicate with that thing if he can get closer to it."

"And?"

"Why would there be anything else, Mr. Riker?"

"Come on, LaForge, I see it in your face. What else?"

"Just a little thing, sir. Because you've been so nice to him, he's gone to find out if he's alive enough for the creature to suck the life out of him."

The bridge shrank away. Riker's eyes tightened until they were aching. He brought a hand to them and leaned the other palm on the bridge rail. "Oh, no," he groaned. "Oh, damn . . . who knew he'd be that sensitive?"

"Did he have to be?" LaForge shot back.

"Damn," he murmured again, this time a whisper. "Worf, anything on that shuttlecraft?"

"Sensors on passive aren't picking up anything at all, sir. I don't understand. Even passive read should pick up something the size of a shuttlecraft."

Riker gestured toward Worf, but looked at LaForge and asked, "Got an explanation for that?"

LaForge shrugged. "Data's not stupid, sir. He probably rigged a sensor shield of some kind to give him time to get away before we could beam him back or hit him with a tractor beam. We could pick him up right away on active sensors, but passives aren't powerful enough and Data knows we don't dare use them."

"Does he have a plan?"

"Not that he told me. He intends to attract its attention, that's all I know."

"Worf, can he do it in a shuttlecraft?"

The Klingon paused, then said, "No problem, sir. All he'd have to do is use the weapons on board."

Pacing away from them, Riker folded his arms tightly, gathering to deal with a problem he himself had caused. "He didn't have to do this. . . ."

"Thanks to you, he thought he did," LaForge said.

Riker struck him with a glare and snapped, "That's enough from you. I know what I did. Have you got something constructive to say?"

LaForge straightened—almost to attention, but not quite—and got suddenly formal. "Yes, sir. Request permission to take another shuttlecraft and go after him. I believe that would put only the two of us at risk and not attract attention to the *Enterprise.*"

"And do what when you find him? Dock up and slap his wrist?"

"I could relay coordinates, and you could beam us both back simultaneously."

Riker paused, and the sarcasm protecting him from his own mistake suddenly flooded away. "That's a good idea," he heard himself say, even though he hadn't meant to say it aloud. He strode back to

215

LaForge and said, "But you shouldn't be the one to go. I'm the cause of this. I'm the reason he's risking his life, and I'm going after him."

"You, sir? You said he was just a machine. That he doesn't have a life to risk."

Stifling the desire to reach out and crush those words out of the air, Riker gazed at LaForge so intently he could almost see through the ribbed silver visor and through the dead eyes to the very core of LaForge's concern for Data. He took a step closer to the navigator and said, "Geordi, nobody needs to be that wrong more than once."

Stiffly LaForge insisted, "How do you know you were wrong?"

But the answer to the challenge was already there on Riker's face, and he even had the words for it. "Machines don't go beyond their programming. No machine has ever sacrificed itself to save others," he said. "Data just did both."

LaForge's stiff posture slackened as he heard Riker's whole-hearted belief and saw the subtle physiological changes that showed him the first officer was sincere. Even through his anger, he couldn't doubt his own vision. "Sir, I don't know if he'll listen to you. You know what I mean."

Softly Riker responded, "I'll make him listen." He started toward the turbolift, then whirled and snapped his fingers. "Notify Dr. Crusher to get the captain out of isolation, stabilize him, and fill him in on this. But give me time to get clear of the ship first."

LaForge took a tentative step toward him. "Sir, could I—"

"No," Riker said. "You stay here. In fact," he added with a gesture that took in the bridge, "take over."

* * *

The bad memories were piling one on top of the other like an avalanche and there was nothing to stop them. Nothing to distract his mind from them or give him something, anything to cling to. Not an itch, not a blink, nothing. He could no longer focus his thoughts voluntarily. His mind moved of its own accord. The more he tried not to think of certain things, the quicker his mind shot to them and lingered there. There was no longer any way to avoid thoughts or deflect the process. After the good memories had been relived, his mind went deeper and deeper into the past he had long ago learned to control; all the terrible things from childhood and even from his adult past came plunging back at him and there was no stopping it. His mind was a wide field on which all these things were wild birds pecking.

Why was he being left in here so long? Why had he been forgotten here?

If only he could wiggle his toes. His fingers. Anything. To feel his own presence would be something, at least—at the very least. To hear himself breathe . . . it was all gone. His sense of time was utterly gone, no matter how he tried to keep control, to keep track. The mind worked at something like twenty-four thousand words per minute, so it probably seemed longer than it had been—but how long? If he could blink, he could begin to judge time again. If he could draw a breath or move a finger, he would have some point of reference. If there was only something, some sense of time or life . . . breathing, heartbeat, anything. It was difficult now to tell if he was awake or asleep, or even to know the difference. No matter how he kept reminding himself of where he was and why he was here, any sense of purpose slid away almost instantly now. Thoughts could no longer take hold in his mind. Then

217

the distortion set in. Doomed to the redundancy of his own thoughts, he felt the horror of the future. Even pain would be welcome.

They've forgotten me. They've forgotten I'm here. But where is here? I'm not sure anymore. Do they know they've left me behind? Have they stopped monitoring? Did they forget having a captain named Picard? Wasn't there an entity?

Riker wanted to leave the area, not attack the creature . . . Has he used this opportunity to do that?

Ridiculous.

But what other explanation?

That thing's out there. It must have attacked again. It's taken all of us and this is eternity for me now. My God, we must all be inside that thing! There's no other explanation. Why else would I be in here for so many days? How can there be such solitude? Man wasn't meant for this. I wasn't meant for this. I don't want it.

My arms. They're falling off. I have no shoulders to hold them on. My elbows are growing . . . my knees . . . how can I still be alive this way? I can't hear myself breathe. I can't swallow. Listen . . . nothing. Nothing. Where is everything? Everyone?

Death isn't supposed to feel unnatural like this. But I'm not dead. I'm not dead. But life isn't like this, and how can there be anything other than death and life? Beverly? Are you checking? They've left me behind. They thought I died and they left my body in space and somehow my mind is awake. This is monstrous . . . unforgivable. I can't touch myself. A human being should at least have himself for company. Where am I? Let me out! Don't leave me in space! It's so cold here. . . .

Chapter Eleven

TROI PACED OUTSIDE the isolation chamber, her arms tightly folded. She couldn't get warm. Frustration picked at her as she tried to find the words to explain her perceptions to the captain, words good enough to make her walk over there and put an end to this chamber experiment. The mind was her professional realm, and this kind of mental distortion had always irritated her. The mind need not be stretched out of shape to be understood, or to be made to understand. Such a man, Picard was—subjecting himself to this on the slim chance that it would help make his decision a bit surer than it otherwise might have been.

"Have some coffee, Deanna," Dr. Crusher said, having lost count of the passes Troi had made between the chamber and the monitor.

Troi cut her pacing short. "How is he? Do you know?"

"Stable, physically. The encephalogram's a little erratic, but nothing I'd call unexpected."

Shaking her head, Troi said, "I must be more affected than I realize, to let him do this to himself. I've never approved of these procedures."

"If the captain comes out of there even a little more sure, it'll all be worthwhile."

"I'm not convinced," Troi said.

"Sit down, will you?" Crusher ordered up a steaming cup of coffee and handed it to Troi, actually having to fold the counselor's hand around the cup. "Drink. And forget about the captain for a few minutes. I guarantee he's forgotten all about you."

"That's what worries me."

Crusher sat back and nodded, checked the monitors again, found them unchanged, then crossed her legs and tried to take her own advice. "What about you? What's it doing to you?"

Troi's black eyes lay unfocused on the pool of coffee. "They're on me every second. They give me no rest . . . these strangers. They're so desperate, Beverly, and it's an intimacy beyond description. I don't think even a full Betazoid could understand it. I tried so hard to make the captain understand . . . and Bill . . ."

Crusher leaned forward and squeezed Deanna's wrist reassuringly. "Don't take it too hard. He was doing what he thought was best."

"Was he?"

"Oh, I think so."

Troi felt her lips tighten as she fought back the rush of emotion. "I wish one or the other of us could be . . . somewhere else."

"I know," the doctor said sympathetically. "It's difficult to deal with someone who reappears out of your past. Especially when you disagree."

"I expected his support," Troi said, her voice cracking. "We know each other better than either of us knows anyone else on this ship. I thought he of all people would accept my judgment."

"It's not his job to accept your judgment, Deanna, you know that. If anything, his duty is to make sure the captain is clear on all angles of a crisis."

"Oh, Beverly, that's not what he was doing. I could feel it. He really believed the things he said."

"He's entitled to," Crusher said soothingly. "Having an affection for each other doesn't mean you have to be joined at the brain. You're allowed to disagree."

"I know that, but . . ."

"How long have you known each other?"

"Oh, nearly five years." A warm tinge of nostalgia mellowed her distraught expression. "We had a lively time together before he decided to devote his life to a long-term mission. There was a time when we planned a future together . . . before we realized we wanted different things from life. He was gallant and gentlemanly, as he is now, perhaps a bit brusque and arrogant—"

"As he is now," Crusher appended with a playful smile.

Troi nodded. "This," she said, glancing around at the wholeness of *Enterprise,* "was a coincidence neither of us foresaw."

"Why do you call him Bill when everyone else calls him Will?"

Troi's cheeks flushed, and she managed a smile. "I didn't know it was so obvious."

"It's not. I'm just astonishingly observant, you know."

Troi's delicate smile widened. " 'Bill' sounds like a word in the language of Betazed. A word I like . . . reminds me of my childhood there. There's no translation, but it had to do with—oh, I shouldn't tell you. I wouldn't want to compromise him."

"Go ahead," the doctor said, a mischievous gleam in her eyes, "compromise him."

"Well, it means . . ."

"Yes?"

"Shaving cream."

" 'Bill' means 'shaving cream' in Betazoid?"

Troi felt a touch of laughter bubble out of her. "That word always reminds me of this particular brand of Macedonian shaving cream my father used to use. It was scented evergreen and—"

"Oh, that explains it!" Crusher said. "Latent childhood impressions of parental evergreenery. There you are! It's not Riker who attracts you—it's pine trees! And I think I'm only a fair psychologist. Move over, Deanna, I think I like this. Wait till Wesley hears about it. Shaving Cream Riker."

"Beverly, you wouldn't!"

"Oh, wouldn't I? It'll spread like wildfire among everybody under twenty years old—"

Her face was alight with conspiracy when the sickbay door shot open. Geordi streaked in and without the slightest hesitation stabbed a finger at the isolation chamber and said, "Get him out of there. We've got trouble."

"Captain? Captain? Jean-Luc, can you hear me? Jean-Luc?"

He heard her voice. Had been hearing it, in fact, for what seemed like years. He moved toward it through a terrible darkness, a spiraling tunnel with glazed walls, and after half an eternity he opened his eyes.

"Jean-Luc?" Beverly Crusher bent over him, concern etched into her features.

He felt the anger working on his face, the effort of trying to speak when his body had almost forgotten

222

how. He felt betrayed and enraged, wanting to demand why they had left him in there so long—why they had put him through that, why they had let the phenomenon devour him and everything he held precious.

"Neurological functions approaching normal, Bev," someone said from behind her. Another doctor. What was his name? Mitchell? Yes, the neurologist.

"Finally." She sighed. "Jean-Luc, do you understand what I'm saying?"

He managed a nod, and his head pounded its protest. He forced it to move, discovered his neck was in no better condition, but he was now able to see Counselor Troi standing beside his bed with another expression like Beverly's. His anger began slowly to dissipate as he began to differentiate reality from dream. As if he was emerging from a vivid nightmare, he had to pick his way through the mist, deciding point for point what was real and what was not.

"My God . . ." he rasped. His voice sounded like gravel. "How . . . how long . . ."

"More than fourteen hours in isolation," Crusher said, "and it's taken us over two more to rouse you. I told you I didn't want to do this."

"Fourteen," he uttered. "It felt more like . . ."

"Hush while we stabilize you. You just relax."

He let his head fall back on the pillow, stared at the ceiling, and whispered, "My God . . ."

He lay still, aware of Troi's unflagging gaze but unable to meet it yet, his mind clogged with confusion. This was like awakening from a long, distorted, unrelenting nightmare and not knowing for sure which parts were only dream. This remained with him in the pools of sweat between his fingers—his precious fingers that he'd thought were gone—and in the coldness of his feet that wouldn't warm up. Finally he heard his own breathing. Ragged, but a joy to hear again. He concentrated so singularly upon it that when the sickbay door hissed open, he wondered why his breathing sounded that way. Only when Lieutenant Worf's massive frame loomed over the counselor's did Picard begin to separate truth from illusion.

"You said you would contact us when he was awake," the Klingon boomed to Crusher.

"I said I'd call you when he was stable," Crusher told him sternly. "He isn't. But I will when he is, don't worry, Lieutenant."

But Worf didn't leave. "Ship's business, doctor."

"I think it'll have to wait."

Picard raised a numb hand. "Lieutenant," he struggled to say, "report."

"Aye, sir. We had to pull you out of isolation early because we have a new emergency. Commander Data has taken a shuttlecraft and gone out into the sector to attempt contact with the entity, and Commander Riker has gone after him in a research dinghy."

"Wha—" Picard came halfway off the bed and was bodily attacked by the doctor, the neurologist, and two interns who actually managed to knock Worf out of the way. "What? When?"

"Two hours ago for Mr. Riker, sir. We're in contact with him, but he hasn't found Data. We're keeping communication to a minimum, of course."

"What kind of absurd—get me up."

Crusher tossed her head and called, "Stimulant."

Picard watched incredulously as she pressed the hypo against his arm. The situation must be even trickier than his foggy mind was putting together.

"Just don't make any fast moves for an hour or so,"

she told him as the two interns helped him find his balance.

"I'm afraid all we may have left," he said, "are fast moves." As he experimented with his newfound legs, his gaze fell on Troi as she watched expectantly a few paces away, her expression taut and hopeful now, wanting to know what he had experienced, what he had decided, yet frightened of asking. Or perhaps she was sensitive enough to know she didn't have to ask; he would tell her when he was ready. Yes, that was it. He saw that now as he looked at her large exotic eyes.

He reached for her hand and firmly said, "Counselor, would you like to escort me to the bridge? This situation has gone far enough."

"Riker to Data. Riker to Data. I know you're out there. Talk to me. Don't make me boost my gain. I'm picking you up faintly on tight sensors, but if you make me expand the sensor cone, that thing'll home in on it and we'll both be finished. Do you copy?"

It was the fourth time he'd made that threat, and the fourth time he'd failed. He was bluffing; he didn't have Data's shuttlecraft on his readouts at all. But if Data *thought* he did . . . well, that was the game. He was halfway to the solar system, traveling at half sublight. On his aft monitor, *Enterprise* hung against black space, regally composed amid these devilish odds, her opalescent hulls and nacelles seeming quite open to attack right now. Even from here he saw how low her energies were running. Her impulse and warp sections normally glowed brightly and were now simply brushed with pale color. The string of lights that shone from her rectangular windows were dim slits now, and there were fewer of them than he cared to

225

see. This was a disturbing picture of the starship for Riker, this muted version of a ship otherwise unafraid to show her power. Today she dared not, at least not yet. Not until they could fight what they were up against.

"Come on, Data, come on, put me out of my misery," he grumbled, adjusting the array of sensory equipment on his helm board. This research dinghy was sensor-heavy, virtually all sensors from bow to stern, including most of its outer skin. It was shaped like a boat, its underbelly designed to skim atmospheres, its two lateral sensory pods designed to pick up readings of astonishing detail, right down to wind shifts, storm patterns, and even microorganisms. Ordinarily it would never be used for anything other than research, but today it was the best bet for finding Data. It was smaller and slightly faster than a shuttlecraft, and its pincer-fine sensors could put out a finer beam and draw in cleaner information on less power than any other vessel at his disposal, including cutting through Data's makeshift cloaking device. First rule of tactics: get a better horse.

Of course, he was ignoring the obvious—that he could be heading in completely the wrong direction and Data could be a million miles the other way. But if any part of Data was human enough to run on instinct alone, that instinct said to head toward a star system, where life originated, where it belonged. Where the thing might be.

And so the swirling gas giant was once again Riker's companion in space, the gas giant, the asteroid belt with its obliterated portion, now just so much chips and dust after the starship's antimatter dump. Funny —in the *Enterprise* this distance didn't seem so big. Without the mass of the starship around him, Riker felt the whole perspective acutely, and even if it took the same amount of time, his search exaggerated the distance he was covering. His dinghy seemed small against the black panorama—seemed, hell, it *was* small.

"Data, come in, please," he attempted again, tightening his communications beam and managing to lengthen it a few more miles. That would take a wider sweep—everything was compromise. Working the controls so delicately he could barely perceive the change on the displays, he licked his lips and murmured, "Come on, Data, don't make me live with this."

"This is Commander Data. Mr. Riker, please turn back, sir."

Riker flinched and gawked at the console for a moment, then pounced on it. "Data? Do you copy me?"

"I copy, sir. Your pursuit is ill-advised."

Riker opened his mouth to snap an insult or an order, but caught his breath and changed gears on the spot. Working as fast as his fingers would go, he tried to force the minimal sensors to draw in on Data's location without putting out enough energy to attract the entity. He paused, took a breath, counted to one, and slowly said, "Data, I know what you're trying to do. Geordi told me. I know this is because of those things I said, and I want to tell you . . . I was wrong. I had no right to say those things."

"Appreciated, sir. That does not change the accuracy of your statements. You did help me to perceive myself, and for that I am grateful. I'm receiving erratic readings on the phenomenon, sir. It seems to be fading in and out of contact. If it probes me again, I may be near enough to it to transmit as well as receive."

227

"That may kill you. Don't try it. We've got other ways to fight this thing."

"Fighting it is impractical at this time, Mr. Riker. It uses our own energy against us."

"Worf may have found a way around that," Riker told him, hedging his bets, "but we need you to help us lock down the theory. Turn around and let's go back while we can."

There was a pause, long enough to make Riker nervous. Finally he tampered with his equipment and said, "Data? I'm switching to visual."

As he said it, the screen to his right flickered and focused, supplying him with a reassuring picture of Data's face, a little staticky because of the reduced power output.

"Data, listen to me. I want you to come back with me. You're too valuable a crewman to lose on this wild scheme to communicate with that thing. Be reasonable."

Data's expression was one of regret but resolution as he thoughtfully said, *"Even if I could not find a way to communicate with it, sir, I must continue my search."*

Even though he knew what was coming and hated himself for sparking it, Riker asked the question he had been steered into. "Why?"

"I must find out if there is anything in me that the phenomenon recognizes as a life essence. I must know if there is enough humanity in me," Data said slowly, *"to be destroyed."*

Riker squinted into the brightness of the screen. "Data, think about that. It's not very logical, is it?"

"No, sir. But this may be my only chance to discover whether I am even alive, much less human. And if the entity fails to absorb me," he said, his impassivity

228

more than disturbing, *"I shall have my answer. I will know my place."*

"Your place is with us," Riker told him. "I know that now. You're doing something no machine would do. That's enough for me."

Then the remarkable happened. Data smiled at him. It was a simple, spontaneous smile, childlike and heartwarming, and it didn't seem he was even aware of it. The android's sulfurous eyes sparkled with a lively quality that Riker had never noticed when he was standing in the room with him, but it was also the kind of smile that was laced with regret. Riker could tell—he'd seen enough smiles—what it meant.

"Picard to Riker. Do you read?"

He flinched again, startled by the completely different voice that suddenly pelted through his com system, and tapped the right pressure points. "Data, stand by." The screen winked off, and he hit another link. *"Enterprise,* this is Riker."

"What the hell do you think you're doing out there, Number One?"

"I'm zeroing in on Data, Captain. I've almost got a transporter triangulation on him."

"Have you got a lock on him? He's out of low-power communication range with us."

"Yes, sir I'm talking to him right now. At least I'm trying to."

"Is he having any success with his hypothesis? He's very likely the only being the entity's happened upon who's walking the line between living being and machine. He may be our only chance to communicate."

"That's true, sir, but I really think there's more risk in that than profit, especially for Data."

"Then don't dally out there. Get a triangulation on him and we'll beam you both in. I can't afford to lose

both of you. We'll have a talk later about those two vessels you appropriated. You can wager on that."

"Yes, sir, I underst—Data! Stop it!"

"Riker, what is it! Report!"

"He's arming the shuttlecraft's weapons, Captain, he's going to fire blind to attract that thing. Data, kill those weapons. That's an order."

"Sorry, Mr. Riker," Data said calmly, *"but I must draw its attack before you come near enough to be caught also. I do not believe the dinghy puts out sufficient energy to draw its attention while you're still at this—"*

"Riker!" Picard's voice shot through the system. *"We're picking up massive energy readings. It's got to be right on top of him out there! Do you see it?"*

"Switching," Riker snapped. Perspiration rolled down his forehead, and became a sheet of moisture when the viewscreen cleared.

In space in front of him, the shuttlecraft's blocky form was dwarfed by the all-too-familiar and too hideous spectral image that had become his nightmare. It closed on Data's shuttlecraft with lightning speed and swallowed it whole while Riker watched helplessly, and it took up half his visible space in the process. As it devoured Data's ship, it reached a long electrical arm through space toward Riker.

A chill streaking down his arms, he smashed his fist on the comlink. *"Enterprise!* Beam us up now! Now!"

The nauseating sensation of beaming began almost instantly. The captain must have been ready for this, must have anticipated it. Riker gave himself to it, as though that would help, and stared into the viewscreen as he felt himself dematerializing. But he was still able to see the viewer clearly enough when the shuttlecraft was torn to bits, its tiny impulse engine blasting outward in a dynamic explosion.

Agonizing seconds later the interior of the research dinghy was gone and the transporter room's dark gray textured walls were forming around him. Above him the soft lighting, below him the glowing platform—beside him . . . another form materializing.

He reached out as soon as he could, but instinctively recoiled from the crackling electrical sheath that enveloped Data once again. This time it seemed to have a sense of purpose—or was he imagining it?

"Data!" he shouted without thinking.

The electricity snapped a few more times, then faded. Riker stepped toward Data instantly. Just in time to catch him.

The platform thumped as Captain Picard and Geordi LaForge appeared out of nowhere and knelt beside Riker and the collapsed form of Data. His android eyes stared up at nothing. His heart still beat dutifully. His pulse still made a steady drum in his wrists. Biomechanics still worked the shell he had called his body. But the essence of life that had possessed a courage no machine could duplicate—

Was gone.

Chapter Twelve

DATA LAY IN a wedge of bright, tight surgical beams in the dimmed main sickbay lab. Physicians, neurologists, microengineering specialists, robotics experts hovered over him, but no one could shake the poisoned apple from his throat. He lay there on the table, his face less placid than a corpse's might have been, his expression caught in a moment of surprise, perhaps even revelation.

To Picard, the elemental darkness rested in the room was like a Poe stanza. He paced around the small group and looked again into Data's opalescent eyes, and longed again to understand what the android had seen at that last moment. The chamber experience was still with him, making him feel somehow separate from these people who hadn't been through it. He thought he knew now what resurrection could be like, what it would be like to be caught by that thing—only to reawaken with new knowledge and be able to use that knowledge. He had reawakened to a monumental difference in his own perceptions. Colors seemed brighter, smells nicer, shapes crisper. There was a sudden wonder to being so consummately alive.

Over on that table, Data's face had that kind of wonder on it, but he hadn't come back.

When Beverly Crusher finally backed away from the table, her face limned with frustration, even anguish, and her willowy body had lost some of its grace. She moved slowly toward the corner where Riker and Geordi were impatiently standing, not too near each other, and Picard turned to meet her there. He lowered his voice.

"No hope?"

The doctor sighed. "Not from us. As far as we can deduce, Data's android brain is still operating all the complexities of his body. But there's no consciousness anymore. We just don't know what else to do."

Geordi turned toward them from where he had been facing the wall. "How'd it get him?" he demanded, his throat tight. For the first time he allowed himself the realization that Data might truly be lost to them, even if his heart still beat. "How could it take part of him and leave . . . that?"

Riker folded his arms and pressed one shoulder into the bulkhead. As he gazed at the floor with a pall of regret over him, new lines cut themselves into his face. "Probably the thing didn't distinguish between Data's body and the shuttlecraft. If he'd been fully organic, his body might've gone up in smoke or whatever that thing does to organics. I guess it recognized something in him," he added, rather mournfully, "that it . . . wanted."

Picard looked at his first officer. He'd never seen Riker so depressed, never heard this stony tone. Vexed that he didn't completely know what was going on

233

between his command officers, he peered now at the engineers and doctors who became more helpless by the moment, who were now beginning to stand back one by one and shake their heads over Data's quiet form.

"For better or worse," the captain said thoughtfully, "Data may have found his answer."

Anger began to burn low in his mind, a layer of heat beneath all other thoughts, making them sizzle and jump. There would be no diminishment of the self on this ship. Rage built within him as he imagined Data forever trapped inside that phenomenon, forever to endure what Picard himself had barely touched in fourteen hours of hell.

His shoulders stiff with his anger growing, he turned toward the exit and flatly said, "I'll be in engineering."

He went, but he went alone. When he was down in engineering, he swept aside each engineer's offer to assist him or escort him, shrugged off their curious looks when he went into special-access chambers and came out again with computer input chips that no one had given him or pulled up for him. Word spread quickly that the captain was here, doing something for himself and not asking anyone to do it for him, and before long curious eyes peeked at him from a dozen hiding places in the engineering complex. Even in the dimness, he stood out simply because he wasn't usually here. Eventually the curious junior engineers who saw him lurking about started trying to track his doings secretly on their access panels. They discovered that Captain Picard knew both what he was doing and perfectly well how to keep them from

234

finding out. They discovered they could trace his activities about halfway at each turn before they lost the pattern of his computer use. So they watched, unable to say anything about it because he was the captain, and if this was anybody's equipment, it was his. They knew there was something going on topside; why wasn't he up there? They muttered among themselves about reporting to the first officer, but nobody volunteered to do the talking.

So the engimatic captain of the *Enterprise* floated around engineering for over an hour, not speaking to anyone, offering only the most ghostly of smiles to those who came too close, lighting here and there like a moth to tamper with the equipment and be suddenly on the move again, and not a living soul dared approach him with a direct question. He was too purposeful in each movement, each pause, each touch.

Then he was gone. Without a word, without an order. He cradled a few computer tie-in remotes in his elbow, and walked out.

Once clear of engineering and on his way through the darkened ship by way of ladders and walkways, Picard paused on one of the upper decks and touched the nearest intercom. "Picard to sickbay. Mr. Riker, you still there?"

Almost immediately Riker's strong voice answered, *"Yes, Captain, still here. No change."*

Picard looked down at the small bundle of remotes he carried. They seemed innocent as they lay in the crook of his arm, small bundles of circuitry inside casings. But they were deadly.

"In ten minutes, I want you and LaForge to be on the bridge. This has gone far enough."

The words chimed through the ship, right through the cloth of silence and darkness they'd swathed around themselves, saying quite plainly that the phenomenon was going to have to deal with the captain now.

Before entering the bridge, Picard quietly and privately plugged his remotes into their proper places in the control layout deep within the bridge maintenance loop, a thin corridor of computer access boards behind the actual walls of the bridge itself. Here, new systems were built into the bridge systems, the great hands of the starship, working all the instructions put to it from the gigantic computer core running through the primary hull.

Picard made use of those access boards now, tying them all in to one single button on the arm of his command chair. He had thought about using a code that he could key in from anywhere on the ship, but at last dismissed the idea and created an actual button to be pushed. And in that one place—the command chair. If he was going to put his finger down on destiny, he would be in his rightful place, at the head of this majestic ship, when he did it.

He stalked back onto the bridge, noticeably somber, and into the audience of expectant faces. Riker. LaForge. Troi. Wesley Crusher. Worf. And others, especially those manning the positions he might have expected to see Data manning. The Ops controls or Science 2. He missed the gold-leaf face and the gently innocuous expression. He missed it a great deal. His deep rage grew.

"I'm glad you're all here," he said ceremoniously, approaching his command chair. This time, however, he didn't reach out and casually touch it as he might have otherwise. This time the chair itself was a source of raw power, and he didn't want to give anything away. "I want to know what you've concluded, what our options are, how we can best deal with this invasion. If we have to drain this starship of every last volt and every last moving molecule, we'll do it. That thing out there has already cost the life of one of us; it will take no more of us. It isn't going any farther into the galaxy. We're stopping it here and now."

Deanna Troi let her eyes drift shut, so deep was her relief and gratitude. Picard saw her reaction and understood it so clearly that he might as well have been the Betazoid. When she raised her head and opened her eyes, they were glazed with tears and she was almost smiling—but then the smile dropped away and her eyes filled with perplexity. She saw into his heart now, he could tell, saw the knowledge and the determination that were foremost in his mind, unhidden from her probing thoughts, saw the remotes now engaged into certain circuits that would carry a certain message to a dozen locations in the lower structures of the ship and do the kind of thing captains thought of only in moments of supreme desperation. She stared at him, then looked down, at the arm of the command chair, at the small patch of controls that tied the captain's own touch into his ship. And that single blue pressure point, like a poker chip. She knew. Picard watched her, without offering either reassurance or a request for her silence. She would be silent, he knew. They understood one another now.

Riker stepped forward—not exactly a surprise.

"We're going to chase it down?" he asked.

"We're going to kill it, Mr. Riker."

The first officer paused, his lips compressing, then said, "That's not like you, sir."

Picard knew what was behind Riker's eyes and that dubious tilt to his head, and he looked right at him now. "Isn't it? Is it more like me to allow that marauder to wander the galaxy freely, sucking up more lives?"

That moment saw a charge of excitement. Even Riker realized suddenly how long he'd been waiting for something to bring that level of indignation to Picard's face. The captain's brown eyes were narrowed, his Roman-relief profile aimed squarely at the viewscreen, his jaw like a rock set upon another rock.

And even so, straight through the ring of Picard's words, Riker forced himself to do what was his duty. "What about the Prime Directive? We can't guard the whole galaxy."

"Even the Prime Directive must have its elasticity," Picard said firmly, and there was no doubt that he had thought about this, had already endured and forded the difficulty of this very question. He paused, and moved forward on his bridge, all eyes on him. "From a distance, this may look like Utopia, Will," he said, broadly enough for all to hear, "but when you're staring right at it, it's something else. It's a tyrant and demands our grappling with it. There will be no tyranny here," he said. "Refusing to make a decision is its own kind of cowardice."

Riker moved to the captain's side, and the two men stood before the vast viewscreen and all it held. "You're that certain?" he asked. He wondered why the rock of resistance still sat in his stomach. He knew perfectly well that Captain Picard was no grandstander, that such a man would turn the ship and run in the other direction if there were a way to avoid using the weapons, yet he still had to make this one last request, that Picard simply say yes, he was certain.

But the captain said nothing. He merely gazed sidelong at Riker, exercising his command right in that simple silence.

Riker nodded and backed off a few steps, making his own message clear.

The captain turned, and standing on the dais with the whole blackness of space as his backdrop, he addressed the faintly lit bridge. "All right, what do you have?"

"Sir," Worf began immediately from the opposite stage, "we've concluded that it backed away from its first attack on us because it reached its absorption capacity. We've calculated its drain on us at the point it moved off, and think it's possible to overload it."

"Risks?"

"We would have risk if we had possibility. Our phasers simply can't put out enough power to do what must be done. It dissipates its energy faster than we could pump it full."

Picard pressed his lips tight and tried to envision such a creature, but all he could do was glare at the undeniable readouts and see that it was true. Behind him, voices buzzed, annoying him as flies annoy a horse. Geordi. Wesley. Geordi. Wesley again, arguing. An exchange of whispers, grating on Picard as he tried to dig out a miracle solution, and finally he spun around, demanding, "Have you two got something to add or not?"

Both Geordi and Wesley flinched, and Wesley's cheeks flared red. "Oh . . . no, sir."

"Yes, sir," Geordi contradicted.

"But it doesn't work," Wesley hissed, tugging at Geordi's sleeve.

"Data told you how to make it work."

"But what if it doesn't?"

"When you're going to die, a one-in-a-million chance is better than nothing, Wes!"

"By the devil!" Picard roared. "What are you talking about?"

Wesley dropped into self-conscious silence while Geordi fought with himself and won. He approached the captain and said, "Wes has an idea how to increase the ship's energy output through the phaser systems, sir."

"All right," Picard said then, "I'm listening. Keep it short."

"Wesley, tell him."

Wesley licked his lips and brought his narrow form up beside Geordi. "Well, sir, it's a phaser intensification system that pulls more firepower with less base energy by breaking down the first phasing cycle into increment frequencies, then reintegrating the phasing all at once in the final cycle. Mr. Data gave me some clues that should make it work, and Geordi thinks we can—"

"The point is, sir," Geordi interrupted, speaking just as fast as Picard had asked for, "if we could modify the ship's phasers to this theory, we could fill that thing up with about five times the energy it got when it—"

"Yes, I understand the science, Lieutenant. That's very radical, what you're describing." Picard stepped down from the viewscreen bank and strode between them. "But these are radical moments." With that he

240

touched the intercom, while all breaths held. "Picard to engineering. Argyle and MacDougal, gather your primary staff and meet me in the engineering briefing room in three minutes. Ensign Crusher, I want you to describe your theory to the engineers and let them decide if it can be implemented."

"Sir," the teenager blurted, "I can build the crystal focusing system myself just as well as any of them."

The captain glared at him. "We're going to let the professionals handle it, Mr. Crusher. What you're describing will take pure antimatter feed, and that's nothing to play with."

He stepped away, but Wesley followed, slipping out of Geordi's grasp at the last second. He snapped the words out like spitballs. "You always treat me like a kid, even though I'm on the bridge."

The captain turned. His voice took on an iron resonance.

"You're on the bridge," he said, "because I chose to put you here, not because you earned it. Your ability exceeds your wisdom, young man. You'll eventually learn the unforgiving lesson that the people around you are worth more in their experience than you are in your gifts, and you shall, like everyone else, have to wait your turn. Now mind your place, close your mouth, and follow me to engineering, where you will put your gift to use and let others do the same."

Wesley was understandably subdued thereafter, give or take the minutes it took him to spell out the phasing idea. The engineers gawked at him, frowned, rolled their eyes, squinted—it looked like a cornea convention. By the time they filed down to the main phaser reactor room, they already had half the me-

241

chanics and most of the formulae worked out in their heads, and Picard stood back to watch the machine of intelligence at work. He watched too as Wesley caught a first glimpse through his own brilliance and youthful smugness of the resourcefulness and conceptual ability of experienced engineers. The boy's face lit up with both amazement and humility each time the engineers shot him a question as part of a discussion that had simply left him behind. Picard could tell from Wesley's expression that the young man didn't even know why the engineers had to know some of the things they were asking. And for every question asked, there were two more problems to be solved that he hadn't thought of. After a time he began to catch a glimpse of why his own idea seemed so foreign. The engineers weren't looking at the phasing unit as a unit. They saw it as part of the whole ship, all the intricate systems, lines, circuits, energies, fluxes, coils, and capacitors, each affecting all the others. It wasn't enough for the phasing unit to work; it had to work in concert with a thousand other units.

As soon as the engineers understood his idea, they were at work troubleshooting it. After several false starts, and even a complete rebuilding of the strange new system, all the theoreticals became applicables. Problems Wesley had never foreseen were discovered, then sidestepped or solved on the spot. The harmonics hummed, the antimatter feed had its safeties hooked up, and all in less time than it had taken Wesley to build his original mock-up. He circled the new contraption, a hulking unit attached directly to the main phaser couplings, and shook his head. It looked like nothing he'd imagined. He could see what parts did which duty, but it simply didn't look the way he thought it would look.

Picard liked that look on a young face. He liked the look of growth.

Finally the chief of phaser engineering came toward the captain and Wesley, wiping his hands on his worksuit, and shrugged. "Good as it's gonna get, Captain."

"Will it work?"

"Can't tell you that, sir. Half of it's theory and the other half's guesswork. All the systems hook up cleanly, it's got power, it's got antimatter flow, and it's got safeties. As for working, only testing can tell."

"We'll test it in combat," Picard said ruefully. "We seem to have little choice. We can't—"

"Riker to captain! Emergency!"

Picard snapped at the nearest intercom. "Picard. What?"

"It's here, sir! Our grace period just ran out."

It had, in spades. When Picard and Wesley spun from the lift and charged onto the bridge, it was no longer dark. Red alert lights bled from every wall, but the main lights hadn't come up. The forward viewer wavered and crackled with the enhanced blue-red false-color image of the entity at its most awful. The port monitors, starboard, aft—every monitor showed this pulsing threat in a great broken circle of electrical light around the bridge.

The bridge crew stared at the monitors, swiveling from one to the other as though looking for a doorway that hadn't been guarded, a single route that would provide escape from the prison, but they knew they were looking at the thing's backup tactic, the one to be used when all else failed.

Picard paused in the upper ramp. "Is it in the machinery?"

Riker whirled past Troi on the lower deck and stepped toward him. "No, sir, it's surrounding us. Contracting approximately twelve thousand miles per minute."

"It hasn't found us, then?"

"It's using this new pattern to find us. It knows we're here somewhere within a specific radius, and it's surrounded the whole area, gas giant, asteroids, and all. It's closing in on us. Obviously, it's a lot bigger than we first perceived."

"Size now?"

Worf straightened up at Picard's right. "Roughly three-point-one AUs in diameter, sir, and contracting."

"My God," Picard snarled. He understood the picture now; they were inside a gigantic fist—and it was closing on them. "Worf, estimation. Can we fire on it?"

A terrible scowl came over Worf's already fierce features. He hated his own answer as he said, "Not while it's in this form, sir. It dissipates energy in direct proportion to its surface area. We couldn't pump enough energy into it fast enough to overload it."

Picard rounded on the tactical station and stood beside Tasha Yar. "Then we're going to have to force it to compact again. Where's that gas giant?"

Yar shook herself and bent over her console. "Bearing point-seven-nine mark three-four, sir."

"Head toward it."

Riker came aft on the lower deck and asked, "Your plan, sir?"

"We're going to hide behind a tree, Mr. Riker," the captain said, moving down the ramp with his hand tracing the shape of the bridge horseshoe. The strange light across the monitors cast a bloody purple glow on his face. "It won't be able to absorb all the energy inside a level-ten gas giant a half million miles across. It's going to have to decide to come around one way or the other. When it does, there'll be a standoff."

Riker turned immediately and said, "Geordi, point-five-zero sublight to the gas giant, tight orbit."

"Point-five-zero, aye," Geordi repeated, avoiding a glance at the Ops position, where Wesley had slipped into Data's seat.

Picard kept his voice steady. "Prepare an emergency warning dispatch to Starfleet, single-pulse and high-warp. If we don't make it, I want to be sure the Federation's ready for this. Shields at maximum," he added, holding a hand up to shade his eyes from the sizzling screens.

"Shields up," Yar said shakily. "Maximum energy available for defensive—" She stopped, glaring at her readouts, and almost instantly had to gasp, "Sir, it's moving in!"

"Keep tight to the gas giant. Tighter, LaForge!"

"Trying, sir . . ."

Across the *Enterprise*'s shields crashed the punishing force of the phenomenon. It knew where the starship was, but discovered it had found two things—a starship, and a massive planet that was virtually a ball of twisting energy. No matter how it contracted, no matter how it closed its fist, the planet confounded every effort to devour the starship. Every time the thing tried to contract upon its quarry, it was driven back by the energy put out by the gas giant. Spasms of electrical energy pounded the ship and flooded through the gas giant's churning atmosphere. The ship defied the attack, shimmying with every pulse of energy that flogged the shields, draining them moment by moment.

"Outer skin heating up, Captain," Yar reported. "We're entering the atmosphere."

Picard ignored her. "Move in closer, LaForge. If it wants us, it's going to have to face us."

"Captain!" Troi shouted. When he neither fired the weapons nor hit that blue button, frustration crumpled her features and she blinked into the bright screen.

Threads of smoke and fans of sparks shot from half the bridge consoles as the ship fought the mauling once again, but Picard made no further orders. He would stand his ground and so would this ship— though he stood now beside his command chair and gripped the arm with the blue button.

"Captain!" Yar shrieked then, and raised her eyes to the main screen. Even as she spoke, every screen dropped its color in a great wash forward, as though all the images had been sucked out of the back to the main viewer. The main screen now glowed with a compact view of the creature, back in its original form.

"Get ready!" Picard shouted, but it was already upon them, dashing around the protective tree and pouncing on the ship alone, while beside them the gas giant spun ignorantly.

The *Enterprise* was taken by a great fist of lightning many times more powerful than that of moments before, and electrical bombardment once again blitzed the bridge.

"Fire phasers point-blank!" Picard ordered over the shrieking noise.

The ship spewed energy. Rocked by each shot, the

Enterprise endured the punishment as the radical new phasing system dragged energies apart that wanted to be together, then shoved them into each other at the last instant. The entity bucked in the assault, shaking the ship. Around him Picard saw his crew attacked by the silvery lights and blue undercurrents.

"Shields draining . . ." Yar shouted from her post above them.

"Keep firing!" Picard responded, hanging on to the command chair as bolt after bolt of intensified phaser energy thundered through the ship and into the phenomenon's heart.

"The thing's output is becoming unsteady, sir!" Worf shouted over the electrical shriek. "It's working!"

Suddenly the ship trembled so deep in her core that everyone felt it through his feet, and the phasers stopped.

"What—" Picard tried to turn, but managed only to twist the upper half of his body around to see Yar.

"Complete phaser meltdown, Captain! The core's blown!"

Picard's heart sank to his knees and rattled inside the electrical sheath that now strengthened on the bridge.

"Captain!" Troi's face appeared beside his shoulder. She was hanging on to his arm with both hands, her eyes tormented. "Do it! Do it, sir! Please!"

He looked at the blue button. He pushed his hand toward it. Even as he moved, forcing his quaking muscles to fight against the electrical attack, he felt himself slipping away. The beginnings of the chamber experience . . . consciousness beginning to float, to let go . . .

Troi's voice pierced his pain and struggle. "Captain!"

The blue button was an inch away from his thumb. He concentrated on it, clinging to his identity and his memories as if they were ropes dangling in an abyss. If only he could find the energy—

"Energy," he ground through his gritted teeth. "The gas giant! Yar!"

But she was helpless, plastered back against Worf by the lightning, which grew stronger with every pulse now that the ship's shielding was strained to its fullest.

"Riker!" Picard roared.

He could vaguely see Riker dragging himself step by agonizing step up the horseshoe rail toward tactical.

A form pressed against Picard's shoulder and a narrow shape came by his elbow . . . a hand. Troi's hand. Reaching for the blue button. He heard her struggling to move past him, to fight off the terrible assault as she promised she would.

He struck out with his left arm and held her back, but her determination made her strength superhuman and she was pressing harder against his shoulder, her hand clawing toward that button.

"Let me!" she bellowed through the electrical blasts.

Picard wrenched her away from the command chair with the last of his energy, and the two of them collapsed across the command arena. "Riker," Picard rasped with a final breath, "hurry! Full power!"

Even as he spoke, glowing photon torpedoes broke from the ship's primary hull and crashed down through the gas giant's atmosphere into its active heart, forcing it to release its energy. Bolt after bolt careened downward, drilling into the compacted energy, which spewed back out in great volcanic blasts. And still the ship didn't relent. It continued sending fully charged photon torps deep into the planetary reactor and forcing explosion after explosion, until finally the greatest of all disruptions came. Half the planet's violent core erupted and shot out into space.

The concussion sent the ship catapulting through open space, blown out of orbit by megatons of exploding matter.

The ship turned in space, gravity gone to hell, tossing its people about like dolls, and finally settled a quarter million miles from the gas giant.

Picard dragged himself to his feet and stumbled forward. An instant later, Riker was beside him. Around them, the crew grabbed for their control boards and tried to accept the fact that they were still alive—*really* alive.

Before them on the screen, the creature fluxed and twisted against the glowing rubble of the gas giant's remains. A million explosions raged around them where it was forced to digest the gas giant's released energy and, finally, in one singular blast, was ripped apart.

Nodules of false-color energy splayed outward across the system, and all the glitter was suddenly gone. Only blobs of dissipating energy remained, cascading by the millions around the ship and outward into open space.

"It couldn't take it. . . ." Riker murmured hoarsely.

Picard rasped, "Status!"

Yar's voice trembled. "Shields down . . . main reactors unstable. The phaser core is a complete burnout.

Totally fused. Nothing but molten metal in there, sir."

"Bet it smells," Geordi grumbled as he pulled himself back into his helm seat and gingerly touched his own equipment. Beside him, Wesley simply held on to the Ops console with both hands, and shook. They both knew. *Fused.* The whole core. All the safety systems had somehow saved the ship from being part of that meltdown. Wesley's model had had no safeties. If he'd turned it on, it would've created a dead short, the reserve antimatter containment would've collapsed, and a thousand people would've disappeared and Starfleet would never have known why. There was a sudden ringing clarity about why a starship had rules.

Wesley continued to stare, to blink, and the color stayed out from his face for a long, long while.

"Report on that thing?" Picard barked as he got to his feet.

It was Worf who finally came forward on the upper bridge and made the stark announcement. "Dissipated, sir. No central mass any longer." He looked at Picard directly now and said, "You did it, sir."

Picard sighed, his shoulders aching. "Collaborative effort, Mr. Worf." He stepped to one side now and reached downward for Counselor Troi's hand.

She sat on the floor, stunned, her face a thousand emotions slowly wringing out of her as she regained control. As her hand closed on his it was weak and shaking.

He lifted her to her feet and privately said, "Well done, Counselor. Your prognosis?"

She swallowed hard, then looked up at him and

forced herself to speak. "I can't feel them, sir . . . anymore."

He smiled. "Congratulations."

Troi nodded, trembling, still working at once again being in total possession of herself. For a fleeting moment, loneliness filled her eyes.

Chapter Thirteen

GEORDI LAFORGE SAT at his helm with depressingly little to do. The ship couldn't move until the warp engine core was stabilized, and couldn't leave the vicinity anyway, at least not yet. As soon as the immediate danger had blown itself to bits, their duty as a main Federation extension kicked in and they were obliged to make sure the area was secure before they even thought of moving on.

He was one of only five people on the bridge now. Worf and Tasha occupied the upper deck, feeding through the intricate readings that correlated the first repairs on the phaser lockup. The meltdown would take weeks to clean up and mend. Mr. Riker was on the upper deck, speaking quietly to Deanna Troi. The two of them had been talking for a long time. Under different circumstances, Geordi might have been more curious to know what they were talking about.

The bridge was ominously quiet now. The pit at the center of his soul wouldn't fill. No matter how many of the helm's light displays flashed and hummed to tell him things were being rapidly put together belowdecks, Geordi merely watched dispassionately. They'd been attacked once before, and engineers were quick learners. This repair would go two times faster than the previous ones. The ship and her complement would proceed to her mission, only slightly bruised from this incident, perhaps even stronger for it, but they would in the end simply move on. Such was sometimes the cost of winning. No real changes.

Except for the empty place beside him, which someone would fill, someone else.

Bitterness filled his mind. What tribute would be made for an android's sacrifice? What memorial would there be for Data? A burial in space, befitting a Starfleet hero, for the body lying empty and pulsing in sickbay, a body not yet dead, never to be reclaimed? Geordi wondered as he sat if he would be left to mourn alone. If Picard and Riker would clamor to define death as fervently as they had to define life. Or if it really mattered at all. Ultimately they had already failed Data, and nothing would make up for that.

He gazed now, through his visor, at the open space on the viewscreen. The remains of the gas giant still boiled in space like the remnants of some primordial explosion, ignorant of their own beauty or their own meaning. Much like Data, who hadn't perceived his own charm or worth.

Geordi slouched in the chair, one elbow braced on the helm, and felt emptier still. He hadn't realized how lost he'd become in his own thoughts until a hand dropped onto his shoulder. Someone wanted his attention, and only the discipline of Starfleet training brought him up through the murk and made him straighten and look.

But it was neither the lordly face of Picard nor

Riker's big-brother expression that looked down on him. What he saw was a warm infrared glow, a gentle face and a welcoming smile.

He spun out of his chair and knocked the helm console aside.

"Data . . ."

Data caught his arm and kept him from tripping over the Ops lounge, and kept grinning that warm little grin.

Behind him, Captain Picard, Dr. Crusher, and Wesley were watching the unexpected reunion as they too came away from the turbolift toward Geordi. On the ramp, Commander Riker was speechless as he broke away from Troi and came toward them.

"Data!" Geordi gasped again, clasping Data's cool hand and looking deeply into the android's eyes to see if it was indeed Data—and not just some weird new science nobody had told him about that could make the body walk around.

"Hello, my friend," Data said, humility touching his tone. "I'm sorry to have put you through this."

Geordi squeezed Data's hand with both of his, desperate to feel the essence of life that simply refused to showcase itself, but he couldn't think of anything to say.

"Captain," Riker blurted finally, "Doctor—what happened?"

"We're not sure," Beverly Crusher said with a one-shouldered shrug. "He just slowly came back and started looking around. He was disoriented for a while, but as you can see . . ."

Riker grasped Data's arm and pulled him around— not too roughly, but not too gently either. "Data? You all right?"

The android nodded generously. "I feel a bit woofled, sir."

"Do you know what happened to you?"

"Yes, sir. I think I croaked."

Riker stared at him, suddenly breathless, and tried to absorb his presence. It simply wasn't normal for the dead to get up again.

Data seemed sympathetic, or at least touched by Geordi and Riker's reactions. "Truly," he said, "I do not know what happened to me or why I returned. I can only surmise that when the creature got in trouble, it had to release those it was carrying and try to fight for its own existence. Of all the millions of life essences, I alone had a place to come back to. Of course," he added, "I am only guessing."

Breathing quickly, Geordi glanced at the others then back to Data, and laughed his relief away.

"All right, all right," Picard said tolerantly. "Riker, Data, and Mr. Crusher, I want you all waiting for me in my ready room in five minutes, clear?"

"Very clear, sir," Riker murmured, but he was still looking at Data. Looking very protectively this time.

Data looked back, and gave him a grateful nod.

The three of them stood in the captain's ready room, admittedly nervous.

For a few minutes they were companionably silent. Riker ultimately approached Data and held out his hand. "Congratulations. You've got the answer you wanted."

Data took the hand, though he seemed self-conscious now. "Not really, sir. The phenomenon's criteria for life was never clear to us."

"Look," Riker said, cutting him off, "as far as I'm

255

concerned, that was the closest we've come to an authority on what life is. You may not be human, exactly, but it recognized something in you as alive. And . . . that's good enough for me. I'm glad you're back."

The android tipped his head and responded, "Thank you for coming after me. That is, as you say, good enough for me."

Wesley folded his lanky arms and commented, "Don't get mushy, guys."

Riker cuffed him. "When you've been dead and come back to life, you can talk about mushy, mister."

"How much trouble do you think we're in?"

With a small shrug, Riker said, "I don't know about you, but I doubt the captain'll be congratulating either Data or me on our ingenuity. Two utility ships lost, disobedience of standing orders—not very pretty."

"At least neither of you melted down the whole phaser core," Wesley commented sullenly.

"True, but we—"

The captain entered, and they all came to attention in front of his desk, simply because none of them wanted to look him in the eye. The captain came around his desk, but didn't sit down.

"Congratulations, Mr. Crusher," he said immediately. "You have the unique privilege of assisting in the three-week rebuild of the entire phaser core. A rare opportunity for one so young."

Wesley perked up and said, "Thanks, sir!"

Picard scowled at him, annoyed that his sarcasm was lost on Wesley, and added, "We'll see if you can still smile in three weeks."

The smile fell off appropriately.

Picard ignored him, glowering at Riker and Data. "And you two, about this propensity for stealing starship property and striking off on your own," he said, his voice growing in intensity and ferocity, "just don't make a habit of it. Dismissed."

Startled, neither Riker nor Data had the sense to get away while they could, at least not for the first few seconds. Finally Riker gestured Data and Wesley out, stepping after them onto the bridge. A sense of relief washed over him as the office door slid shut behind the three of them. Together, they turned toward the bridge itself, and stopped short.

Only Riker was able to make a coherent movement —he touched the ready room door and it slid open again. As he stared out onto the bridge, he called back, "Captain . . . you'd better come out here."

A moment later, Picard was at his side.

They and the command crew looked out over the large expanse of the bridge—a bridge crowded with human forms. A hundred human forms, all in uniform. Sailors. Command officers from a time past. Some uniforms were blue, some green.

At the center of the rows of naval officers from an age gone by, Arkady Reykov and Timofei Vasska stood together in ghostly silence and gazed at Captain Picard.

On the lower bridge, Deanna Troi gazed at them, tears breaking from her lovely eyes. Finally, she found her comfort.

Captain Reykov raised his hand to his forehead in salute. A moment later, every one of the hundred Earth sailors also raised their hands.

Picard cleared his throat. "Attention," he called.

His command crew snapped straight.

He brought his own hand up and saluted those for whom he and his ship had nearly destroyed themselves.

Captain Reykov's eyes twinkled like those of a living man, and he nodded in gratitude. His hand snapped down. His men did the same.

Slowly then, from each end, the crescent of sailors began to disappear, one by one.

The *Enterprise* was once again a ship for the living.

STAR TREK®
THE NEXT GENERATION
IMBALANCE

by V. E. Mitchell

The Jarada are a mysterious race of insectoid beings with an extreme devotion to protocol. When this usually reclusive race offer to open diplomatic relations with the Federation, Captain Picard and the U.S.S. *Enterprise* are quickly ordered to Jarada to negotiate the exchange of Ambassadors.

When the ship arrives, the Jarada seem uncharacteristically friendly. They invite Picard to send down members of his crew and negotiations proceed both quickly and smoothly. Suddenly, however, the Jarada change. They cut off Commander Riker and his away team from the U.S.S. *Enterprise* and initiate an unprovoked attack on the ship. Now Picard must unravel the aliens' mystery before it's too late for the away team - and the U.S.S. *Enterprise*.

DREADNOUGHT!

Star Empire is the Federation's most powerful new
weapon - a dreadnought, first in a class of super-
starships - capable of outgunning a dozen Klingon
cruisers, or subduing a galaxy.

On the eve of her maiden voyage, Star Empire is
stolen by terrorists who demand a rendezvous with
the *Enterprise* - and with Lieutenant Piper, stationed
aboard Kirk's ship on her first training cruise. Now
Piper must discover why her friends from Starfleet are
among the terrorists... and why they insist that the ship
was stolen not to attack the Federation - but to save it!

STAR TREK®
THE NEXT GENERATION
CHAINS OF COMMAND

by Bill McCay and Eloise Flood

While exploring a group of devastated class M planets in a remote sector of space, the crew of the U.S.S. *Enterprise* is shocked to discover a group of human slaves on a forbidding, glacial world. When the slaves revolt against their human overseers, Captain Picard and his crew sympathise with the slaves plight but cannot interfere in the conflict.

After the revolt is a success, Captain Picard learns that both the slaves and the overseers were controlled by a mysterious bird-like race called the Tseetsk, who are coming to reclaim their property. With time running out, the rebels kidnap Captain Picard and Counsellor Troi - drawing the U.S.S. *Enterprise* into the middle of their deadly plan of vengeance.

For a complete list of Star Trek publications, T-shirts and badges please send a large SAE to Titan Books Mail Order, 19 Valentine Place, London, SE1 8QH. Please quote reference NG1.